BLINDSIDED

JOHN MAHAFFEY

NEMESIS SERIES BOOK 4

Blindsided
Published by Crosswind Press
The Woodlands, TX

ISBN: 978-1-7375093-3-2
FICTION / Thrillers / Suspense

Cover by Donna Cunningham
Interior design by Wolf Design & Marketing,
wolfdesignandmarketing.com. Copyright owned by John Mahaffey.

CROSSWIND PRESS

FROM THE AUTHOR JOHN MAHAFFEY

Blindsided is a work of fiction. Any resemblance to persons, alive or dead, is purely coincidental.

Special thanks to these wonderful folks at My Word Publishing who bring their book magic to make it all happen: Polly Letofsky for her book business smarts, Donna Cunningham for her amazing cover design skills, Jennifer Bisbing, for her dedication to making this book series flow, Carly Catt for her keen eye for editing, Victoria Wolf for making the typeface jump off the page, Mary Walewsky for reaching readers, and Ralph Scott and Kendra Murray at Squeaky Cheese Productions for giving voices to my characters.

PROLOGUE

WITH THE PASSAGE OF TIME, as happens with all good things, Trey McCall's reign at the helm of Nemesis was coming to an end. He and his wife, Tara, were opting for a simpler life in the Texas Hill Country. Fresh faces were on the horizon to carry on the McCall family tradition, both at the cybercrime-fighting giant and on The Circle M ranch. Groomed for the top position for years by Trey McCall and backed by the full support of the Nemesis board of directors, Molly Elizabeth (Liz) McCall assumed the chairpersonship of Nemesis at twenty-one-and-a-half years old. No one, including Trey—who stayed on as a consultant—knew the Nemesis organization better than Liz. *Nobody*. It had been the entire focus of her life since Liz was a child. Like her great-grandfather Mac McCall, it was in her blood to fight injustice.

CHAPTER 1

IN AN INSTANT, SHE WAS FLUNG from the frying pan into the fire. No sooner had Molly Elizabeth (Liz) McCall been sworn in as the head of Nemesis than one of her most valued agents handed her a missive.

Dear Liz,

Sorry to rain on your parade, but this was too important to put off. We just now confirmed what we've long suspected: Desiree Richards was the supreme leader of the Nobilis Familia. I say "was" because she is now incarcerated in a mental ward outside Montreal, suffering from diminishing cognitive capacity as a result of habitual overuse of an addictive substance. She's delusional and incoherent, and she keeps mumbling the name "Millicent." Doctors say there is little chance Desiree will ever recover from her current state. If you wish, I will stay here and keep you informed of any change. By the way, congrats. You are going to make an awesome chairperson!

Tina Tremblay

LIZ NOTIFIED THE NEMESIS STAFF of this unexpected turn of events. Most had assumed that the Nobilis Familia's supreme leader role would pass to Ari Moon, head of the international firm Moon Enterprises, or Miles Stewart, the overseer of The Castle in Albania. But Liz had a different take—a gut feeling. The new leader had to be a person groomed by Desiree. Someone Nemesis had previously vetted. An individual far removed from what they portrayed.

For days, Liz examined Nemesis files of archived photos and videos taken at major gatherings held by the noble clan organization. But she came up empty in her search for anyone who fit the profile. Even so, she believed in her theory and plodded on.

MEANWHILE, IN CANADA, an orderly at the hospital where Desiree was admitted contacted Boris. The employee recognized Desiree from the old days, when he'd participated in several scams she and Boris masterminded. Without delay, Boris flew to Montreal to visit her and was horrified at what he saw and heard. Adverse side effects of caida libre, a potentially lethal and addictive drug discovered by the ancient Mayans, were clearly present in what remained of a once vibrant, brilliant individual. Confined to a padded room, semicomatose in a state of partial consciousness, and with eyes staring straight ahead, Desiree monotonously uttered one name—"Mil-la-cent." Boris picked up on the reference as a relative he assumed Desiree had invented to bolster one of her hoaxes in the past. Except for that, nothing else registered.

Therefore, when her doctor asked Boris if he recognized the name, he shook his head. "Hmm, no, I don't believe so. Although, for some strange reason, that name seems significant in some way."

While he strolled the grounds of the hospital, Boris searched his memory for the one individual Desiree catered to more than any other. Then it hit him. He knew exactly who Mil-la-cent was and where he could find her. What an incredibly simple feint. No one would ever suspect that it was Millie Snowden, his Natasha from back in the day. Especially since nobody believed Desiree might actually have a long-lost daughter. There was no record of her anywhere. Still, it was Desiree—and she was devilishly clever.

Motivated by curiosity, Boris let himself into Desiree's place with the key she'd sent him shortly after she'd moved into her condo. Donning latex gloves, he gathered all incriminating evidence tying Desiree to him, Millie, and the Nobilis Familia organization. After he burned unrelated documents in the fireplace to make it look like a perpetrator had found and destroyed pertinent evidence, Boris removed the SIM chips from the phones and expertly swept clean the computer hard drives. Then he shuffled files with damning evidence among a cluster of existing documents in his briefcase. Finally, he slipped a lone letter addressed to Millie into his jacket pocket. On the outside, across the flap of the envelope, Desiree had written at an angle, *FOR YOUR EYES ONLY.*

After an in-depth look around the condo for anything he might have missed, Boris took the elevator down to the ground floor. As darkness approached, he drove in bumper-to-bumper traffic through a city ablaze with bright lights and queued-up nightspots, past ancient cathedrals and historic sites along his way to the Montreal International Airport. On the perimeter, he turned in his rental vehicle, cleared customs, and waited in a café across from his gate for his two-hour-and-forty-minute flight to Minneapolis in the States. In less than twenty-four hours, Boris had assembled a slew of key information about the ambiguous Desiree—much more than he'd ever expected.

NEMESIS AGENTS TINA TREMBLAY and Rose Conner were in separate cars on a stakeout near Minneapolis, surveilling Talley Marsh and Millie Snowden. Nothing of any consequence had taken place for days, and it looked as though today was no different.

"Hey, Rose. Did you catch that on the bug our techs planted in our subjects' office? Millie's got a doctor's appointment today," Tina said over their Bluetooth earbuds. "Strike up the band. It's another rip-roaring, event-filled afternoon. I remember when we couldn't keep up with those broads. Now they're about as exciting as elevator music on hold."

Rose chuckled. "Yeah, ditto that. How about—Whoops, here comes Millie. Gotta go."

Tina stayed put, and Rose followed Millie at a safe distance. At the hospital, Millie walked to a central nurse's station, picked up her lab forms, and proceeded through a set of double doors that opened toward her. A sign on the door read, PATIENTS ONLY, ABSOLUTELY NO EXCEPTIONS. Without a legitimate reason to follow her suspect, Rose sat and waited for Millie to return.

As soon as she cleared the double doors, Millie made for the rear exit. In the stairwell, she reunited with Boris. At first glance, she barely recognized her old lover. His transformation was a pleasant surprise. Now a sun-bleached blond, twenty-five pounds heavier, and mostly muscle, Boris appeared to be more confident and caring. When they embraced, suppressed feelings rushed back, and their kiss was longer than she expected it would be. Millie realized she missed him more than she would've thought.

Unsure if he should give Millie the whole story all at once, Boris shared only the sad news about Desiree's condition. This was no fabrication. Desiree *was* totally out of her mind, fixated on repeating the same name over and over.

"Oh, I feel so bad for her. With all her faults, she was a strong-willed woman with an obsession for what we believe in. Out of curiosity, what name does she repeat?" Millie asked in a quavering voice.

Hesitant to reply, Boris took a deep breath. He had no choice. "Millicent."

"I, ah, really don't understand why she would, ah … Unless you don't think she meant me? I mean, how could it be? Maybe. It's gotta be somebody else. I mean … Oh, that's just too farfetched to be real. Although, I've had this funny feeling about her ever since we met. I never found out who my birth parents were. As deep as I dug, nothing ever surfaced. Boris, do you think *Desiree* could *be my mother*?"

Boris reached inside his coat pocket and, without another word, handed her the envelope he had taken from Desiree's condo.

Millie stared at it for what seemed an eternity, then carefully opened it and gently removed the letter. It read:

My Dearest Millicent,

Please find it in your heart not to hate me. Oh, how I wanted to hold you close to my bosom and tell you how much I loved you, but I couldn't. You were my Achilles' heel. The one who had to be kept a secret from the world of diabolical souls who wished to destroy us. I left you alone to make your own life decisions, but I always kept an eye on you—to help out the best I could. Whatever road you pick from here on out is up to you. Take your time. Choose carefully and wisely.

Love always,

Your Mother, Desiree

AS BEAUTIFUL AND PEACEFUL as Puerto Vallarta was to take refuge in, Ari Moon yearned to get back to his old stomping ground in Hong Kong, with its vibrant city atmosphere and the comforts of his elegant penthouse. A timely getaway to Mexico had enabled him to dodge the fallout from the caida libre catastrophe and the fray created by the ongoing arrests of the ill-respected Nobilis Familia members. But that was six months earlier, long enough for the smoke to clear. Besides, Ari missed his two ladies, Eva and Victoria. He missed not just their romantic energy but more—they were simply delightful to be around. Both were bright, personable, easy to talk to, and definitely not the average bimbos you find in their business. Like fine wine, they became more desirable as they matured. As a precaution, Ari had not kept in touch with them since he took to ground in Mexico. Once he got settled back at his penthouse, he intended to summon them from Albania. They were his eyes and ears when it came to Miles. It wasn't that he didn't trust his associate. To him, there was no such thing as being too careful.

A fortnight later, on the afternoon of his clandestine return to

Hong Kong, Ari had his chauffeur let him out on a busy downtown street corner. From there, he casually walked into a pub and sipped a Tsingtao beer while he checked to make sure he wasn't being followed. Assured he hadn't been, he ambled out the back door to a Western Union office and wired Miles to send the girls home.

Of course, when they arrived, Ari would fib about where he had been—a compassionate tale to paint himself as a true humanitarian. Perhaps he would say one of his school chums from university had fallen gravely ill and needed a friendly face to cheer him up. Then, after a few days, Ari would approach the girls with the new proposal he had come up with.

While in Mexico, Ari Moon had seized upon an idea for expanding his influence in the Middle East. Suliman Kumar, an extremely wealthy prospective client in Qatar, was in the market for an agency to promote and distribute his wares worldwide. As for the nature of the goods, Ari suspected they were contraband.

It was an ideal way to make use of Eva's and Victoria's persuasive talents. Step one was to fly them to Qatar as envoys from Moon Enterprises to meet with Suliman and explore the possibilities. After a few days and nights with the ladies, if the outlook was promising, Miles would swoop in to make his pitch and close the deal. And Ari Moon would not have to make in-person contact with Suliman at all.

It was a glorious reunion when the girls arrived in Hong Kong and had a whirlwind week of wining and dining with Ari. Certain the ladies were comfortably back in familiar surroundings, Ari invited Victoria and Eva to sit down while he explained a scheme he had dreamed up for a gentleman in Qatar. At first, they were hesitant. But as he continued, their interest grew.

"But, darling. We barely got here! And you already want to send us away? I don't understand," Victoria cooed, a pouty, hurt expression on her face.

Eva chimed in, "What? You don't love us anymore? Qatar, of all places?"

"Believe me, nothing would please me more than to spend the rest of my days in the company of you both," Ari said. "However, this fellow looks to be an easy mark. With the persuasive talents you both possess, frankly, it's too great an opportunity to ignore." He laid it on thick.

After they heard him out, the lure of easy money, along with the prospect of getting back into action, appealed to the two smooth operators. They glanced at one another, then replied in unison, "We're in. When do we go?"

"A week from today. I'll make all the arrangements," Ari confirmed with a huge grin. Then he popped the cork on a bottle of Dom Pérignon champagne to celebrate.

A WEEK LATER, IN QATAR, Suliman frowned as he paced the floor of the lobby at the private airport, waiting on the arrival of the Moon Enterprises jet from Hong Kong. Forewarned that the two delegates Ari Moon assigned to him were women, he had resented the fact he was not held in higher esteem as a prospective client.

Moments later, when he got a look at the two knockouts Ari sent, Suliman moved those thoughts aside and stared. In similar fashion, the two women were pleasantly surprised that the photo Ari showed them back in Hong Kong did not do Suliman justice at all. In person, Suliman Kumar was a handsome man in his late fifties—fit, trim, and just under six feet tall, with long, wavy jet-black hair.

He greeted them in English, delivered with a slight British accent.

Mesmerized by his brilliant smile, the women's eyes lit up as they both reached the same conclusion—their assignment had just taken on a much more appealing aspect.

Judging by the delighted expression on his face, Suliman couldn't agree more.

FOLLOWING A THIRTY-MINUTE DRIVE to Suliman's vast estate, the ladies were shown to their quarters and were momentarily stunned at the opulence of their accommodations. Eva and Victoria quickly snapped out of their trance, excited to explore the spacious two-bedroom suite on the third floor, resplendent with gold fixtures, crystal chandeliers, priceless Persian rugs strewn on Brazilian hardwood floors, and sliding wooden plantation shutters that opened onto a balcony overlooking the Persian Gulf. Matching bathrooms featured massive, carpeted walk-in closets, wall-to-wall marble floors, a walk-through shower, and a jetted Jacuzzi tub. To top it off, a remote control fob opened a retractable ceiling skylight to let in fresh air and pure sunlight or moonlight.

Resting in a gold letter holder on a vintage desk was a printed invitation to dinner at nine p.m., allowing the new arrivals a few hours to rest after the almost ten-hour flight from Hong Kong. Customarily, the dress for dinner was formal. However, Suliman made an exception to allow casual dress for all that night.

Eva and Victoria arrived on time for dinner and were awestruck at the spread laid out before them. Between oohs and aahs, oh mys and yummys, the girls cruised the lengthy serving table from opposite sides, filling their plates with a smidgen of each item from a smorgasbord consisting of Russian caviar, Maine lobster tails, fruits and salads,

Kobi beef, and an assortment of vegetables as sides, along with table-side cherries jubilee and bananas Foster for dessert. Afterward, the trio slowly sipped drinks in a canopy-covered seating area that afforded a pleasant breeze and a view of a private marina, where massive yachts bobbed gently up and down in the docile water. Suliman could tell by the expressions on Eva's and Victoria's faces that they were taken aback by the setting.

NOT ONE TO WASTE TIME or an opportunity, Suliman got straight to the point. "Ladies, I'm hoping you two can be of assistance in promoting my new discovery, the one I vaguely alluded to when I contacted Ari Moon. Specifically, it's a radical pharmaceutical breakthrough I financed at a lab in a remote part of the desert. My scientists created a catalyst that, in synergy with the body's own immune system, attacks deadly viruses. To date, our antivirus enzyme, InnoVita, has a success rate of nearly 100 percent in the treatment of all viruses, including mutations. Only one pesky issue stands in our way—approval by traditionally accepted regulatory agencies that perpetuate their existence through insatiable greed, endless delays, and vast incompetence.

"Since I've already invested heavily in InnoVita, I'm anxious to bypass the years-long nightmare of dealing with fools. My concept is to introduce it on the Asian black market, where I'm assured by trusted colleagues that it will take off. Ari Moon confirmed that former Nomad facilities could produce the basic formula in North America and then ship it to Qatar for completion, packaging, and global distribution. It was Ari who also recommended that I consider you two as international ambassadors for InnoVita—and I can certainly understand why. I would be honored if you would accept that role."

Victoria gave him the once-over *twice* before she responded. "We appreciate your blind faith in us to endorse such a remarkable medical miracle. But, frankly, you have taken us completely by surprise." Eva nodded as Victoria continued. "I think it best, before we make any decisions on such an important matter, that we find out more details about the product in question, then talk it over with our employers. I hope you understand."

"Beautiful, smart, and vigilant," Suliman thought. Then he commented, "Of course, ladies. I wouldn't have it any other way. Perhaps then we might move on to less pressing matters and get to know each other on a less professional, more personal basis—if you are so inclined."

THE NEXT DAY, VICTORIA PLACED a call to Talley and Millie. The Nomad duo had just returned to their office from a road trip to remove any trace of caida libre from their manufacturing facilities and were excited when they heard what Suliman Kumar proposed, whereby Nomad handled the manufacturing of a solution composed of legal ingredients they shipped to Suliman in Qatar—nothing more. All Talley and Millie needed from Suliman were the specific components and ingredient percentages.

AT NEMESIS HEADQUARTERS IN TEXAS, Liz paid close attention to the conversation. Afterward, Nemesis added Suliman Kumar to their list of international suspects to watch closely. The more principal players they had eyes on, the better their chances of getting to the head of the snake. If InnoVita was half as successful as it was hyped up to be, the lure of easy money was sure to pique the interest of gluttonous entrepreneurs. Following the money had always proven to be a useful tactic.

As far as Talley and Millie were concerned, Nemesis regarded them as clever, timely, and more fortunate than most con artists. Throughout the years, every time they were in jeopardy, the Nomad duo managed to cash in before the scam self-destructed. The only downside was they became permanent residents on Nemesis's list of usual suspects.

SHORTLY AFTER EVA AND VICTORIA LEFT QATAR, Suliman signed a deal with Moon Enterprises to distribute InnoVita on the black market. As expected, InnoVita became an instant success. In the first business quarter, it was phenomenal, and to the delight of the initial investors, the second quarter surpassed the first. Word spread rapidly about the wonder drug, resulting in a rush of new international capitalists knocking at the door. To keep up with demand, Talley Marsh added half a dozen US production laboratories. Money came in faster than they could count it. However, all was not what it seemed.

SULIMAN WAS NOT ONLY AN ACCOMPLISHED ENTREPRENEUR, but he was also the leader of a radical international group. A far cry from how he portrayed himself to Ari Moon or Ari's two lovely female ambassadors, Suliman's aspirations were diabolical. A true believer in his cause, he took only a small percentage of the InnoVita profit for himself. The majority went to finance missions of mass murder and destruction dealt out by his ruthless cult of veteran mercenaries. His delusional destiny was written in the stars: to reign over his sect of followers and spread their message throughout the world.

CONVERSELY, ARI MOON'S AMBITIONS were egocentric, based purely on his quest for acquisition and power to secure more control. Ari skillfully manipulated his highbred associates. Using threats of exposure thanks to incriminating videos he accumulated at The Castle shindigs, he turned them against one another while claiming to be an ally to each.

BECAUSE LIZ MCCALL SPENT MOST of her adult life preparing to take over for her grandfather at the helm of Nemesis, she had little room for a social life. As concerned grandparents, Trey and Tara spoke to her about getting out some with her friends, which Liz promised she would do. But she never found the time.

In her youth, when she joined her parents on the Tour, she had loved the outdoors, walking on the lush grasses and sandy beaches while her father, Jefferson, played. Those memories stayed fresh in her mind and were easily recalled at will. When her dad asked her if she would like to go to Pebble Beach with him and Reanna, Liz, now in her early twenties, cocked her head and slowly nodded. A week in Carmel would do wonders to clear her mind. Trey, Tara, and Liz's great-aunt, Miranda, could watch the store. The chairperson was only a phone call away.

A giddy Liz McCall was all smiles as they loaded up the last of their gear in their G5 aircraft for the three-plus hour flight from their airstrip at The Circle M to Monterey, California. Forty-five minutes after landing and transferring their luggage to a courtesy car provided to them by the tournament, they arrived at a beautiful home Jefferson had rented for the week on 17-Mile Drive. It overlooked the Pebble Beach Golf Links. Ravenous, the McCalls dropped their bags inside the foyer and drove to The Lodge at Pebble Beach to grab lunch in The Tap Room.

Liz remembered the room well from a past visit. It was a gathering place as well as a world-renowned eatery and bar. Its walls were adorned with pictures and memorabilia of years gone by. Famous people from all walks of life, lovers of the game of golf, participants in Crosby Clambakes, PGAs, and US Opens were depicted in action on the famous Pebble Beach Links.

Although the restaurant was packed, as soon as the maître d' recognized Jefferson, a table miraculously became available. Seated by the window facing the entrance, Liz had just placed her order when she noticed a handsome man stroll through the door to a table directly across from theirs. The man was thirtyish, close to six feet tall, and well-groomed. He had a radiant smile. Their eyes met as he eased into his seat. Liz quickly turned away, embarrassed that she had been caught staring at him. He caught her gaze a couple more times as he glanced over casually. After the man finished his meal, he flashed her a smile when he exited the restaurant.

Her heart sank, and Liz finished her meal in gloomy silence. It was the first time in forever that a man had had that kind of effect on her.

After lunch, the McCalls walked across the driveway to the putting green. And there he was. Liz spotted the handsome stranger sitting on one of the benches in front of the Pebble Beach retail shops. He was chatting with a couple of celebrity participants in the event. Laughing and joking, the stranger looked at ease with these movie stars and TV idols. It was like they were good buddies. When he noticed her ogling him, he begged their pardon and walked over to where Liz stood with her parents.

"Hello. My name is Bryce Lonagon. I don't mean to appear forward, only ... I was wondering if maybe we'd met somewhere before. I saw you eyeing at me in The Tap Room like you were trying to place me from somewhere," the man said as he stuck out his hand in greeting.

Liz turned bright red as she shook his hand, found her voice, and weakly replied, "No, I don't think so. I'm sure I would remember you. I mean, well, you know. I don't know what I mean. Oh, this is all coming out so wrong. My name is Elizabeth McCall, though I prefer Liz. I'm here with my mom and dad. He's competing in the tournament."

Having paid little attention to the two figures standing next to this glorious creature, Bryce apologized for his rudeness and shook hands with her parents. He was a bit embarrassed that he had barely glanced at Jefferson McCall. Frankly, his attention had been directed solely toward their gorgeous daughter, Liz McCall—a stunningly attractive woman in her twenties who was blessed with a natural, sultry voice that bore a hint of a Southern accent.

Sensing they were in the way, Jefferson said, "Well, looks like I better make good on my promise to go shopping with my wife. Reanna has already scoped out some cashmere sweaters she wants me to check out. Great meeting you, Bryce, and hope to see you again soon."

With that, Reanna and Jefferson excused themselves and wandered into the shops to browse while Bryce and Liz sat by the green. Two hours later, they were still there chatting, and her parents stopped to ask if Liz was ready to go back to the house.

Glancing at Bryce, then back at her parents, Liz said awkwardly, "It's such a beautiful afternoon, and, ah, well, Bryce and I thought we might go for a walk on the beach and … Anyway, I'll call you guys after a while, okay?"

Jefferson smiled at his daughter and said, "Of course."

Reanna whispered in Jefferson's ear as they walked away, "Told you it would be a good idea to bring Liz to Pebble Beach."

CHAPTER 2

LOST IN EACH OTHER as they tripped over and around driftwood, with a constant need for eye contact, Bryce Lonagon and Liz McCall walked along Carmel Beach until the sun hovered above the horizon. They waded barefoot in the chilly water that lapped up on the sand, mesmerized as they watched dog owners bond with man's best friends on the beach.

Hand in hand, the duo worked their way back to The Lodge as the sun threatened to slide into the Pacific. Liz was about to call her mom when a text message appeared from Reanna, saying she and Jefferson were at The Bench restaurant at The Lodge. They had saved Bryce and Liz each a seat if Liz and Bryce would care to join them—an invitation the pair readily accepted.

Huddled together around a large propane heater for warmth, the four of them watched ocean waves crash over the seawall at Pebble Beach's famed eighteenth hole. The smell of salt water hung heavily in a misty breeze, and shrieks of hungry seagulls pierced the air while they circled for dinner in Stillwater Cove. The McCall party, plus Bryce, ate, drank, and talked until the sun vanished over the horizon and the chill in the air became too imposing.

On their way out, Bryce asked Jefferson if he had a fourth player for his practice round the next morning. Jefferson replied that he did not and invited Bryce to join the group for their nine-a.m. tee time at Pebble. Then Bryce gave Liz a gentle kiss good-bye and disappeared to his room at The Lodge.

All Liz could talk about on the drive back to their rental house was how wonderful Bryce Lonagon was and what a lucky happenstance it had been to meet him.

Maybe not so much chance, thought Reanna as Jefferson held back a chuckle. Later that night, with bedrooms on opposite sides of the rambling ranch-style house, Reanna made sure Liz was well out of earshot before she snuggled up to Jefferson and whispered, "What have you done?"

Jefferson replied, "This matchmaker stuff is complicated. If I didn't know Bryce so well, I would have never mentioned anything to him. It's just that he seems so perfect for our girl. I've played golf with him enough times in tournaments to know what he's all about. You can judge a guy's character pretty quickly when you play golf with him. Golf presents a player with endless opportunities to stretch the rules. Never have I seen Bryce fudge an inch, which confirms his rock-solid reputation as a trustworthy individual in my book."

"Why didn't you tell me you were planning all of this?"

Jefferson hesitated momentarily, then explained. "Well, Bryce was devastated when his wife died in a car crash, going back ten years now. She was the second car going through a green light when a drunk bitch in a Mercedes ran the red and T-boned her. It was only minutes after she had phoned Bryce with the news she was pregnant with their first child. She was on her way home to celebrate the good news with him. The drunk walked away with only a few scratches, and her rich lawyer husband got her off on a legal technicality. It tore Bryce up for years. He just recently got back to being his old self, playing golf again with his buds—even cutting up a little—while masking the huge void that remains in his life. That man is too good to go through life being lonely. He doesn't deserve it."

"Still, I would have helped."

"The plan just came together. A while back, I mentioned our all-work-and-no-play daughter to him. Even showed him a picture of her. After Bryce took a long look, he said he would think about calling her. Unfortunately, he never did. That's why I arranged an invite for him to the clambake here at Pebble and partnered him with one of the up-and-coming rookies—a personable kid who I think has what it takes to be something special on the Tour.

"Anyway, when I told Bryce you and I had convinced Liz to take a break and come with us, he seemed genuinely interested. He even told me he was ready to step back out socially. Bryce agreed to act like he had never laid eyes on us before, so their meeting would seem coincidental. And now here we are, and I'm proud to say I'm glad we did it. I just hope she doesn't find out until much later."

To hush her husband, Reanna held her finger to his lips, then put her arms around Jefferson and kissed him passionately. One thing led to another … Soon they were lost in each other.

DURING THE WEEK, BRYCE AND LIZ spent every possible moment together. She followed him every step of the way through four rounds of golf on the Monterey Peninsula. Every night, they had dinner in a different restaurant in Carmel, then walked off their meal by sightseeing and window-shopping around the quaint township. Sunday came way too soon—especially for Liz, who wanted the magic to last forever.

TO LIZ'S SURPRISE, WHEN THEY ARRIVED at the airport in Monterey, Bryce was waiting inside the private aviation terminal. Jefferson had asked him to fly back to Texas with them to talk about a blue-chip golf resort project on a piece of property Bryce owned in Central Texas, halfway between San Antonio and Kerrville. To make it extra special, Bryce wanted Jefferson McCall's name associated with the golf course. While they discussed the details, Bryce agreed to stay at The Circle M.

LIZ COULD NOT BELIEVE HER GOOD FORTUNE. Her dad couldn't believe she hadn't figured it out yet. On the three-plus-hour flight back to Texas, Liz and Bryce sat together in the back of the plane, chatting and laughing uncontrollably. Reanna and Jefferson glanced back at the ecstatic couple, certain Bryce and Liz were that rare perfect fit.

After they landed, Bryce helped load their bags into a waiting SUV. In only a week, Liz's life had changed dramatically. No longer did she pine for that one, someone special in her life. To show her appreciation, she ran up to her father, threw her arms around his neck, and whispered, "Oh, Daddy, thank you so much. I don't know if you had anything to do with this or not. And I don't care because you made it possible for me to meet this incredible man. For that alone, I'll love you forever."

Unable to contain her excitement, Liz McCall was up early on Monday morning to meet Bryce for breakfast. Afterward, he walked her to her office on his way to meet with Jefferson and Trey at the golf complex to discuss his Central Texas project.

WHILE LIZ DAYDREAMED THROUGH WORK, Bryce filled Trey and Jefferson in on his plans for his property west of San Antonio. After a tour of The Circle M golf facility, Bryce expressed his admiration for the Matt Bremer design.

"It's brilliant," he said. "Especially his resourcefulness in configuring a nine-hole course on such a small plot of land. Matt's use of multiple tee boxes and double greens is clever as well as functional, and the condition of the place is impeccable. With your blessing, I would like Matt Bremer to become an integral member of my design team."

Beaming with pride, Trey replied, "You won't be sorry. The man is a genius when it comes to design and construction. I'll relay your message to Matt posthaste. I'm sure he'll be thrilled."

Matt was over the moon when he heard the news. Thankful for the opportunity to show off his skills, he accepted the position on the spot.

THE NEXT MORNING, AFTER TALKING ABOUT nothing but golf, the men broke for lunch and were surprised to see Tara, Reanna, and Liz seated on the patio at the driving range. It was Tostado Tuesday, one of the McCalls' favorite days at the bar and grill. Following lunch, Liz and Bryce made their way to the ever-expanding motor pool to grab a Jeep so they could tour as much of The Circle M as they could before dark.

A landscape architect by trade, Bryce was impressed with Molly McCall's creative genius brought to life on The Circle M.

"I can't say enough about Molly McCall's talent. Everywhere I look, I see things in the right places with the proper proportions. She had an eye for symmetry that I haven't seen in decades. Beauty and functionality do not always coincide, even in the works of the most renowned architects. Molly incorporated them both in a no-nonsense use of common sense. Just look at the main ranch house, for instance. No wasted space, no outrageous fingerprint to brand the architect, solid construction built to last, not for show. Simple, comfortable, yet elegantly designed structures. Molly was special. I wish I could have met her and picked her gifted, artistic mind."

Liz and Bryce made their way through the pastures and around the lake, past the golf complex and the oil wells pumping black gold, then up to the crest where Molly Elizabeth McCall's namesake was buried. They got out of the car and prepared a picnic of cold cuts and iced-down beers. Liz beamed at the comments Bryce made about her grandmother's ingenuity and creativity. Bryce glanced over at Liz, who was trying desperately not to cry.

Unable to hold back, she blurted out, "Oh, Bryce. She was such a strong woman who saw all of this in her mind and was determined to build her dream. I never knew her, but she's a part of me. And now that I'm in charge of all this, I don't ever want to let her down."

Leaning over, Bryce kissed her gently on the lips, then spoke softly in her ear. "Liz, you're a strong, disciplined woman. Your family would never have put you in charge unless they had total faith in your abilities. From what I have seen so far, nobody is better equipped to handle the job than you. Period."

For uncountable minutes, she stared deeply into his eyes, then kissed him, holding on to him with all her might. Gently, she pushed him over on the blanket and lay on top of him, kissing him passionately, sloppily, hungrily.

"Are you sure you want this?" Bryce whispered in her ear.

"Oh, yes. More than anything in the world," she moaned as she pulled him closer.

In front of God and memories of family on that ridge, they made love. They'd found in their intense passion a bond each had been searching for. Clinging tightly to each other, neither wanted to disturb the enchantment of the moment.

At last, Bryce broke the silence. "Liz, oh my God. That was wonderful. You are truly amazing in every way. I feel like I've known you for a lifetime."

"I know what you mean. Isn't it wonderful?" Liz echoed as they watched the sunset bathe the landscape with a golden hue.

On the drive back, a full moon and a billion stars lit their way.

ON FAR DISTANT SHORES, ARI MOON in Hong Kong and Suliman Kumar in Qatar used the capital InnoVita had generated on the black market to embark on quite different routes to achieve their goals.

With his share, Ari bought influence with the Nobilis Familia. He never ceased to be amazed by money's power to change the mindset of the greedy patrons in the elite body of the *family*. Most would forsake anything for a price. Many of the privileged people born into a political dynasty with considerable clout had no conscience or morals. They possessed only the desire for more wealth and power—the perfect vessel for manipulation. And that gave Ari a gigantic pool of fools from which he could pick and choose to scam.

Unlike Ari, Suliman funneled his share into creating chaos inside governments across the globe—instigating coups and social unrest and employing mercenary brigades notorious for using deadly force and intimidation to achieve their goals. Targeted countries were those with huge oil reserves and accessible ports for conducting international trade—ones that provided basic staples, like produce, meat, poultry, and fish, to feed the masses. Others were targeted for their natural resources, precious metals, and rare earth minerals. Once Suliman gained control over human *essentials*, forcing the world to comply with his demands would be child's play.

A COUPLE OF DAYS AFTER ARI'S DAMSELS LEFT QATAR, Warlock intercepted emails, faxes, and conversations conducted between three parties, all of whom were on the Nemesis watch list. Miles Stewart (emissary for Moon Enterprises), Suliman Kumar (Qatari Acquisitions), and Talley Marsh (Nomad) kicked around marketing strategies to persuade worldwide authorities to approve InnoVita.

In the Nemesis cybercrime lab, Liz, Tara, and Miranda listened to the conversations Warlock captured. Other than a vague suggestion of a felonious act, little else of significance was discussed. Impressively, Liz saw an opportunity to exploit the situation. It had been a good three months since Talley or Millie had made any contact with their two Canadian stakeholders, Tina Tremblay and Rose Conner.

Time to shake things up, Liz thought. So, without hesitation, she sent for her agents in Banff. Within twenty-four hours, Tina and Rose were in Liz's office, where she equipped each of them with a diamond-stud spy cam recording device to be worn at all times. Nemesis needed bodies on the inside at Nomad.

Wasting no time, Liz had her operatives on a flight to Minneapolis by nightfall. Having performed a minor miracle, she sighed and fell onto her office couch to crash. Before she closed her eyes, she chuckled to herself. Blindsided, Millie and Talley had little choice but to agree to meet with Rose and Tina, since the Canadians were not only investors but majority stockholders in the company as well.

At ten o'clock sharp in Talley's office the next morning, the four women had barely taken their seats when Tina blurted out, "Been a while, eh? We were beginning to think Nomad had forgotten about us. We certainly haven't forgotten about you. Sorry about all that shit with caida libre. That cost us all a bundle in future profits. But hey, there's light at the end of the tunnel. Right? Rose and I were wondering if you two have heard anything about a product called InnoVita."

Rose watched the two directors' reactions closely as her colleague asked the question. It was instantly apparent that neither had expected the question, as they helplessly looked at one another, hoping the other would answer.

After an awkward silence, Talley chimed in. "Well, hmm. As a matter of fact, Millie and I are in the process of preparing a prospectus on InnoVita for you both to peruse. Sorry for the delay, but we've been overwhelmed by caida libre fallout and the sudden success and popularity of InnoVita. What with having to retool and expand on the run, frankly, it's been a chaotic nightmare."

It was an obvious cover-up. Talley never intended to allow the Canadians anywhere near InnoVita. Now, with no way out, she promised to have details of the new venture by the end of business Friday for Tina and Rose to scan over the weekend.

It was all much to Liz's delight as she watched and listened in, along with the Nemesis team. At Nemesis headquarters, she was impressed with how her Canadian team bulldozed their way into the subject of InnoVita in their Nomad meeting. Thanks to them, the cybercrime software at Nemesis could identify and locate companies participating in the production and distribution of the "miracle" drug.

WHILE LIZ MCCALL FOCUSED ON BUILDING evidence to destroy the cabals that threatened the world's decent populace, Ari Moon and Miles Stewart concentrated on something quite different. Thanks to mass promotion in the media, on the internet, and through social media, InnoVita was the first remedy to come to mind for millions when they heard mention of viruses. The many methods of delivery—vaccine, capsule, syrup, or lozenge—made the product versatile and thus more popular. In anticipation of a huge windfall, Ari's most avaricious Nobilis Familia members stood in line to finance additional promotions for InnoVita. What Miles and Ari failed to realize was that for each new elite person they enlisted, they created another avenue for Nemesis to investigate.

MEANWHILE, IN TEXAS, BRYCE LONAGON signed an agreement with Trey and Jefferson McCall and Matt Bremer, Bryce's recent hire as the architect on their golf course project. Afterward, the four of them flew down to walk the Hill Country property called Whispering Canyons Resort and Spa. Suitably named, it referred to the winds that swirled eerily around and through the draws, howling and groaning in an almost human timbre.

Bryce had set aside an impressive piece of property for the golf course. Topography-wise, it was a designer's dream. Featuring hills, valleys, gullies, ridges, lakes, trees, and streams, along with elevation changes to work into the layout, it gave the architect a canvas on which to shape a masterpiece.

Matt Bremer was almost salivating. Bryce noticed. So he reassuringly put his arm around his architect and looked down at him as he spoke. "Whispering Canyons merits a designer who's not only innovative and knowledgeable, but who has an appreciation for the beauty of nature and the land. I believe we have that in you, Matt Bremer. *If we're smart enough to leave you alone to do your magic.*"

Everyone laughed except Matt, who blushed at the compliment.

FOCUSED ON MAKING BILLIONS, pharmaceutical entities in bed with Moon Enterprises pumped out InnoVita products as rapidly as possible. Stores could not keep them in stock; shelves emptied as soon as they were filled. Accumulating more airline miles than he could remember, Miles Stewart bounced about the globe, meeting with opportunists who sought to become rich and powerful on the coattails of InnoVita. Clients handed him buckets of money to buy in. Due to an unforeseeable miscalculation, it wasn't long before he had sold more InnoVita than actually existed, creating a huge backlog.

WHEN MILES REPORTED THE ISSUE to Ari Moon, his boss just laughed and said, "Screw those greedy bastards. Let 'em wait. Those dumbasses are getting exactly what they deserve. Keep selling, my boy, keep selling."

It was astonishing how the purchase and renovation of an Albanian castle, referred to as The Castle, had paid off for Ari. Used as the venue for over-the-top, risqué shindigs for the privileged, it was equipped with a state-of-the-art spy cam surveillance system. What boggled Ari's mind were the people he captured on the hidden cameras. Even more remarkable were their sexual proclivities. So-called beautiful people, federal judges, politicians, evangelists, priests, athletes, and actors believed they were invincible. All were sitting ducks, wide open to discovery and humiliation. None seemed to understand that the price of their anonymity would be paid back in favors—done to preserve their secret lives while owned by Ari Moon.

Blackmail became a useful tool. Ari's coffers filled so quickly that he would soon be able to buy and sell most of his members. Cringeworthy films involving dignitaries were the most damning and most lucrative. In time, Ari would have enough clout to dictate policy to some of the most strategically positioned rulers in the world.

LIKEWISE, SULIMAN KUMAR saw contributions to his mercenary corps soar. With the windfall from sales, he was able to increase the number and scope of his followers. His crusading armies were now a presence on every continent, concentrated en masse in metropolitan areas. Ari sought to control influential people through extortion and intimidation. But Suliman chose to control the populace with false promises and indoctrination.

ON-SITE IN THE TEXAS HILL COUNTRY, Bryce Lonagon came up with an out-of-the-box idea. *Since there is more than enough property to support two courses, why not have two McCall signature golf courses?* Trey and Jefferson could each consult with Matt Bremer on their respective course. An unconventional marketing tool, no doubt. But with the McCall family endorsement, it was sure to land Whispering Canyons on the international list of must-play golf destinations.

At breakfast one morning, Trey casually asked, "Hey, Bryce. Would you mind if Novél Vargas joined us to have a look at our project? Her father, Jorge, has been our ranch manager for decades at The Circle M, and his wife, Sidney, is our chief legal advisor. Since they're part of the McCall extended family, I think it would be a great experience for her to see a golf course under construction.

"We haven't seen much of her around lately since she's been on the road, making quite a name for herself on the LPGA Tour. With her incredible start—two wins, a second, and a third in her first five events in her rookie year—Novél is already a popular household name in the world of professional golf. From a female golfer's point of view, I think we could benefit by utilizing our budding LPGA star's experience and perspective in our course designs."

Bryce replied, "Hmm. If she's interested, I'd welcome her input. Come to think of it, there's a strip of land butting up against a canyon wall with a magnificent waterfall backdrop that would be perfect for a nine-hole par three course. We'd name the course after her, and she could help design it with Matt."

When Trey relayed this conversation to Novél, she was over the moon and couldn't wait to contribute. Trey snickered to himself and thought, *Now Whispering Canyons will have three signature golf courses for Bryce to promote.*

Winding around the property—following the terrain of rolling pasture land, limestone-sided canyons, and the banks of a wide, meandering creek—the golf courses gradually took shape. Huge oak trees hugged the sides of the fairways and snuggled up to and hung over the corners of challenging, undulating greens. Natural spring water filtered through limestone bluffs and outcroppings, then collected in retention ponds, providing scenic beauty and additional irrigation. Novél's par three course proved to be a dazzling gem that complemented Trey and Jefferson's championship venues.

FARTHER NORTH AND EAST, at The Circle M golf range, Tara, Reanna, and Liz met for lunch to chat about the miracles of unforeseen happenstance. All of a sudden, Reanna felt queasy and light-headed, then excused herself to go back to her house to lie down. Neither of the other two women gave it much thought. It was a boiling hot day, and chances were Reanna just got overheated.

Reanna, in her early forties, knew exactly what was going on inside her body as she remembered that wonderful, romantic night she and Jefferson experienced at The Lodge at Pebble Beach. Not long after that, she sensed a hormonal change deep within. Only last month, Reanna and Jefferson had discussed taking permanent measures to ensure they'd have no more children. Then they both got busy and never followed through. It was too late now, and she knew it. The next day, her family doctor confirmed her suspicion.

Jefferson was all smiles when he returned from the Hill Country on Friday afternoon. Not sure how he would take the news, Reanna sheepishly asked him to sit down in their living room. Confused by her behavior, Jefferson cocked his head and gave her a quizzical look. Guardedly, she gave him the news. It was clear that what she told him was the last thing he had expected to hear.

For a moment, Jefferson stared out the plate-glass window at little whitecaps on the waves slapping across the lake. Anxious and afraid, Reanna didn't say anything else or make a move, petrified by what might happen next. Then a huge grin spread across his face, and in a flash, Jefferson leaped off the couch and swept her up, twirling her about the room and knocking nicknacks off tables, overturning lamps, and upsetting potted plants. It was not at all the reaction she had expected. Yet she should have known that Jefferson would see it as another gift from heaven. But this was insane. He kissed her long and hard, then held her out in front of him, meeting her eyes, drawing her close, and kissing her again.

She was so relieved. Reanna was laughing and crying, even though Jefferson was holding her so tight that she could hardly breathe. When she whispered in his ear, he bashfully put her down gently and called a family meeting to share the good news.

The news spread like crazy across the Hill Country. Reanna was going to have a baby. Of course, the men of the family were overjoyed, hoping for a boy, only to realize that another male in the family created a slight problem. All the males in the family since Mac's father had been named Jefferson Davis McCall—from senior to junior, all the way down to the fourth. A discussion ensued between Reanna and Jefferson. He contended that naming a boy Jefferson Davis McCall V would add to the confusion. Reanna calmly settled the issue by suggesting that if it was a boy, they address him by his middle name—Davis.

CHAPTER 3

NOMAD FOUNDERS, TALLEY AND MILLIE, assumed a role they had played before—that of manufacturer and supplier. Just like in the past, they found it boring as hell. All they seemed to do was fill quotas and coordinate shipping dates.

One night, Talley used Millie's college nickname and said, "Hey, Sissy, how about you and I team up with those two Canadian bitches who are always up our asses? You know we're not getting any younger. And I don't know about you, but I miss those wild nights of getting high and letting go. So, what do you think?"

Millie feigned excitement. "You know, I've been thinking about the same thing. What the hell. Let's do it. What's your angle?"

"What if we go behind Ari's and Suliman's backs and distribute a *same-as* version of InnoVita to independent groups? Say we substitute a serotonin-type derivative to instill euphoria instead of caida libre with its adverse side effects. I have beaucoup contacts in my files from the old days we can solicit. It would require more manufacturing plants and additional dockside storage space, which we can afford. All could be done with the utmost secrecy under the guise of a dummy corporation that's untraceable to Nomad. We can call it Legacy Pain Remedies or whatever." Talley spoke in a disjointed rant, took a breather to settle herself, and went on.

"As long as we keep up with the components we supply to Ari and Suliman, they have no reason to suspect we're working our own racket. As long as our product performs, rogue pharma cartels don't care where they get their supplies, especially if they can save a buck. And the best part is that we can put Tina Tremblay and Rose Conner in charge of the fake corporation. With the Canadians' names on the legal documents, we stay in the clear."

MILLIE LIKED THE IDEA BECAUSE IT GAVE HER cover for a bizarre undertaking she had been giving a lot of thought to lately. The grown-up hide-and-seek game she had been part of for years had lost all its luster. As had the potential role of supreme leader of a ragtag collection of fools. The Nobilis Familia could have it all—with her blessing. For her to vanish, Millie needed the strongest allies possible, and she knew where to find them.

With whom and what she knew, Millie was sure Nemesis would give her sanctuary in return for the incriminating information she possessed. To guarantee their collaboration, she had to stay in character until she found out the actual name of the global grand puppeteer. Then Millie could sit back and chill out.

TINA AND ROSE LOVED WHAT TALLEY PROPOSED. Only a few days before, Tina admitted to Talley that she and Rose were tired of being handed crumbs in what appeared to be a bonanza with InnoVita. So much so that she and Rose were actually thinking about cashing out of Nomad to explore other avenues. But as soon as Talley suggested they head Legacy Pain Remedies, Inc., the Canadians seized the opportunity.

Nemesis now had two of its best agents running the show for one of Nomad's newest interests. In the months it took to get the new enterprise operational, Tina and Rose proved to be efficient and trustworthy. While Talley congratulated herself on her excellent choices in managing the company, the Canadians were feeding information back to Liz—names, numbers, and addresses to be cross-referenced with incoming data on Moon Enterprises and Qatari Acquisitions. By comparing the similarities, Warlock eliminated a mountain of data that didn't pertain directly to their quest and concentrated solely on persons and logistics most heavily involved with InnoVita.

LIKE ARI MOON, SULIMAN KUMAR STRIVED to keep his personal life a secret. It wouldn't do to have his followers know he profited greatly from the very entities they vowed to destroy. As a result of the resounding success of InnoVita, Suliman found it increasingly difficult to keep his identity obscure. His involvement with Ari Moon and Nomad added to his concern. Consequently, Suliman diverted from his current endeavor to work on something that was quite the opposite of his lifesaving virus formula.

For decades, scientists in Suliman's employ had experimented with and perfected deadly bioengineered agents that were tasteless and odorless. Recently, Suliman's scientists had created a versatile bioweapon designed to incapacitate and given it the Spanish name Muerte Lenta (slow death). The contagion, which had a short incubation period, could be dusted over targeted groups with drones or blended into over-the-counter remedies used to combat disease. Initial symptoms mocked those of a common cold. By the time a patient exhibited the full set of symptoms two to three days after exposure, they would be violently ill or near death.

Suliman needed the invisible ally in his arsenal, since his youngest and most enthusiastic followers were woefully inexperienced in actual combat. He would immunize his people against the effects of the contagion so they could simply walk in and take over from the debilitated victims. With the ability to destroy entire armies in the field and infect entire populations, Suliman was well on his way to his ultimate goal of worldwide superiority.

NOW THAT DESIREE RICHARDS WAS NO LONGER a factor, the rumor mill in the underworld wagered that either Ari Moon or Miles Stewart would take on the Nobilis Familia supreme leader role. Liz McCall put everyone at Nemesis headquarters on high alert to pay close attention to the activities of Miles and Ari. In the meantime, she revisited the history Nemesis had amassed on the two major players and their confederates. What she found was shockingly vague.

In his teens, Miles Stewart had numerous run-ins with the law and was known as a flimflam artist who dazzled and charmed his way out of trouble. Although he was picked up half a dozen times, the young man was never booked after his victims fell under his beguiling spell and dropped all criminal charges. Even though Miles attended classes at several colleges, he never graduated. However, he did accumulate enough on-the-job training on the street to support a reputation in the underworld as a learned, skillful operator. As his acumen blossomed, so did his notoriety as a guy who got things done. Shortly after his twenty-fifth birthday, Moon Enterprises hired him to be their chief facilitator, and he had been there ever since.

Ari Moon was a genuine enigma. Considering the kinds of lowlifes he did business with, Liz found it uncanny that Moon remained anonymous and free of scandal. Obviously, he was a master manipulator and delegated all the dirty work to others.

As she thumbed through the data on Ari and Miles, an interesting pair kept popping up—Eva Moreno and Victoria Novak. Liz noted that both had been promiscuous in their youth, lost their virginity in high school, and carried on to higher levels of sexuality in college in Northern California. They were not the most studious, but they were smart enough to make excellent grades. While attending Chico State, two-and-a-half hours by car from Napa, the two sexually adventurous lasses met up with Talley Marsh, who, in addition to her horse farm, ran a prosperous house of ill repute known as Slice of Heaven. Eva and Victoria joined Talley's stable of working girls and, before long, were the most requested pair.

What impressed Liz most about the two was that through thick and thin, Eva and Victoria stuck with Talley Marsh and her partner, Millie Snowden. Their loyalty paid off, and now the quartet sat on a pile of money—millions of dollars generated from caida libre and their newest venture, InnoVita.

After she studied their histories, Chairperson Liz McCall concluded there was an avenue she could use to peel back the layers of duplicity created by the genius behind it all—if the two vixens and Miles Stewart agreed to help. Eva and Victoria also had mercurial relationships with Ari Moon, Suliman Kumar, and Miles Stewart. Liz had to convince the bombshell beauties that they were in mortal danger from one or all of them and could be saved only if they clandestinely sided with Nemesis.

Liz suspected that the courtesans knew more about the rogues than any of the perps would have wished. From Liz's experience, statements made to individuals in the heat of passion or shared under the influence of alcohol or drugs were parked in the recipient's brain, on recall when needed. In search of advice, she shared her perspective with her grandfather. Trey listened without interruption, then added his own twist to entice the girls to cooperate.

"Why don't you mix things up a bit? Haul the girls in on international prostitution charges and assorted felonious activities," Trey suggested to Liz. Then, with a wry smile, he added, "That ought to stir the pot."

"I knew I could count on you to have the perfect solution." Liz chortled and gave her grandpa a hug.

JUST BEFORE DAWN THE NEXT MORNING at their chateau in Albania, Eva and Victoria were taken prisoner and flown to a safe house outside the beltline in Dallas. Clueless about where they were or why they were there, they were kept in seclusion for a couple of days. Frightened, confused, and isolated in separate rooms, the prisoners had no idea who their captors were.

The timing of the abduction could not have been better. The night before the girls were removed from Albania, they were involved in a vocal altercation at The Castle. Without forewarning, Ari Moon had rudely informed the aging hussies that they were being replaced with younger models. Their pleas fell on deaf ears as they were unceremoniously shown the door. For the girls to be treated in such an irreverent manner after giving body and soul to the cause was unforgivable. Neither spoke a word on the ride back to their quarters, their minds too occupied with thoughts of vengeance.

With all that transpired in such a short period, it was understandable that the captives were completely thrown off balance. When Liz and Trey McCall showed up, Eva and Victoria were guided into the interrogation room, where their blindfolds were removed.

Victoria straightened her rumpled clothes and began to rant. "Okay, assholes. What in the hell is going on here? If you're some kind of cops or feds, nobody read us our rights or any kind of shit like that. We're going to sue your asses until they bleed, you got that? And if this is some kind of sick joke of Ari's, he can just fuck off."

Liz countered in a tone that demanded respect. "Whoa, hold your horses there, sweetheart, before you step in it any deeper. We know you two have been consorting with some of the world's most despicable international underworld figures. You best pay close attention to what I say from here on out. We've followed nearly every move you two have made, from Slice of Heaven to Sister Nation to Nomad and more," she exclaimed as she waved a handful of documents in Victoria's face. "We're willing to overlook the crimes in these reports, allegations that could land your happy asses behind bars for the rest of your lives. Now, do I have your full attention?"

Not a single peep escaped from the captives as they perused the legal documents Liz handed to them. From time to time, they looked up, trying to imagine how these two agents had been able to find out so much about them.

When Eva and Victoria finished reading the material, Eva

responded. "To be frank, before recent developments, Victoria and I would have fought you tooth and nail over your *allegations*. We might've even won. However, since we were rudely kicked to the curb by the most unappreciative bastards ever, we'd be willing to consider a reasonable deal—with one nonnegotiable caveat. Talley Marsh and Millie Snowden have been nothing but kind to us over the years. We'll cooperate if you extend your leniency to those two as well. That's it. Ball's in your court. Who are you guys, anyway? I recognize you from somewhere."

"*Wow, that was easier than I ever dreamed,*" thought Liz. Then she replied, "We used to be your biggest pain in the ass. I'm Liz, and this is my grandfather, Trey McCall of Nemesis. We're your new benefactors. So, if you have no objections, let's get you two to The Circle M and your new surroundings."

WHILE LIZ AND HER AGENTS CELEBRATED THEIR GOOD FORTUNE, Ari moped about in The Castle, suffering from a rare case of guilty conscience over how he had treated the girls. He decided to apologize. When his calls went unanswered, he got concerned and sent Miles down the mountain to the babes' chalet to bring them back to The Castle.

No one was there, and there was no note—nothing left to suggest where they went. There were just a couple of unmade beds and some dirty dishes in the sink. Miles rushed back to The Castle to deliver the news. Before he could finish, Ari went from concerned to rabid—ranting and pacing the great room.

How dare they go without letting me know? he thought, incensed to have the shoe on the other foot. After he drank a couple of double vodkas to calm down, the alcohol worked its way slowly through his system.

Somewhat sedated, Ari relaxed in his comfy, overstuffed leather chair in front of the fireplace. For an inordinate amount of time, he stared at the flames, which flickered as they swayed on the wooden logs, burning them down to smoke and ash in the belly of the fireplace. Shadows waltzed across the walls in rhythm to the music of an imagined symphony, imitating twirling couples circling the room.

Eventually, he spoke to his assistant. "Miles, what do you make of their abrupt departure? Think I'm blowing things out of proportion?"

"Can't say. I mean, they didn't take it well. That's a given. Still, it doesn't make sense that they would leave all their belongings behind. Even their suitcases were in the storage closet."

Ari raised his eyebrows, then remarked, "You don't think they would do something stupid, do you?"

"No clue. But there is that old saying about a woman scorned and all the malice that goes along with that," Miles countered.

"So, how much do you figure they know about us and our operation?" Ari asked in a petulant tone.

"My guess, it would be pretty much everything. You've got to remember that we sent them all over the world to promote caida libre and InnoVita brands. Hell, they probably know almost everyone we do business with, and on a personal basis."

"Oh my God. We are so screwed. If they squeal on us, there's nowhere on Earth we can hide. It's imperative that we locate them ASAP," Ari Moon said with a lost expression frozen on his face.

FOLLOWING A RECORD-BREAKING MONTH of InnoVita sales—well over $40 million—Suliman Kumar seized on an opportunity to expand the presence of his global movement in the United States. Bellevue,

Washington—a suburb of Seattle—was one of the fastest-growing areas in the Northwest, home to some of the most cutting-edge cyber-related companies in the world. It was also Rife with a radical attitude that, in no time, made it a mecca for young, obsessed anarchists and the malcontents that Suliman's extremist army vetted as new members.

Before long, the movement had established its own headquarters on a piece of property east of Bellevue near Snoqualmie Ridge. It had been purchased by a subsidiary of a faux company owned by an international syndicate in Eastern Europe. The recruits were lodged in condo-style dormitories with modern amenities in what amounted to a country club for terrorists.

CHAIRPERSON LIZ MCCALL LEARNED of the compound from data Warlock picked up while monitoring Suliman's recent conversations. With InnoVita's overnight success, Suliman's revolutionary movement gained popularity exponentially. Liz's instinct was to infiltrate Suliman's mercenary training camp as soon as possible. It was imperative that Nemesis monitor the progress of this menacing force. She selected two of her youngest looking agents, Seth Collins and Rebecca (Becca) Evans, for the mission. Both were experienced retired military veterans in their late twenties who could easily pass for college students on the GI Bill. Following a brief strategy meeting in her office, Liz dispatched Seth and Becca to Bellevue.

It was pouring down rain when they landed in Seattle. A normal half-hour drive from SeaTac Airport to Bellevue took over an hour in the deluge.

At least they were dry—that is, until they exited their car at the downtown Westin and were drenched by a sudden flurry of windswept rainwater. Uncomfortably chilled by the wetness, they gratefully checked into the hotel and went up to their connecting rooms on the third floor, which faced downtown. Each room had a spacious balcony from which to enjoy glorious sunsets covering picturesque Lake Washington in a soft pink glow.

Anxious to get down to business, Seth and Becca were up with the sun in the morning. Most of the day, the agents appeared to hunt for jobs while they familiarized themselves with their surroundings and established landmarks to map out escape routes. In keeping with their cover, they visited several cyber-tech company websites, where they submitted their personal information and resumes. They received the same response from each company—if management was interested, they'd receive notification via text within five working days.

While making the rounds of the websites, Becca and Seth made it a point to check out the companies' dress codes. Pacific Coast casual was the main theme. Guys wore mostly button-down shirts (no tie), khakis, loafers (no socks), and casual jackets. Women wore jeans or pantsuits, pullover sweaters, Italian designer boots, and designer jackets. A chichi vibe of laid-back poise and certainty mixed in with arrogance prevailed among the companies they contacted.

On their fourth night, Seth's phone vibrated on the nightstand. It was a text message from one of the biggest and most popular companies in the cyber world. Short, sweet, and to the point, it informed him that Mr. Frost would like to meet with him and Becca at ten sharp the following morning in his office on the top floor, suite 1051, of a building only a short distance from the Westin.

At nine forty-five a.m. the next day, the properly attired couple parked their car in a visitor's slot in the company parking garage, passed through security, and took the elevator to the top floor. Dressed to fit the role, Seth had gone with a light-blue patterned shirt, khakis, tan loafers, and a tan suede-and-leather jacket. Becca had donned tan pants, a tight baby-blue cashmere sweater, beige Italian loafers, a dark-blue soft leather jacket with a faux fox collar, and Maui Jim sunglasses.

At the stroke of ten, Mr. Frost's secretary opened the suite door to find the two expected visitors seated on bench chairs across from the suite. With a fake smile pasted on her face, she motioned for them to come inside and have a seat in Mr. Frost's office while she hunted him down, then went to make coffee.

Moments later, Mr. Frost walked in. Seth introduced himself and Becca, which Frost acknowledged by nodding. Then he took his seat behind his desk. Patiently, Frost waited while his perky little secretary set a tray of coffee on a table in front of them and left through a side door. After they each fixed a cup and retook their seats, Frost cleared his throat.

"Alrighty then, where to begin. First, let's get down to why I invited you here today. My team took a detailed look into both of your histories. I hope you don't mind, but we need to be extremely thorough in this day and age because of what may be asked of you if you accept our offer. We noticed that both of you are veterans of a war that, by your own admission, neither of you believed was necessary. Your welcome home was nonexistent, as if the country you fought for had no appreciation for what you sacrificed to preserve its beliefs. Am I right so far?" Frost studied their reactions.

Secretly thankful to the Nemesis team for adjusting their histories, Seth and Becca hung their heads as they nodded yes.

Frost continued. "No one likes to be taken for granted, used, then discarded like yesterday's garbage. We understand and empathize with your plight. I've been given the honor to invite you both to join an incredibly elite team where you can use the skills you've honed over the years for the good of humanity. If you are interested, I would be happy to show you our brand-new campus, which is a bit of a drive from here but worth it. Think it over, discuss it between yourselves, and let me know within the next twenty-four hours. I realize the details are vague at this point, but I can assure you both that my offer is tailor-made for your talents. Here is a number you can use to deliver your answer. Address your text message to Frost. Then I'll get back to you at the Westin within the hour."

Before he ushered them to the elevator, Frost handed Seth a card with only a phone number on it. From a meeting that lasted less than half an hour, it was clear the man was not interested in having a conversation. He was only feeling them out for a third party. No doubt the meeting had been recorded, and their reactions were probably already being studied. Frost's knowledge that they were at the Westin proved they were being surveilled. This was the real deal. The reason Nemesis had sent them to Washington State.

SHORTLY AFTER SETH AND BECCA DEPARTED his office, Frost was off to the compound, where Suliman Kurar waited to hear firsthand what Frost made of the couple. By the time Frost arrived, Suliman had listened to the recording and reviewed the video. He was pleased with how smoothly Frost handled everything. From what Suliman observed, Seth and Becca were an ideal fit for their program. Since they were a bit older and had a great deal more real-life experience than most of the recruits, the novices would look up to them for advice and counseling. Since they had been scorned by their country, it would be simpler to indoctrinate the couple into the fold. As an additional precaution, Frost had their rooms expertly swept for electronics and weapons, and their possessions were thoroughly searched. Documents found in the room safe were photographed. Everything checked out. No red flags.

As the conspirators ended their conversation, the burner phone in Frost's pocket vibrated. A smile crossed his face, and then he read out loud, "Frost, we've decided to 'tentatively' accept your offer pending more in-depth disclosure from your side."

"I like these guys. They got balls. I want them on our side. Whatever it takes. You got that, Frosty?" Suliman exclaimed as Frost left to make it happen.

WHILE BECCA PUT THE FINISHING TOUCHES on a BLT from room service, the hotel phone on the nightstand rang. Not to appear too anxious, she answered on the third ring. It was Mr. Frost with good news.

"Congratulations, my dear. My superiors have accepted you two. I've rearranged my schedule to meet with you at ten a.m. tomorrow in my office to fill in any blanks. It will be nothing you probably haven't heard before in training. Although, we do owe you an explanation of what we expect. See you at ten?" Frost inquired, more as an order than a request.

"Yes, sir. We'll be there at ten sharp. Oh, and thank you, sir, for this opportunity," Becca replied in military fashion.

MR. FROST WAS SEATED AT HIS DESK when his less-than-efficient secretary showed Seth and Rebecca into his office. He stood up to welcome them back, sat back heavily into his chair, and immediately got down to business.

"I'm so glad you two have tentatively joined us. It's now my duty to seal the deal, if you will. Please allow me to outline our mission and what part you two will play to achieve our goal," Frost articulated as he set up the agenda for the meeting.

For the next twenty or so minutes, Mr. Frost went into vague details about what the movement stood for and hoped to bring to the world. It was a massively distorted, flowery description. Complete bullshit covered with whipped cream. And Seth and Becca pretended to eat it up. They looked back and forth at each other, smiling and nodding approval at every selling point the man emphasized. At the end of his dissertation, Frost asked if they had any questions.

"Since you asked, I have a few questions," Seth said. "First, just as a point of protocol, how are we supposed to address you? Second, when will we have an opportunity to meet the leader of the movement? And finally, what exactly will our responsibilities entail? Becca and I are highly trained operatives. We don't want to sign on as babysitters to a bunch of pansies looking for a safe place to hide when the shit hits the fan." He responded in a manner he expected Mr. Frost would respect.

"I'll answer your questions in the order they were given. You're to address me as Mr. Frost or just plain Frost. I seriously doubt you'll ever meet the leader face-to-face or even know his true name. I've been with the movement for nearly five years and still have no idea who the leader is. Finally, Seth and Rebecca, you can rest assured that, with your experience, there's no way you'll be delegated to babysit anyone. You could possibly be bodyguards but never babysitters." Frost spoke matter-of-factly, then abruptly adjourned the meeting with a call to his assistant.

On their way back to the Westin, Seth and Becca rehashed the brief meeting with Frost. Neither bought one single word of his recruiting speech. If one-tenth of it was true, it would be miraculous. No matter. They were in, and that was all that counted. Before they left for their mission, Liz had cautioned them not to contact Nemesis on their personal devices or the hotel phones. Whichever company hired the two agents, there was no doubt that it would be child's play for them to monitor cell phones, personal computers, and hotel telecommunications. Which is exactly what the company Mr. Frost represented did. But since their arrival, Frost's goons had found nothing in the couple's communications that was remotely unusual or suspicious.

AFTER A FEW WEEKS OF INGESTING INTENSE, mind-bending propaganda, Seth and Becca were disturbed by what was passed off as a peaceful movement. There was a vast difference between what the Suliman cause promised and what it delivered. Indoctrination counselors pressed a constant cynical rhetoric to convert the unenlightened. They said it was imperative to disregard the old ways that no longer fit the new societal norm. To implement change, the movement enlisted force and fear. Their utopian ideal could not be achieved unless the unworthy were severely dealt with. The doctrines were contradictory to everything Seth and Becca believed in; it would take all the discipline they could muster to maintain their ruse.

Maintaining their cover, Liz's agents pursued their mission by slowly and systematically tearing down the terrorist instructors' hold over the recruits. Then they subtly created doubts, questioned flaws in the doctrine, and confused issues. Seth and Becca worked one-on-one with trainees, out of earshot of the crowd. It was not a simple assignment, being under a microscope held by a skittish upper tier. It was for that very reason that Liz chose them—they had the patience and the moxie to pull it off.

Confident the Northwest situation was in good hands, Liz turned her attention to undermining the Nobilis Familia.

ON THE HOME FRONT, LIZ HANDED her new informants over to Tara and Miranda, Nemesis's cybercrime experts. Delighted with their agreement for immunity, Eva and Victoria worked tirelessly with the cybercrime experts. Complaining of paper cuts and broken fingernails, the four of them meticulously sorted through files on Moon Enterprises clients the escorts had made contact with over the years. Between the caida libre and InnoVita, the volume of names was staggering. Eventually, they whittled the list down to fifty solid individuals of interest. After that, Warlock stockpiled loads of useful business and personal data on each of the contacts in question, gathering details from deep-web search engines and social media. One contact in particular was a sitting member of Parliament who supplemented his income by supplying prostitutes from different parts of the world to the wealthy aristocracy. Another sold arms to the highest bidder on the black market.

Miranda fed the contact names and data into a separate Warlock AI program to organize a POI (person of interest) dossier on each name. Tara and Miranda then worked up a profile for every person. The sisters completed half the files before they ran out of steam. By midmorning the next day, they finished the remainder and delivered them to Liz's office. As she perused the rogues' gallery of files, Liz chuckled to herself and wondered if Ari and Miles had any idea what a shitstorm they had created for themselves and their associates when they canned Victoria and Eva.

Liz figured she had piled up enough dirt on the most influential Nobilis Familia members and decided it was the right time to anonymously leak it to the media—her first step in building distrust between Ari and Miles. It wouldn't take much since Miles already sensed an unsettling change in Ari's attitude.

CHAPTER 4

AT THE CIRCLE M, REANNA APPROACHED their second child's due date. Liz McCall was going to have a little brother two decades her junior. The entire ranch population was atwitter, expecting Davis McCall to make his appearance any day. Reanna was the most excited of all. Having carried him to full term, she was ready for some relief.

There would be no shortage of love for the newest addition—not in this family, that was for sure. Born on October 25, Davis was a Scorpio, giving the family another stubborn personality to deal with in the future. He received the same welcome to the community his older sister had, and he responded much like Liz had by frowning, burping, and soiling his diaper. The most astonishing thing about Davis's appearance was that the boy was the spitting image of Mac McCall.

After a few weeks, Reanna suggested that Jefferson and Trey take a break, such as playing a tournament or two on the Tour. She had Liz to help with Davis, and they would all be fine. Plus, the guys could see if what they'd been working on at the range stood up under the gun.

It was obvious to her that they were antsy, as both had doted on her throughout her pregnancy. They needed a hiatus. Minutes after Reanna made her pitch, Jefferson was on the phone to the Tour office to commit for the next two events. Then he headed to Trey's office to tell him the news. The first event was at Westchester Country Club in New York; the next was outside Memphis, Tennessee, at the TPC Southwind.

A CLASSIC OLD-SCHOOL COURSE DESIGNED by Walter Travis that opened for play in 1922, Westchester Country Club had all the ingredients both Trey and Jefferson wished to incorporate into their golf courses. It was built on rolling, rocky terrain, offering few level lies in the fairways. The poa annua greens were tiny, with subtle undulations and minute plateaus tucked in the corners. It was a shotmaker's golf course and right up Jefferson's alley.

The two men stayed in one of the two-bedroom suites at Westchester Country Club's hotel. News traveled fast that the McCalls were on-site. Jefferson spent the first part of the week accepting the congrats and ribbing from fellow players on the birth of Davis. He had never heard himself being referred to as the "old man" so often. It was a blast to be back with the guys again. Jefferson was overjoyed to have two weeks without the pressure to win or the sound of a baby crying. He was there to just freewheel it and let it fly. It felt so liberating.

Early on, Jefferson showed a bit of rust at Westchester but managed to make the thirty-six-hole cut on Friday. He and Trey stayed on the practice ground until dark, working on a move that Don January suggested to Trey when he was on Tour. It had to do with having the right hand on the takeaway to set the club properly at the top of the swing—a little something Ben Hogan mentioned to January back in the day. The tip worked marvelously for Jefferson for the weekend. The "old man" held up nicely, finishing off his final round with an eagle three on the last to win by four strokes over a stellar field.

The following week, he and Trey traveled to TPC Southwind. Memphis had always been one of Jefferson's favorite stops since it was there. As a rookie, he had secured his Tour card for the next year with a second-place finish. During the week, Jefferson maintained his free swinging style, only to lose to a birdie on the last—a second brides-maid finish for him in the event. Nonetheless, *it was an awesome two weeks of golf.*

On the flight back from Tennessee to the airstrip at the ranch, Jefferson asked his dad candidly, "So, why didn't you tell me about that right-hand stuff years ago? No telling how many more tournaments I could have won."

Trey snickered as he replied, "None, I would wager. You see, I've watched you use that move most of your entire career. Don't you see? That's why it was so easy for you to incorporate it back into your swing. Your mind just needed a gentle nudge back in the right direction."

AS HE SAT IN HIS JEEP out on his Texas Hill Country property, Bryce Lonagon studied the majestic landscape. The Central Texas under-taking at Whispering Canyons was Bryce's boldest venture yet. Two eighteen-hole golf courses and a nine-hole par three in the works was a lot on anyone's plate. Even he agreed that any more would be too much. That was before he discovered a heavenly spot tucked away among a series of draws and canyons nearly invisible from the air and ground. Created by nature at the end of a box canyon, a spectacular two-hundred-foot waterfall spilled spring water into a collection pool twenty feet deep. It was shaded by ancient cypress trees sprinkled along its banks, and he had never seen a more bewitching place to beat the heat of a summer day or escape from the world for a while.

He envisioned himself swinging out on a rope securely affixed to a sturdy tree limb and dropping like a stone into the cool, clear water, then enjoying a picnic in the shade on the grassy bank. He imagined what it would be like to hole up in a log cabin along the shore and let the burble of the waterfall gently lull him to sleep. *The Cabin.* That's what he would call it—a secret hydro-powered sanctuary reserved for family. He thought it might come in handy one day. Lord knows he didn't need another project, but this one wouldn't be a chore. It would be a pleasure.

BACK FROM THE TOUR AND ANXIOUS TO RETURN to their consulting roles at Whispering Canyons, Trey and Jefferson sat down in the construction site office to discuss some fresh design ideas with Matt Bremer and Bryce Lonagon. Only Bryce wasn't there.

"Where's the boss?" Jefferson asked Matt.

"I don't rightly know," the architect replied. "He hasn't been around here much at all. Seems to be preoccupied with a new project somewhere else on the property. That's all I know. Oh, he did say that we were doing a bang-up job and he didn't want to get in the way."

CHAPTER 5

MEANWHILE, THERE WAS GOOD NEWS on the home front for Liz and her cybercrime-fighting team. Based upon her intuition, expert profiling, a little luck, and just plain human nature, Liz's prognostications proved to be spot on. Sinister factions threatening the free world began to experience what their organizers referred to as growing pains that, in reality, were carefully orchestrated maneuvers by Nemesis meant to wreak havoc and discord.

Seeing as they were more interested in quantity than quality, the extremist groups didn't foresee what was coming. Nemesis took advantage of the situation. Little things began to go wrong. Messages were lost or misplaced, deliveries were sent to wrong destinations, directions to rallies were altered—and all were cause for concern among the ranks. Singularly, these were a nuisance. Collectively, they posed an issue as to the competence of the founders, directors, and staff. The leaders of the guerilla forces could ill afford to have their members question their leadership. Any hint of rebellion within the ranks could easily result in mass mutiny. Once the impatient generation of anar-chists abandoned a cause, they lost interest entirely and turned their attention to the next *breaking news* crisis.

As Liz expected, Ari Moon and Miles Stewart were pressured by their elite clients and hit hard by the upturn of negative publicity aimed at their cause and demographic. Supposedly, the Nobilis Familia controlled the media; if so, Ari and Miles wondered where the hell all this unfavor-able propaganda was coming from. In the past, Miles would have gone straight to Ari about the issue. However, as of late, he had lost faith in his mentor. Frankly, he did not trust the man. Miles suspected Ari was setting him up as the fall guy. Ari Moon was so well insulated that he was invisible. Miles Stewart was totally exposed—out front and on point.

ARI'S CHOICE TO REMAIN IN THE SHADOWS worked to near perfec-tion for a tremendously long time. The biggest drawback was the loneliness that accompanied it. He had no family, no true friends, no intimate significant others—nothing but a pipe dream and a pot full of money to fund his folly. The unbearable loneliness contributed to costly miscalculations on his part. Stirred by the feminine wiles of Eva and Victoria, Ari had taken them in, believing they had genuine feelings for him. He had confided in them and shared far too much sensitive information. Now that the girls were on the lam, he was not only lonely but extremely angry and depressed. Angry that he had let his desires dominate his common sense. Depressed because he had been taken in so easily. He no longer trusted anyone, including his right-hand man, Miles Stewart.

The irony was how rapidly they distanced themselves from one another, considering how beautifully Ari and Miles worked together in the past. Due to the adverse information that the Nemesis Warlock program fed to the media, animosity between and toward Ari and Miles spun exponentially out of control. Ari and Miles, like so many others who were unceremoniously cast aside, no longer held any status in the world of the advantaged elite.

Reacting to the law of unintended consequences, Nemesis provided an avenue of retribution for persons snubbed by the Nobilis Familia. For those willing to present irrefutable evidence of criminal activities within the organization, Nemesis would see to it that the respondents received protection and relocation.

A fair number of the renegade contingent realized the jig was up. In addition to Nemesis, international law enforcement agencies and the mob were closing in on them from every corner of the globe. Most of the elitist clan who'd protected the maverick operators in the past were in deeper trouble than the operatives and left them high and dry. Suspected felons with no viable alternatives turned to Nemesis for sanctuary in exchange for inside information on the Nobilis Familia. In the majority of interrogations, when perps were asked who ran the organization, the answer was Miles Stewart—not Ari Moon.

MILES'S GREATEST FEARS WERE COMING TRUE. Groundwork was in place to cast all the blame on him. He had stayed too long, his greed was too great, and his face was known to almost all the people standing in line to identify him as the ringleader. He could ill afford to resign himself to surrender. It would be his word against scores of clients who had never had the pleasure of meeting or talking to the mysterious Ari Moon. For all they knew, the man was no more than a figment of Miles's vivid imagination. He could describe the man to them, but he had no pictures; he could swear the man was the owner of a villa in Puerto Vallarta and The Castle in Albania, but Miles's name was on both bills of sale and the title documents. There was no mention of Ari Moon anywhere. Over the years, Ari visited his office suites alone and only at night. Save for Eva and Victoria, there were no other employees who could vouch that they'd laid eyes on the man. Had it been Ari's objective all along to set up Miles Stewart as the fall guy? If not, it was one hell of a coincidence.

Where on earth could Miles go to vanish? California was a pleasant place to get lost for a while. So Miles flew privately out of Albania to Palm Springs. From there, he rented a car and drove to Indio to lie low while he transformed his appearance. He was letting his hair grow, as well as his beard, and he decided on hazel-colored contact lenses. At a thrift store, Miles replaced his wardrobe with secondhand garments, a well-worn pair of boots, and a cracked leather bomber jacket. On the way out of the shop, he spotted sneakers in a barrel marked half-price, and he purchased a pair with the most tread on the bottoms. Next door, in an Army Navy store, he bought two pairs of dark aviator glasses, a Swiss army knife, a knapsack, and a duffle to carry his gear.

Then he checked into a dated but clean one-story mom-and-pop motel, making sure his room was not visible from the street. He slipped inside to leave all his purchases, except for the duffle, until his return. Systematically, Miles made the rounds to various banks where he had accounts and took out substantial but not alarming amounts of cash so as not to raise any questions. Back inside his car, he stuffed the money into a large pillowcase and placed it in the duffle.

After his last withdrawal, Miles left his rental car running with the keys in it on a side street a block and a half from his motel, hoisted the duffle over his shoulder, and walked back to his room. Then he sorted out his things and put most away in drawers and the small closet near the bathroom, wanting the room to look tidy but not overly so—as if its occupant was ex-army and still used to old regimens while blending back into society.

Earlier, Miles moved the bed over a few feet from its original position and carefully pried one of the wooden floorboards away from all sides until he could lift out the four-foot-long board. There was enough space underneath to place the majority of the money, along with his weapons and ammo, which he had bought from one of the dudes at the Army Navy store after hours. Miles checked the exact position of the two nine mils, magazines of ammo, and the cash in his hidey-hole. Then he replaced the board, swept some of the dust that had been under the bed to cover the top, and slid the bed back to its original position. He checked closely to make sure nothing was out of place.

Satisfied all was well, he pocketed some cash and went out to explore the area on foot. Midafternoon, he walked into a bar along the strip to escape the heat and grab a beer. He spied two used car lots across the street where he could scope out a new ride. There was no big hurry—his hair and beard still had some growing to do. Miles kind of liked his new hippie façade, as did a weathered floozy at the end of the bar. She sashayed over in slow motion to make sure he took her all in. The bartender rolled his eyes as he recognized a scene he had witnessed on too many occasions. This time, the old boy was in for a surprise.

Miles shook his head as she approached, got down off the barstool, and vamoosed out the door. The woman stopped mid-stride and flipped him off, too late for Miles to see as he headed outside. The last thing he needed at this time in his life was a woman clouding the picture even more. He cleared the door just in time to hear a glass break as it smashed into the doorframe. Hurriedly, he scurried down the street into an old-fashioned hamburger joint and ducked inside.

The smell of cooking beef and greasy French fries reminded him how hungry he was. He ordered two jumbo cheeseburgers and fries, along with a large chocolate shake. Miles glanced out the window in time to see the woman from the bar cruising the boulevard looking for him, the top down on her pink Cadillac convertible as she scoped out both sides of the road. Miles ducked down just in time. The cute girl behind the counter burst out laughing as he watched the insane fool in the pink Caddy make one more pass before the driver gunned the engine, laying rubber as she skidded out of town.

Sensing his anguish, the waitress informed Miles that the madwoman behind the wheel of the pink Caddy was the mayor's daughter Rowena—a woman used to getting her way.

Miles took his time eating. Every so often, he checked outside to see if the Pepto-mobile was back. He had ordered an inordinate amount of food and was surprised he finished it all, making that recognizable sound of finality when the last of the shake left the bottom of the glass. Miles gave the cute girl a nice tip and a thumbs-up, then strolled back to his room at the motel, staying mindful to look and listen for the pink Caddy.

Once inside his room, he locked and bolted the door. Then he moved the bed to make sure no one had messed with his stash in its hiding place. Everything was there just as he had left it. Miles removed a nine-mil Glock and two magazines to keep under his pillow, then replaced the board and moved the bed. He called the front desk and asked if he had any messages or inquiries.

"Only one, sir. Rowena, who inquired if we had someone matching your description staying here." The clerk chuckled. "When I said we didn't, she left in a huff, mumbling a tirade of profanities under her breath."

Miles laughed and thanked the clerk profusely, reminding himself to leave a genuine token of his appreciation.

THE NEXT MORNING, THE DESK CLERK was all smiles when Miles slipped him a crisp one-hundred-dollar bill. Then Miles Stewart was off with a pocket full of cash, ready to buy one of the cars that caught his eye in Big Earl's Quality Used Cars lot. Big Earl was more miniature than giant and had a gift of gab that mimicked a Bourbon Street barker in New Orleans. After bartering for close to an hour, Miles took a 1998 Lexus LS 400 coup for a test drive—a cream-colored beauty with two hundred thousand miles on the odometer.

Miles stopped at Chen's Automotive to get it inspected before he shelled out the asking price of $3,750 cash. Tobias Chen ranted on about hating Earl for stiffing him on a number of previous deals, so Miles knew he would get an honest appraisal. The mechanic told him that two hundred thousand miles on a Lexus was just getting it broken in. After he checked the car stem to stern, Chen found a couple of minor computer chip issues, but he assured Miles he could easily fix. He told Miles that for less than $1,000, he could have the Lexus running like a top. As his form of revenge, Tobias recommended Miles offer Earl $3,000 cash for the car.

The sale went down for $3,500.

As Miles pulled onto the street, he passed the pink Caddy going the other way and ducked down instinctively. Rowena Graves, the mayor's daughter, was a woman unaccustomed to being shot down. Lucky for Miles, she did not recognize him in the Lexus; it was obvious she was still on the prowl. Miles would have to play this cat-and-mouse game for a few more days. As soon as Tobias Chen finished refurbishing Miles's new wheels, he would move on down the road.

He asked the motel manager to inform him if the mayor's daughter made any further inquiries, promising a generous tip for the service. For two-and-a-half days, Miles remained in his room, dining on fast-food deliveries, until Chen phoned to tell him the Lexus was ready. For a nominal fee, Chen agreed to deliver the car to his room at the back of the motel.

When Chen asked him where he was headed, Miles replied honestly. "Haven't given it much thought, my friend. Not a clue, really. Just someplace east of trouble."

Two hours later, Miles Stewart was halfway through southern Nevada on his way toward Arizona. He was in no hurry, figuring he would know where he was going when he got there. His physical appearance had changed drastically. His beard and long hair were now thick and unruly. Fat had turned to muscle, giving him a wiry, healthy physique. And his wardrobe more closely resembled a down-and-out man's than a multimillionaire's. He could comfortably pass as a bereft soldier returning from foreign wars with no job and little direction, able to easily melt into society where nobody noticed, nobody cared. With the boring hum of the road, a thought popped to mind. He had come up with an idea—a way to disappear.

Miles had a massive amount of money from his and Ari's scams that he had squirreled away, distributed in major banks across the country under assumed names—with a flawless fake ID for each.

He pulled off the interstate at the next rest stop to think without distraction. The more he thought about it, the better he liked it. Why not stop into branch offices of those banks and withdraw as much money as he could without raising suspicion? He put his scheme to work in small towns along his route east. By the time he crossed the Texas state line, he had accumulated over $5 million in cash to add to what he already had with him. In a few cases, he had to hang around for a day or two for them to corral such large sums of money, but since he kept a sizeable amount in each bank, no one complained or became suspicious.

For the bankers who questioned his appearance, he gave a sad story about being a rich kid who'd volunteered for the army and was sent to Afghanistan to fight. His outfit was caught in an ambush, his buddies were massacred in front of him, and he was left for dead. Fortunate to be discovered in a pile of bodies, Miles suffered from severe shock and exposure. The army expedited him back home to a VA hospital for treatment and released him only a few months earlier. He lost track of his family during the confusion, only to be told they'd all died in a private plane crash while he was deployed. His parents were well-to-do and left all their worldly goods to their children, which meant him, since his siblings perished in the crash. All he wanted to do now was find a quiet place to nestle down and figure out what to do with what was left of his life. It was a moving *tale*. However, it was an excellent way to silence further queries.

Heading northeast on I-10 outside Kerrville, Texas, Miles noticed a sign for a town called Comfort. *Interesting name for a town*, he thought, then took the exit to check it out. On the feeder road, he pulled into a Dairy Queen to get a burger and a shake. While chowing down on his lunch, he glanced across the street. Could it be fate that he spied a real estate office right next to a Chase Bank (an institution in which he had his largest account)? He had been looking for a Chase branch office to make his final withdrawal, so when he finished his meal, he drove over and walked in.

Astonished at the size of Miles's withdrawal, Charley Granger, the president of the bank, introduced himself and invited Miles into his office. Charley took a seat behind his desk and graciously apologized that his bank did not keep that kind of money on hand. But he assured Miles that he would be happy to have the cash for him by noon the next day. While they waited for the money, Charley offered to put Miles up in a bed-and-breakfast for the night and show him around the charming historic burg.

Miles took the man up on his offer, found the area to be charming, and ended up staying longer than one day.

As it turned out, Charley owned the real estate business next to the bank. To pass the time before the money arrived, he showed Miles some of the ranch land that was available around Comfort. One particular property caught Miles's eye: close to a hundred acres sitting high above a tributary of the Guadalupe River. It belonged to one of the original families that had settled outside Comfort. The most recent owners had passed away, and their kids were not interested in the ranch or the sedate pace of small-town life. The property came with a brand-new barn and a beautiful, refurbished two-story main house updated with modern fixtures and appliances.

Miles picked up his money from the bank the next afternoon. But instead of leaving town, he decided to stick around for a while. Something about that land perched up above the Guadalupe captured his attention. So much so, he came back to the property every day for a week. Each time he walked around it, Miles discovered more he liked about the location. It was remote, and all points of entry could easily be monitored from the high ground.

Charley Granger didn't have to put the hard sell on Miles. But he sealed the deal by offering the property to him at its lowest asking price with a very attractive 3.5 percent interest rate. It wasn't that Charley liked him that much or wanted to do him any favors; it was a hard piece of land for the real estate agent to move because it was a major pain in the ass to get to. Which made it perfect for what Miles had in mind and way too good an opportunity to pass up.

Charley drew up the papers, and Miles became the proud owner of Riverview Crest. All the transactions were done using the alias attached to his Chase account.

IN HIS MAD SEARCH FOR MILES, ARI MOON hoped to find him in Mexico, but he didn't. First, Eva and Victoria went MIA. Now, he couldn't raise Miles Stewart. He had sent encrypted messages as well as private investigators to every location he thought Miles might be, but no dice.

Ari wasn't used to making his own arrangements for anything. He was lost and very much alone. *Perhaps a drink would calm me down*, Ari thought. He went to his bar, poured two fingers of eighteen-year-old Jameson whiskey neat, and downed it. Then a second. Woozy, he went to Miles Stewart's quarters to search them thoroughly for a cell phone, an iPad, anything connected to Miles's name that he had used to communicate with the outside world.

In a drawer in Miles's closet, he found an old address book. In it, he located the name of a travel agency he recognized. He called to book a private jet and arrange auto transportation at both ends, from Puerto Vallarta to Tirana, Albania. The person taking the reservation mistook him for Miles Stewart because of the phone number and asked if he wished the transaction to be billed to his personal account for reimbursement from his company as per usual. Ari nodded vehemently and mumbled a positive response.

In Ari's safe, he discovered an about-to-expire passport issued to an alias he used sparingly. Pressured from all sides, he was running to the only place left in the world where he felt safe and secure—Albania. Surely, he could coax a few of the old guard who had power, money, and influence to join him.

The first order of business was to get to The Castle. After a six-thou-sand-mile, nine-hour flight from Puerto Vallarta, the G550 landed in Tirana, Albania. A customs agent met the private jet on the tarmac and came aboard to check Ari's passport and ask him the usual ques-tions as to why he came to Albania and for how long. While studying Ari's passport, the agent stared at the document for an uncomfortable length of time—as if something was amiss. Finally, the customs official stamped the passport and handed it to Ari with a warning that the passport was about to expire and that Ari needed to renew it at his earliest convenience. With another private plane taxiing in, the agent gruffly wished Ari a good day and quickly hustled down the exit stairs to meet the new arrival.

An hour later, Ari Moon sat in front of a roaring fire in the great room at his Albanian sanctuary. The service staff who warmly greeted him upon his arrival were paid handsomely for their allegiance. Ari inquired about Miles, but the staff had nothing to add to the mystery. Miles was not at all popular with the help. The fact was, most of them hated him for how he maligned and berated them while he pranced around giving orders during the outlandish shindigs he hosted at The Castle.

After a while, Ari went to the bedroom suite to lie down. He asked to be awakened at eight thirty p.m. and requested a beef steak and fresh vegetables, accompanied by a hearty red wine. Dinner was served in the great room at nine p.m. sharp in front of the fireplace to cut the chill. Famished after a long, tension-filled day, Ari devoured the extra-rare steak, the sides of asparagus and new potatoes, and most of the red wine. Afterward, he enjoyed several snifters of brandy and a Cuban cigar by the fire. A grandfather clock in the great room chimed ten times when an inebriated Ari Moon retired to his bedroom, where he fell asleep as soon as his head hit the pillow.

Following nine hours of undisturbed shut-eye, Ari woke up early and attempted to contact Miles Stewart to no avail. No doubt the man was in the wind. Ari then called members he believed to be loyal followers of the Nobilis Familia but was shocked at how few took his call. He had become a pariah, put on ignore, hung out to dry, and left to fend for himself. That's when he realized how much he had grown to rely on Miles Stewart over the years. Miles handled everything from exotic parties to hiring mercenaries.

To add to Ari's angst, all of Miles's files were encrypted and password protected, and Ari didn't have the passwords to unlock them. Luckily, he remembered the combination of the safe down in the dungeon that held millions of dollars in currency reserves—enough to hire a small army to defend the Albanian fortress. It was always a huge gamble to deal with mercenaries. Historically, their loyalty was to the money, not the person or the cause. If he couldn't recruit enough faithfuls from his declining membership, he would have no choice.

Only a handful of ardent followers agreed to come to The Castle to discuss a plan to reinvent the family and pursue their abject beliefs—a dismal turnout for such a grand cause. None of the loyalists wielded enough power through wealth or influence to make much of a difference. However, one did have ties to the mob—meaning access to arms and soldiers for hire. It was the only dim light at the end of a lengthy tunnel, but at least it was a beginning. All could be turned around.

THE CYBERCRIME LAB PICKED UP a lot of unusual chatter back and forth from Albania. In the past, all communications from that number were handled by Miles Stewart, but the most recent calls were initiated by Ari Moon. One curious aspect piqued Liz's curiosity. A majority of the parties Ari called were far beneath the status of characters with which Ari would usually associate, which suggested the Nemesis propaganda barrage launched against the Nobilis Familia was having its desired effect. It could be that Moon had taken refuge to retreat and rebuild. It was obvious by the number of times he tried to contact Miles that Ari considered him an essential element in any restructure scheme.

WHEN HE OPENED THE SAFE DOOR next to the dungeon and looked inside, Ari noticed that quite a bit of the cash was missing. But he had no idea how much. Miles was in charge of accounting and cash flow for The Castle. Another *How could I have been so stupid?* Ari added it to all the other crap cascading down upon him.

CHAPTER **6**

NEMESIS UNDERCOVER AGENTS Seth Collins and Becca Evans worked behind the scenes to undermine the mind-bending agenda conducted by Suliman's instructors on the recruits near Seattle. Oblivious to their traitorous actions, Mr. Frost praised Seth and Becca for going the extra mile to deal with the most difficult cadets in their spare time. Because of their perceived devotion to the movement, Frost gave them permission to leave campus if they cleared it with him. The first few times they ventured out, they were surveilled. But then their quarters were no longer searched. Scanning their environment at every turn, the agents didn't see a tail but knew not to let their guard down with people like Frost, who could turn on them in an instant.

LIZ MCCALL WAS PUZZLED when she received a call from Seth on a number she did not recognize. She was about to read him the riot act about secrecy when he explained how and why he had called. While he and Becca were browsing in a mobile phone store in Bellevue, Seth got the idea to ask the person waiting on him if he could call his mother in Texas to hear how the reception compared to his old phone. The girl smelled a sale and gave him the okay. She even let him take the phone into the back for some privacy.

On the other end of the line, Liz smiled about the freedoms Seth and Becca had earned from Frost and lauded her agents on their progress. Then Liz updated Seth on her plan to use on Suliman's crew a propaganda blitz similar to the one she had used on the Nobilis Familia. Her goal was to hit Qatar Acquisitions squarely in the pocketbook. Before she signed off, Liz instructed Seth to report to her if he or Becca observed any new and unusual activity on the campus.

SULIMAN WAS TAKEN COMPLETELY BY SURPRISE when the stock price of InnoVita tanked. It started slowly at first, then it sunk like a brick. Calls came in from irate investors asking him what was going on and why he hadn't notified them that this was on the horizon. Rogue drug manufacturers and dealers were rabid. Some even made death threats if he didn't resolve the situation immediately. His assets were dwindling faster than Suliman could have ever imagined. He had been blindsided. At this rate, he would be broke or dead by the end of the month.

By the time Suliman got through to Millie and Talley, the internet was going ballistic about another drug scam. Bombshell alerts claimed the product misled the public into believing a major step in virus elimination had been discovered. Unnamed sources found InnoVita to be just another overhyped fake cure. Millie reassured Suliman the claims were nothing but lies. The damn drug did what they promised it would. Somebody was messing with them, and the dumbasses out there in the cyber world believed the disinformation.

How ironic that the same internet strategy that made InnoVita the drug discovery of the century was responsible for labeling it a sinister hoax. Once the damage was done, it was irreversible. Society now conditioned to soak up anything posted on the web and treat it as the gospel. It mattered not that InnoVita might well be the cure for deadly viruses that scientists had been seeking for decades. If the web said it wasn't, then it wasn't. Period.

Armchair scientists piled on, many with vast personal investments in competitive products battling to replace InnoVita in the marketplace. They were like sniveling scavengers circling their prey and grabbing whatever piece they could from its weakening carcass. The people Suliman dealt with in the pharmaceutical business took a dim view of being bushwhacked. Even though it was not his fault, the blame fell squarely on Suliman. He would try to salvage what he could from the devastation, but he knew deep down he was finished.

Perhaps he could locate Eva and Victoria. Maybe they could give him some cover from the upcoming onslaught. He always felt they had a soft spot for him, and he hoped he could count on that. Try as he might, Suliman could not find his two playmates from the past. They seemed to have vanished into thin air. The final straw—his only chance—was to contact Ari Moon.

ARI WAS IN HIS STUDY WHEN HIS PHONE BUZZED. Surprised to see Suliman's name pop up on the caller ID, he hesitantly answered and struggled to discern what Suliman was jabbering about. When he heard the name InnoVita, Ari paid closer attention. Upon hearing the bad news, his first reaction was to wonder, *Is this ever going to end?* Now, underworld thugs from pharma would be coming for him too. After an hour of trying to absolve one another of responsibility for the crashing stock, they settled down to formulate a strategy. If either one had a chance of coming out of this fiasco, they would have to join forces.

SULIMAN KUMAR HAD ACCESS TO WEAPONS and an army of minimally trained fanatics; Ari Moon had a defensible fortress. The dim light at the end of the tunnel got a bit brighter. It was not quite a marriage made in heaven, but it was all they could muster on short notice. The wolves were not yet baying at the door, but time was not on their side. At the moment, the only uncommitted force available to Suliman was in Washington State; the more experienced combatants were heavily engaged in conflicts elsewhere. Suliman called Mr. Frost at the training compound east of Bellevue to round up as many raw recruits as possible for transport to Albania ASAP. Accelerated training would commence at their destination. Frost didn't question the orders. Instead, he set about making it happen.

Seth Collins and Becca Evans were among the assemblage deployed to Tirana.

SULIMAN CONTACTED A MUNITIONS DEALER from his past who agreed to send him the supplies he requested at a price three times the going rate on such short notice. A day later, a chartered C-130 transport plane loaded with Suliman's forces landed on a private strip at the Tirana International Airport. From there, they were transported to the base of the mountain, where they were shuttled up the mountainside on the lift to The Castle's entrance. It took several hours to get all the new arrivals situated in their living quarters. What had once been sex suites now housed soldiers.

While everything was being shuffled around, Seth and Becca worked out a temporary plan of action. It would take days for the new arrivals to get acquainted with their surroundings—just the kind of disorder the Nemesis agents needed to locate and familiarize themselves with the communications center in The Castle. Anyone milling about wouldn't be out of place since they were all essentially out of place until order was established. The minuscule number of reinforcements from Ari's side were nothing more than hindrances who, at the moment, were less than useless. It was time for the Nemesis agents to take advantage of the disorder.

Frost spied Seth and Becca checking out the operations center. Pleased that they'd stepped up and taken some initiative, he put them in charge of communications at The Castle. Then Frost made it a point to praise their leadership prowess in front of The Castle's population. As a further reward, he moved them from the general quarters to a small suite with its own bath. Seth and Becca looked at each other in amazement, thinking, *If this fool only knew what we are really up to.*

It took a week to somewhat organize the motley army. As far as castles went, the fortification was spacious, although not designed to be a multifunctional training facility. Instructional areas inside the walls were limited. Classes were done in shifts, which tried the patience of overworked instructors who had to bark the same orders repeatedly day and night. It was less than ideal, but it was private, secure, and, for now, off everyone's radar. Or so Ari and Suliman believed.

MEANWHILE, AT NEMESIS HEADQUARTERS, Liz held a meeting in her office with her inner circle to bring everyone up to date on their good fortune concerning Seth and Becca. Liz believed it to be a desperate undertaking by Ari Moon and Suliman Kumar to combine the remnants of what was available from their dwindling followers. It was the classic fox-in-the-henhouse scenario that so rarely happens. But when it does, you've got 'em right where you want them.

Tirelessly, Liz kept the pressure on by providing negative InnoVita propaganda generated by Warlock to the web. Internet junkies believed what they read, and sales of InnoVita dwindled to a trickle. Meanwhile, Nemesis cyber-lab gals cunningly bypassed the gatekeepers to slip news of the Albanian merger directly to the drug kingpins. The info caused quite a stir among the drug bigwigs. Nemesis agents closely monitored greedy captains of the drug industry, who were too overwhelmed with the success of InnoVita to pay attention to Ari or Suliman. The two men were merely a means to an end for the pharmaceutical moguls, and nothing more. Now that the shit had officially hit the fan, they looked at Ari and Suliman as their primary scapegoats to use as prime examples of what can happen if you screw with the organization.

Thanks to gossip on several underground websites, Nemesis learned of an organized initiative by drug bosses to assemble an army of trained mercenaries. Their mission was to destroy the merged forces at The Castle. Warlock confirmed the rumors to Liz, who warned Seth and Becca and instructed them to vacate The Castle at the first sign of a potential attack. To keep the pressure on, Nemesis continued the barrage of misinformation.

USING ONE OF NOMAD'S MIDWESTERN LABS, Talley and Millie challenged the authenticity of the InnoVita lies that were flooding the internet, destroying their business, and ruining their lives. They ran every test they could think of to discredit InnoVita but couldn't find anything wrong with the antibody-enhancing enzyme. Plain and simple, the compound neutralized viruses. Somebody was pulling a fast one on the web—one really smart son of a bitch.

Without success, Millie tried every backdoor cyber tactic she knew to find an IP address for the clever asshole perpetuating the falsehoods. It was like the anti-InnoVita blitz came out of nowhere and retreated back. Meanwhile, Talley was on the phone, putting out fires and rebutting indignant accusations of theft and fraud. All Millie could do was throw up her hands in frustration and shake her head in disbelief. To top it off, it seemed everyone, but the paperboy, was suing them.

To think that not too long before, Millie had commented to Talley how wonderful it was to never have to worry about money again. Now this. Their legal fees promised to be astronomical. If they lost, they would be old and dead broke by the time they got out of jail. Yet if they won, they would be free and dead broke.

How could anyone be cold and callous enough to do something like this to us? Millie wondered. It just wasn't right. How easily she overlooked the fact that, for most of their adult lives, she and Talley had done the very same thing to so many others. The irony was that InnoVita had been the first and only legit product Millie had ever promoted. And it was going to be the one that brought them down.

CHAPTER 7

ON A MILD, SUNNY SPRING DAY in the Hill Country, Bryce Lonagon toured Whispering Canyons Country Club and Estates to take in the finished products. His dream had been to create a resort that included golf, tennis, lawn bowling, hiking, hunting, fishing, boating, swimming, sightseeing, shopping, theaters, and concert facilities that were readily available to guests and residents. And he did it. Plus accommodations, including a Four Seasons hotel, clusters of luxurious casitas, and private homes. Gourmet restaurants dotted the outskirts of a boutique shopping mall. Two world-class golf courses and a classic nine-hole par three course wound their way through an exceptionally conceived community that offered a country lifestyle second to none. Across the highway from the development, Bryce built a theme park with rides, slides, and games for youngsters of all ages to enjoy.

For opening weekend, Trey, Jefferson, and family arrived from The Circle M ranch, joined later by a bevy of their friends from the Tour for a golf clinic and pro-am to christen the McCall signature golf courses.

Country music and rock stars performed on stage at The Glen behind the Four Seasons. Bars and food stations set up inside the hotel spilled out over a spacious lawn with seating for a small army.

Judging from the comments and the huge turnout, Bryce had a winner on his hands. Most guests stayed the entire weekend to soak up the sunshine, enjoy the amenities, and embrace the relaxed vibe surrounding Whispering Canyons.

With all the property had to offer, there were no hard-sell tactics necessary to procure memberships. There was already a waiting list. The seven-member board of the Whispering Canyons' megacomplex consisted of four charter members who'd invested heavily in the venture, along with Jefferson and Trey McCall. Bryce Lonagon was chairman of the board and the deciding vote in case of ties. By order of entry on the waiting list and after being heavily vetted, hopeful members would be invited to join. The board did not want a stuffy, snobbish membership but one composed of individuals who shared respect, interests, and comradery.

On the flight back to the ranch in East Texas, Bryce, Jefferson, and Trey compared takes on the opening weekend. Their ladies were engaged in heavy conversation about the food, shopping, and cute musicians who'd played at The Glen on Saturday night. There were a few minor snafus, mostly with food and beverage, that could be easily remedied with time. Little things like inexperienced waitstaff or temperamental chefs usually took care of themselves. There were no major problems with plumbing, leaky roofs, heating and cooling, or other utilities. Bryce's best building contractor had handpicked the subcontractors for the project. Bryce did not ask them for a rush job. He wanted it done right, not fast. He got what he asked for. The golf courses were pristine—Matt Bremer had the three layouts in tournament condition. From the reaction of the touring pros in atten-dance, the Whispering Canyons courses would make exceptional venues for a Tour event.

IN THE MEANTIME, AT THE CASTLE IN ALBANIA, things were quite the opposite for Ari Moon and Suliman Kumar. Rather than cohesion, there was confusion. The consolidated forces did not see eye to eye. Suliman's force outnumbered Ari's by ten to one. With such an over-whelming advantage, the larger contingent felt the need to impose their beliefs, expecting the others to fold and comply. The Nobilis Familia did not take kindly to being told what to do, much less what to believe in—especially by some snot-nosed punks dressed up so neat and tidy in their matching razor-creased fatigues and spit-shined boots.

As the two factions trained on the grounds of the mountain fortress, it became abundantly clear to Ari and Suliman how unpre-pared their forces were. A troop of Cub Scouts could outmaneuver and outfight the majority of the bozos currently mixing it up in the confines of The Castle. Somehow, and in short order, they had to shape the beta castle defenders into a respectable fighting force. To add to their woes, only a third of the arms, munitions, and supplies arrived from Suliman's black-market dealers. He had expected a small amount of thievery from merchandise handlers and government officials. That was part of that game. But two-thirds of the shipment was egregious.

SETH AND BECCA PICKED UP ON the negative mojo. It was a tool they could use to magnify uncertainty and distrust within the melding troops. Seth sent a coded message to Nemesis outlining the current state of affairs in Albania. He disguised the dispatch as an inquiry for supplies to a well-known arms dealer, one who went by the name Mother in the underworld. Mr. Frost saw the memo, recognized the moniker Mother, and again took a moment to applaud the young man's initiative. However, in this case, Mother was an alias for Liz. Unable to speak to the man's naïveté, Seth smiled his appreciation.

AT NEMESIS, LIZ READ BETWEEN THE LINES and understood that The Castle dwellers were in dire straits. She decided not to make the situation public on the web. She wanted to give the pharma mercenary forces plenty of time to build a complement of soldiers to storm The Castle fortress. *What will the pathetic members of Ari and Suliman's forces do when we overrun them? The poor darlings will probably curl up and whine,* she thought.

INNOVITA'S INEVITABLE CRASH put a huge dent in illicit drug company revenues and raised doubt in the minds of consumers as to the competence of management in the pharmaceutical industry. It was generally accepted that one did not put all of one's eggs in one basket; it was a terrible business practice. But apparently, that was exactly the strategy many of the neophyte pharma concerns used. Greed and poor judgment placed a majority of those same drug outfits into bankruptcy. Unwilling to take responsibility, the drug lords looked for scapegoats for their misfortune.

A committee of cartel bigwigs earmarked Ari Moon and Suliman Kumar as the fall guys for the InnoVita fiasco. The fact that the two men were holed up in a fortress with their most ardent followers made them even more attractive targets for the drug cartel army. Under the ruse of getting justice and revenge for the poor consumers who were taken in by these men and their confidants, the multinational drug trust sought to permanently remove the guilty parties. Their underlying goal was to silence Ari and Suliman before they could defend themselves in the public arena. The pharma czars sorted out the most violent mercenaries to be part of their assault group—ones who would show no mercy and take no prisoners. All occupants of The Castle would have to perish for the mission to be a success.

MEANWHILE, IN TEXAS, LIZ TOOK time to reflect on more pleasant matters. It seemed like yesterday that preschooler Davis McCall began to walk and talk a mile a minute. Always on the move, he kept things lively around The Circle M—a diminutive hellion on wheels. Similar to his older sister, he got into everything. Sis (Sith), as he called her, took him everywhere she went, pointing out this, describing that, as if Davis was an adult. The little man just grinned at her as if he understood it all. For all she knew, he might have. They adored each other. You could see it in their eyes and their faces.

Liz recalled her little brother at the golf complex. Totally captivated by the game, Davis had sat focused for hours on his father and grandfather while they practiced. The youngster was mesmerized by the sound of the clubhead contacting the ball and the swoosh as the sphere leaped into flight. With each shot, Davis let out an excited gasp followed by that infectious, happy, giggly chortle little kids own that cracks adults up.

Grandpa Trey cut down the shaft of a Wilson 8802 putter, similar to the one Ben Crenshaw used, so Davis could putt along with the others on the practice green. The youngest McCall had the greatest reaction when he heard his ball hit the bottom of the cup. He would crouch over with a determined expression on his face and raise his putter in the air just like Jack Nicklaus did when he won the 1986 Masters. It tickled the grownups no end to watch him imitate the Golden Bear. They were delighted that the young man had found an interest in the game on his own.

His sister vividly remembered the look of shock and disbelief on the nine-year-old grade-schooler's face when Trey presented Davis with his own set of custom-made golf clubs that the granddad had painstakingly built for his grandson in his workshop beside the driving range. It was a labor of love that did not go unnoticed by the youngster. Davis would have slept with the clubs if his parents had let him.

Every day after school, Davis would rush home to meet his grandpa at the driving range. They practiced, talked, and laughed for hours. It was not unusual for Liz to look out and see the two sitting on their golf bags while the old man told a story. Davis took it all in as he stared up into the eyes of wisdom. The boy was in the spring of his journey in life; Trey was in the late autumn of his. Liz held these treasured moments near and dear to her heart.

AS HE AGED, TREY'S ACHES and pains were more frequent and the relief less effective.

The love of his life, Tara, braved her way through her own age-related ailments. On her daily hike, she smiled and waved at the people she passed. She and Trey shared a wonderful life, regretting only that they had not gotten together sooner. Coupled with the McCall family's determination and the grace of God, they'd overcome the mistakes of youth to become a salvation to so many innocent souls who had nowhere else to turn. They were pleased with what they'd accomplished in their day and proud that their granddaughter, Molly Elizabeth, carried on the tradition.

Trey held Tara close and whispered in her ear, "Darlin', you wanna' know how I see things right now? Our memories are as fresh as the moment they took place, the present is for making new memories, and the future remains as mysterious as ever. We gotta treat each day as a gift, count our many blessings, and never take anything for granted."

Misty-eyed, Tara tilted her head, gave him a loving kiss, and whispered, "My love, no one could have said it better."

AS PART OF HIS GRATITUDE for and admiration of the McCall family, Bryce Lonagon designed a special homestead at Whispering Canyons exclusively for the McCall family. It was an elaborate single-family dwelling—a ranch-style structure with 8,500 square feet of living space. Built on a butte overlooking a three-hundred-acre spring-fed lake, it boasted a panoramic view of the entire Whispering Canyons complex, save for The Cabin in a box canyon in the distance. During construction, the impressive residence was off-limits to all but the contractors and Bryce Lonagon. Barricades blocked the entrance, and temporary fencing around the perimeter obstructed the view from curious lookie-loos down below.

SHORTLY AFTER THEIR SO-CALLED HAPPENSTANCE meeting at Pebble Beach, Bryce and Liz fell madly in love, got engaged, and, just over a year later, were married. Respectfully, Liz chose to have the wedding at The Circle M in honor of her great-grandmother and namesake, Molly McCall. In a simple yet moving ceremony, Bryce and Liz said their vows on the front lawn of the main house in full view of Molly's resting place. Tears of joy streamed down Liz's cheeks as she glanced up at the rise where her great-grandmother was buried. In reverence to Molly, Liz blew her a kiss.

Bryce arranged for the wedding reception to be held at Whispering Canyons, where he provided gratis accommodations for the guests. After the marriage ceremony, the McCall family quickly changed and flew privately to the Hill Country to join the throngs of attendees who had accepted invites to the reception. The vetted guests were sent picture IDs with lanyards, issued wristbands, and had their hands stamped as they arrived at the entrance. After several close calls with the criminal element in the past, the McCalls no longer took chances.

A pair of stretch limos from the resort met the wedding party at the Whispering Canyons' airstrip to drive them to the festivities. Security was tight but inconspicuous, and Nemesis agents blended into the crowd as they were trained to do. It was a precautionary measure taken due to the nature of the McCalls' business. Fortunately, it proved to be unnecessary this time. Liz's propaganda offensive kept their adversaries too preoccupied with bickering among themselves in Albania to bother with Nemesis at the moment. The limos passed the entrance to the resort, continuing on the paved road up into the hills.

Unaware of the impending surprise ahead, Liz was getting seriously concerned until they rounded a curve and arrived at their destination. All the barricades and temporary fencing had been removed. There, with lights blazing and a huge ribbon tied across the front door, sat the most inviting residence she had ever seen. Liz looked over at her new husband, and Bryce had a grin from ear to ear. The others were amazed at what they saw—speechless, with eyes and mouths wide open in admiration. Liz started to say something, but Bryce put his finger to her lips to silence her. He got out and escorted everyone to the front door, where he presented his bride with an oversized pair of scissors to cut the ribbon.

Once inside, he assembled everyone in the foyer. "Before you all die of curiosity, let me explain. I am honored that you have so warmly welcomed me into your wonderful family. I didn't think a simple thank-you was enough to express my true feelings. My crew and I have been up here for months, building our family a special place where we can all feel at home and enjoy the beauty of this magnificent Hill Country setting, away from everything and everyone else. This is my wedding gift to you, Elizabeth, and to all the McCalls, who have taken me so warmly into your family."

Tara was the first to approach him with her arms outstretched to embrace him. She hugged him with all her might and kissed him gently on his cheek. Each of the others in the family embraced him with generous hugs. Finally, Liz threw her arms around him and kissed him tenderly.

Once they pulled apart, Bryce clapped his hands. "Alrighty, then. Shall we?" he asked as he motioned for the family to follow him inside.

As they walked around to take it all in, the overabundance of oohs and aahs made all the hard work worth it for Bryce. The Cabin's nearly 10,000-square-foot-imprint—including basement, wine cellar, and storage—was impressive enough. But the craftsmanship and detail were phenomenal. There were six spacious suites, each with a walk-in shower, spa tub, and walk-in closets, in addition to four guest rooms. Centered in a 750-square-foot great room, a double-sided fireplace provided enough heat to warm the space easily. Sandwiched between the great room and a dining room King Arthur would be proud of sat a massive gourmet kitchen. Game rooms across from the library provided entertainment for kids and adults. A screened porch that circled three-quarters of the structure offered clean, fresh Hill Country air with majestic vistas of Whispering Canyons sunsets.

Outside, there was a saltwater swimming pool, complete with a spa with room for eight people. Dressing rooms and bathroom facilities were conveniently located near the pool area. For a touch of nostalgia, there was the cantina modeled after the eatery at The Circle M practice facility. It sat alongside a perfectly manicured putting green and a ninety-seven-yard par three hole over a pond to entice short-game challenges or late-evening practice.

Bryce left the pièce de résistance for last. Not far from the main house sat a smaller dwelling. It was fashioned somewhat like the cabins at Augusta National Golf Club, only larger and ranch-style. There was a nameplate above the door that read The Mac and Molly McCall Cabin—reserved in perpetuity for the eldest McCalls while in residence at Whispering Canyons. Amassed inside were treasured memories of the family history. In addition to walls covered with timeless photos, Bryce and his IT team had filled memory sticks with memories for generations of McCalls to share.

Trey and Tara watched, swept with emotion, as their luggage was moved in. They were visibly moved to be the ones to christen the distinguished cabin. The rest of the party took residence in suites in the main house. The limos were scheduled to return within an hour to deliver them to the grand ballroom at the Four Seasons at Whispering Canyons for the reception.

The event was more a gala than a wedding reception, providing choice locations for the patrons to celebrate. The crowds spilled out over the hotel grounds. Some enjoyed a stroll on a clear, warm summer night with a light breeze cooling the air, while others took in a George Strait concert or checked out the Hill Country theme park, which was guaranteed to entertain kids of any age.

Davis McCall camped out with the other kids at the amusement park, barking out orders and taking full command of his make-believe army. Cassie Drakos, a longtime agent and trusted Nemesis bodyguard, volunteered to watch over the little man for the evening. The tiny dude had stolen her heart. She loved every minute of her assignment and participated along with the children in all the games and rides.

Davis was allowed to stay up well past his bedtime, and the youngest McCall took delight in running poor Cassie to exhaustion. Just past midnight, he crashed. One minute, he was dancing silly like a clown, and the next, he was passed out, sound asleep in her arms. Cassie carried him back to his room and stayed the night to make sure the little fella was safe.

TARA AND TREY WERE BACK at their cabin by twelve thirty, worn out but so happy for their granddaughter and her new husband. It would take some getting used to, calling her Elizabeth Lonagon. They fell asleep holding each other, just like they had every night since they reunited almost fifty years earlier.

THE PARTY OFFICIALLY BROKE UP after George Strait and his band played their final song at one a.m. Bryce and Liz occupied the *preeminent* suite in the main house, where they made passionate, unhurried love until they were totally drained of energy. Liz looked over at Bryce one more time just before closing her eyes to see a smile on his sleeping face. That confirmed it. Liz fell asleep knowing she had the right man beside her.

After sneaking away from Whispering Canyons at daybreak to jump on a Nemesis Cessna Citation to fly south, the Lonagons spent a two-week honeymoon in picturesque Puerto Vallarta, Mexico. One evening after dinner, they had a serious talk about starting a family. Both wanted children, but at some point farther down the road when things were less hectic. Until they were ready, Liz could stay on the pill.

Now, with Davis on the scene, their sensible plan was put on indefinite standby. With the two-decade difference in their ages, Davis was more of a son to Liz than a brother. She and Bryce agreed it was a blessing from above to have Davis in the family. Furthermore, Liz, still in her twenties, was young enough to bear children later on if they wished. Both were good with their decision.

Bryce couldn't have picked a more spectacular spot in Puerto Vallarta—a rented villa on a ridge overlooking Banderas Bay. The golden-sand beaches and emerald-green water, complemented by pastel-accented sunsets, were breathtaking from their veranda. He mentioned to Liz that he had lucked into a great deal on the rental while searching for honeymoon destinations. It popped up as a recent foreclosure, owned by a wealthy fella who also had a castle in Bulgaria or Albania, one of the two. Anyway, the bank foreclosed on the guy for defaulting on past-due taxes and wanted potential prospects to get a live-in look at the place.

When Liz heard *Albania*, her ears perked up. She asked Bryce who the previous resident was. He didn't know but said he could find out easily enough. All he had to do was feign interest in the villa, and he could get its entire history. Liz asked him to check, although it seemed too farfetched that the villa might have belonged to a person of interest Nemesis was investigating.

It did not take long for the bank's real estate agent to get back to Bryce. Sure enough, the former owner was Miles Stewart, Ari Moon's colleague.

Bryce and Liz poked around inside the villa, on the grounds, and in town to find out all they could about Miles. Liz knew for sure Ari Moon was in Albania at The Castle. As for Miles Stewart, he was long gone—without a whisper of a clue where. Ari and Miles must have kept records. A secluded villa in Mexico seemed a logical place for the hustlers to stow documents and the like.

Jumbled up in the makeup of the criminal mind, there must have been a special gene that enabled them to concoct the most unusual places to hide their valuables. After days of exploring obvious spaces for safes—undersides of drawers, toilet tanks, and behind paintings—Liz and Bryce started probing and prodding floors and walls. Finally, on the fifth day, they found it, quite by accident, under a loose Mexican floor tile that supported the corner leg of a seldom-used leather couch. Coming around a corner, Bryce skidded on the damp floor. To steady himself, he grabbed hold of the couch and, in the process, dislodged a twenty-four-by-twenty-four thirty-pound porcelain tile.

The former occupants must have been in an awful hurry to leave what they did in the hollowed-out space below. There was a treasure trove of evidence, including notebooks packed with individuals' names, addresses, and telephone numbers; detailed ledgers with company names and private contact numbers; sexual orientations of attendees of Moon-sponsored blowouts; and, finally, the most damning proof of all—video evidence filmed during The Castle shindigs in Albania.

How bizarre was the chance discovery? Bryce Lonagon considered it an unintended wedding gift from Moon Enterprises. Liz believed it was something altogether different and much more powerful—karma.

AFTER A HONEYMOON THAT COULD, at best, be considered bizarre, Liz was back in her office at Nemesis, taking inventory of what she and Bryce had discovered. Names and personal data Nemesis agents obtained from Eva and Victoria, coupled with the records from Mexico, gave Liz and her team verifiable ammunition she could use to dishonor and discredit some top executives in the pharmaceutical game, along with their magnanimous donors.

It was gratifying for Liz to watch social media warriors turn on the likes of Miles and Ari, who were being verbally slaughtered on the web and exposed for crimes ranging from larceny all the way up to murder. Former untouchables were tumbled off their pedestals, torn to pieces like the ancient, historic structures they destroyed all over the world. When the mobs who once supported them turned against them overnight; the initiators ducked and ran as far from the mayhem as possible.

CHAOS REIGNED AT THE CASTLE. The only possible salvation for the divergent factions inside was to unite. If they didn't, nobody was going to walk out of The Castle alive. Frost and Vlado, the Serbian commander in charge of Ari's forces, communicated their grim message to their squads. There would be no surrender. Only life or death. The most fragile of the assemblage slinked away to the darkest recesses of The Castle to hide. The others understood their dilemma and got busy training side by side with their new comrades. Hampered by the fact that they were short two-thirds of the weapons and ammunition they needed, the drills were bare bones.

A worried Mr. Frost took Seth Collins aside to ask him in private if he had heard anything back from Mother, the arms dealer he believed Seth messaged earlier in the week. Seth frowned and said he had not but was still hoping.

Frost gave him a concerned look and said, "If Mother doesn't pan out, I fear we are done for. Unless, by chance, you have any other connections."

"Sorry, sir. Mother was my one and only contact. But I can put out some feelers on the dark web if you would like," Seth replied. He shook his head, sighed, and awaited further orders.

Frost thought about it for a second. "Better hold off on that. I'll talk to Suliman first to see what he thinks."

After Frost left the communications center, Seth posted a coded message to Liz, aka Mother, with an update.

OUTSIDE THE ALBANIAN REFUGE, THE CARTEL forces relaxed. Recon over the past month indicated that the occupants of The Castle were hunkered down inside. No one had come or gone from the stronghold. No longer were weekly supplies delivered by helicopter. Behind the walls of the massive cold and damp gray stone structure, the residents were getting antsy. Fear and anticipation of impending battle scenarios permeated their thoughts, adding to their angst. The reduction of gunfire from inside The Castle initiated a change in strategy for the mercenary force outside.

Instead of storming the castle, the merc troops decided to employ an ancient tried-and-true tactic—starvation and isolation. By jamming radio and microwave signals, the mercenary force cut communication with the outside and rendered radar useless for The Castle dwellers. The confined horde shivered in the cold, startled by every unfamiliar sound and shadow.

IN CONTRAST, ARI MOON WAS COOL, calm, and collected. He had an ace up his sleeve. At the end of the underground passage, past the entrance to the dungeon, was a concealed door that only he had the code to open. Behind the door was a cavernous fail-safe haven blasted out of solid rock by demolition experts early on during The Castle's renovation. Loaded with essentials to survive in a luxurious setting designed for comfort and function, it was tailored to easily accommodate two persons for three months—twice as long for one. Over the years, upgrades and accessories, including an escapeway, were added at Ari Moon's whim.

If The Castle was ever overrun or burned down, flames and smoke would never make it through all the layers of rock and soil to the cavern. Courtesy of a fresh mountain stream that flowed swiftly down the mountain year-round, water was piped to tankless heaters and filtering systems located inside the mountain refuge. Electricity was provided by a water-wheel-powered generator fed by the same stream.

AT PRESENT, ON THE SURFACE, VLADO had the onerous job of whipping the wusses and misfits of the combined squads into a respectable fighting force. That had been hard enough when they could train properly. What with the shortage of ammo, recent rationing of food, and the arrival of torrential storms of bone-chilling sleet and rain, it was nearly impossible. The fragile trainees were trapped in a world where they were forced to face reality head-on—something they were helplessly ill-equipped to do. Leaks developed in the ancient fortress, and water poured out of every crevice, turning to ice in the most exposed areas. Existence inside The Castle walls was miserable and growing worse by the day. Rather than a glorious refuge, it had turned into a prison of adversity.

COMMUNICATIONS WERE IFFY. Seth Collins managed to get his last coded communique out before he and Becca initiated their escape from the leaking death trap. As planned, they left at dusk, concealed in a light fog that surrounded The Castle.

Once outside, the Nemesis agents made their way through a gap in the wall near a pathway leading to the service road. Seth retrieved the rope and climbing gear he had stowed earlier in a hole at the base of a tree, and they were on their way. A light fog sheltered them from sight from above. There was just enough light to make their way down the service path. As they neared the bottom, Becca grabbed Seth by the arm to alert him. He stopped and looked around in time to see the glow of a cigarette, accompanied by the unmistakable smell of tobacco. They kneeled behind some brush and listened to garbled voices down below speaking in a foreign tongue Becca picked up on. Scouts from the pharma mercs were checking the perimeter before an all-out assault on the poor bastards in the fortress above. Tired of waiting, the mercs were eager to get it over with.

After an agonizing fifteen-minute wait, the men below crushed out their cigarettes and moved farther around the mountain. Seth and Becca slowed their descent, alert for signs of more unwanted company.

Without further incident, they stepped out of the brush and onto the main road into Tiana, where they thumbed a ride to the outskirts of town. A mile down on the left, they checked into a small hotel. As soon as they had washed away the stench of the dank, drafty castle, Seth placed a call to Liz in Texas. He let her know he and Becca had escaped from The Castle just in time. And it wouldn't be long before all hell broke loose on the mountain.

ARI MOON WAS IN HIS UPSTAIRS SUITE at The Castle when the first salvo hit the courtyard below. An M73 LAW-type rocket took a huge chunk out of the once pristine lawn. Shrapnel ripped into a dozen soldiers milling around on the grass, shredding them like lettuce. More rockets followed.

Ari thought about Suliman for a split second, said, "Screw it," and made a hasty retreat to his reinforced underground shelter. Once inside, he smiled as he swung the chromium steel door closed and engaged the locking mechanism. He was now completely secluded from the outside world. When it was time for him to leave his sanctuary, all he had to do was press a button on a remote control device to open a garage-style metal door expertly camouflaged to blend with the side of the mountain.

Outside, a narrow pathway curled its way down the mountain to an obscure hunting cabin veiled by a cluster of tall black pine trees. Inside the cabin, he kept clothes, weapons, money, and travel documents under an alias. His getaway vehicle, a refurbished Mercedes coupe with its battery on trickle charge, was parked in a padlocked barn fifty yards from the domicile.

With a sigh of relief, Ari wandered over to his floor-to-ceiling glass-door beverage refrigerator to get a Stella Artois and a chilled beer mug. Then he sat down in his leather recliner and turned on his giant-screen television to surf his apps for a good movie. A flashing red light on his control panel indicated a loss of power up above. He figured by now it must be hell on earth up there. A quick glance at his CCTV monitor revealed the massacre in progress.

Seconds later, he switched off the gruesome scene, reclined his chair, took a sip of beer, chose a comedy, and pondered what he should fix for dinner afterward. Twenty minutes later, he was sound asleep.

PREDICTABLY, THE FEEBLE ATTEMPT to defend the fortress was short-lived. The pharma army destroyed their opposition like they were swatting flies. Those begging for mercy were cut down where they stood, kneeled, or hid. The pharma group sustained only a few casualties dealt from the likes of Suliman, Frost, and Vlado, all three of whom went down fighting insurmountable odds. Suliman's last words cursed his luck and that little bastard Ari Moon, wherever he was.

Following their orders to the letter, the invaders smashed and burned The Castle to the ground. Several of the rocket blasts toppled cinder blocks and huge timbers that now covered the entrance to the storerooms and dungeon below, sealing them off forever, with no way in or out. The mission's primary objective had been to make sure Ari Moon and Suliman Kumar did not survive. They had the body of Suliman as proof and could only assume Ari's body was buried somewhere under the smoldering rubble.

AFTER AN HOUR-LONG NAP, ARI AWOKE with a marvelous idea. In that he could stay comfortably where he was for six months, there'd be loads of time to modify his appearance without surgery. Ari laughed out loud. He had always wanted to shave his head, and he couldn't imagine a more perfect opportunity. His underground lair had a fully equipped gym with tons of workout CDs to keep him busy and a tanning bed to give him a perpetual tan. Minor cosmetic adjustments, like contacts, could be easily taken care of at a later date.

Assuming his training program was successful, he would test out his brand-new appearance on a Caribbean cruise to validate whether rumors about shipboard romances were true. First thing in the morning, he would begin his transformation. But tonight, he was going to splurge on a bone-in filet, loaded baked potato, and green beans almondine, all washed down with a full-body Opus One cabernet.

True to his word, at six a.m. sharp the next morning, Ari shaved his head in the shower. When he glanced in the full-length bathroom mirror, he was floored. His head resembled a cantaloupe resting on the neck of a silverback gorilla. It was a sight that spurred him on to attack the gym with vigor and stick with a low-carb, high-protein diet to regenerate his flab into sinewy muscle.

After eight weeks, he had dropped thirty pounds and two inches off his waist, which, along with his slim, tan face, gave him a much younger appearance.

Ari watched television and perused social media apps. He got a kick out of the pundits who gave him up for dead, buried under the crumbled remains of The Castle. They were so sure of themselves; reliable sources assured their listeners it was fact. At least this time, they got it half right. He *was* currently under tons of earth and bedrock at The Castle. He made it a point to pay close attention to trends in business, political realms, and current events. In the future, when he left his retreat, Ari wanted to be fit—mentally, physically, and emotionally.

LIZ AND HER TEAM PICKED UP AN UNUSUAL amount of chatter between two radical pharma czars Nemesis believed to be instrumental in the Albanian raid. The drug chiefs wanted actual proof that Ari Moon was dead, which posed a problem. Anxious to avoid outside intervention, the pharma group greased the palms of Albanian officials to treat the incident at The Castle as an accident, defaulting to the conclusion that defective wiring and a gas leak caused the extensive damage. Access to the scene for anyone other than their own investigators was prohibited.

How convenient! Liz thought. *What better way to support a cover-up?*

Shortly after Seth and Becca arrived back in Texas from The Castle, they met with Liz in her office. Liz was eager to hear firsthand about life at The Castle just prior to the pharma army attack. Although bummed out by the devastation and loss of life, Liz was preoccupied with the whereabouts of Ari Moon, convinced the man was far too clever to fall victim to the cartel force.

"What do you two think happened to Ari Moon?" Liz asked. "It bugs me that his body has yet to be found."

Becca glanced over at Seth and chimed in. "Hard to say, ma'am. We rarely saw the man. He was a very private person who spent most of his time in his suite, including meals. Occasionally, Ari came out to stretch his legs and visit the storerooms below. Can't imagine what for."

Seth nodded. "Exactly. What puzzles me is why he would go down there in the first place. It was all but empty save for an old safe and an ancient dungeon. If he sought refuge down there when the attack started, they may never be able to dig through all the rubble to get to his body."

Hmm, Liz thought. But her intuition screamed, *That slimy bastard is still alive. I know he is!*

WHILE TREY AND TARA TOOK LIFE EASY at the McCall cabin at Whispering Canyons, Trey made it a point to check in daily with his granddaughter, Liz. As soon as he heard the news about the devastation at the Albanian castle, he rang her to get her reaction.

Her eyes narrowed as she replied assertively, "Glad you asked. There's something mighty fishy about the investigators' assessment of the damage and the cause of the explosions. None of it makes sense to me. Sounds like the Albanians want to wash their hands of the whole mess. And to top it all off, I've got this feeling in my gut that Ari Moon is still alive."

Trey put the call on speaker mode. "I admire your spunk. Reminds me of the hunches I got back when I was chairperson—most of which paid off, I might add. Want some sage advice from a couple of seasoned veterans?"

"Of course I do."

"Stick to your guns and trust your instincts. We think you're on the right track. Tara is nodding in agreement and wants to chime in."

"Hey, kiddo. Here it is, short and sweet. Without exception, every one of the elite slimeballs we encounter in our business follows the same pattern without giving any consideration to the end game. It begins with envy, then jealousy, followed by greed, on to wealth and power, and finally to solo control—which is their end game. What they fail to see is the fatal flaw. No *one* human being has the capacity to pilot that ship on a global scale. As history bears out, it is destined to fail. Over time, it dismantles itself from the bottom up. We at Nemesis strive to speed up the process. Hang in there. Trey and I have your back. Call if we can help in any way."

"Thanks. You already have. Just knowing you two share my suspicion is an inspiration," Liz responded with renewed confidence.

WITH NO MENTION OF HIM IN THE MEDIA for months, on a foggy morning, almost six months to the day after he took refuge, the new Ari Moon left his safe harbor. Using the obscure pathway down the mountainside, he entered the same service road Seth and Becca used for their escape. Near the bottom, Ari took an arcane path through the forest to his cabin, where he loaded his go bag full of money, weapons, and IDs, along with a few clothes, into the trunk of a stashed Mercedes. As he opened the driver's side door, Ari heard a rumble and felt the vibration from the timed implosion he had set as he departed his underground lair at the castle.

Midday, the fog lifted, and Ari took a moment to breathe in the fresh air and relish the feel of real sunshine on his face before he drove away. Given that he resembled a scarecrow with ill-fitting garments draped over its body at the moment, he made a stop in the village to buy some new clothes.

Ari strolled into a tailor shop he had frequented for years. The owner, whom he had personally done business with in the past, did not recognize him and ushered him into his shop, believing him to be a new customer. Positive reinforcement that his transformation was indeed successful, Ari Moon discarded his old clothes and donned new threads. Then he was off in search of a hotel where he would spend a few days getting used to his alias. First thing in the morning, he would book that Caribbean cruise he promised himself. Then Ari would make an extremely important phone call to an old friend.

MILES STEWART, AKA TED MILES, KEPT HIMSELF busy after his split with Ari Moon. Life in Comfort, Texas, suited him. The new resident of the Lone Star State single-handedly tackled most of the repairs needed on his property, from mending fences to changing out toilets and upgrading fixtures. Miles sanded the existing hardwood floors in the manor house, then varnished and polished them to a brilliant, glossy shine. The homestead took on a whole new personality when he and a couple of locals put the finishing touches on the outside paint job. Folks didn't see him much around town. Miles stayed mainly to himself and minded his own business, even having his groceries delivered.

Acting on a blueprint he dreamed up, Miles leased a Bobcat long-reach excavator to dig out a thousand-square-foot storage seller in the rundown barn across from the main house. He poured a concrete floor, waited two days for it to set, then added eight-foot cement walls he let cure for a month. Satisfied they were solid, he installed two-inch-thick Brazilian walnut flooring to cover the substructure and rigged a trapdoor floor entrance with a retractable ladder. So far, so good.

His vision was to convert the old barn into a carriage house for guests with private storage underneath for *whatever*. With the floor in place, Miles needed help to complete the redesign. He decided on a construction firm recommended by his banker. Hoping to secure more work from Miles, they finished well ahead of schedule. They'd followed his blueprint to a tee. Even close inspection during his thorough walk-through turned up nothing of concern.

When he was sure the workers were all gone, Miles ventured down into his finished cellar. He had been liberal with the overhead lighting and seen to it that each of the floor-to-ceiling storage cabinets along the walls was equipped with a sturdy padlock. He felt a swirl of cool air and glanced up at the fluttering ribbons attached to the vents in his climate-controlled space. Miles grinned as he sat down at the metal table in the center of the room, proud of the underground home for contraband. Back up top, he checked out the polished floor and the trapdoor latch pull, which was recessed into a pocket in the wood and blended perfectly with the grain of the flooring.

Pleased with it all, he locked the carriage house doors and walked back to his house to grab a beer. As soon as he sat down and clicked on the evening news, Miles heard a reporter say the investigation into the disaster at a castle in Albania was officially over. The consensus by those in charge deemed it a tragic accident in which there were no survivors. For safety concerns, the area around the demolished castle would remain closed to the public indefinitely. It was a timely mandate since, on the six-month anniversary of the assault, a huge explosion blew out the side of the mountain beneath The Castle where the dungeon was located. The reporter signed off with a sad note. The final blast ended any further search for Ari Moon, whose body had not been discovered and whose fate might remain a mystery forever.

Miles cracked a smile and raised his glass in the air to toast his old friend. Just then, his burner phone buzzed in his pocket.

QUINTON (QUIN) LUNA—Ari's new nom de guerre—enjoyed the attention he received from the bevy of available single women while on his two-week Caribbean cruise. At the rate he was going, he would need a holiday from his vacation. When his cruise ship docked in Miami, Quin rented a four-wheel-drive SUV and drove west—through parts of the United States he had missed on his numerous visits to America. Quin was in no particular hurry. The fellow he was traveling to see was busy tidying up last-minute details.

Pent up in the urban world of big cities most of his life, Quin had never before experienced the true freedom of the wide-open spaces he witnessed while driving through Texas. People were flocking to what had become the new land of opportunity, where a person could realize the American Dream. Riding the coattails of this mass migration were the opportunists and malcontents seeking to fleece their share of the bounty. It was from that lot that Quin Luna would recruit his new followers. He hummed along with the radio as he drove on, admiring the changing landscapes as he made his way to the central part of the state.

The magnificent contrast of topography and vegetation astounded him as he continued west on I-10 from Houston. Live oak trees replaced tall pines, and flatlands gave way to rocky limestone hills. On the western outskirts of San Antonio, Quin pulled off the interstate to call his friend for directions on the last leg of his journey into the foothills of the Hill Country. As he bounced over the bumpy caliche-surfaced road and drove through low-water crossings on his way to the ranch house, Quin understood why he had been advised to rent a four-wheel-drive vehicle.

When he came to a stop in the gravel drive, a vaguely familiar face came out of the house to greet him. After an arduous journey, Quin Luna exited the SUV into a bear hug from a scruffy Ted Miles. They unloaded the SUV and moved Quin into one of the guest suites in the manor house. The weary traveler settled in, washed up, and joined Miles in the front parlor for a beer to revisit their last eight months apart. The first order of business was for them to agree to refer to each other by their aliases. Any slipup or references to former aliases would likely end in disaster for both.

Each commented on the physical transformations the other had managed since they last saw each other. With all its moving parts and unforeseen obstacles, both were surprised their charade had succeeded at all. Between Miles leaving in a huff to parts unknown and Quin playing the wounded lost soul looking for sympathy, they had pulled off a masterful performance.

After a few beers, Miles went outside to light the mesquite logs in the firepit grill. On his first night, Miles wanted Quin to experience the taste of Texas beef cooked over an open flame. Afterward, they stayed outside to enjoy the warmth of the fire and continued their chat as the sun dipped over the horizon.

After the abject failure of the Nobilis Familia, they'd jumped through hoops to devise and then execute their grandiose façade. Each worked his way to Texas via indirect routes. Desirous to preserve their shared vision of global preeminence, they'd made the Lone Star State their backup, just-in-case strategy all along. Whereabouts in Texas didn't really matter as long there were enough trusting folks to fall for their scheme. The Hill Country west of San Antonio fit the bill.

TEXAS MAINTAINED A STEADY INFLUX of transplants eager to start a new life. Quin and Miles devised an avenue for them to chase their dreams using Riverview Crest as the vehicle. They intended to build a college of sorts, a two-year preparatory institute, with its mission to help new arrivals adjust to their surroundings and work their way into the community. In reality, it was an elaborate scam to infiltrate the community with reeducated and indoctrinated citizens aligned with the founders' philosophy. The junior college, to be known as Riverview Institute, was free, financed by philanthropic donors, and open to all, offering language studies, classes in agriculture, business, mechanical engineering and shop, and finally, cultural mores. History, civics, and objective thinking were missing from the curriculum, an intentional oversight that did not immediately occur to anyone. The only subject required for all was cultural mores, where social persuasions would be force-fed into hungry, malleable minds eager to absorb knowledge— any knowledge.

Communities in the areas surrounding the new college were elated at the thought of an institution of higher education in their backyard. Quin Luna and Ted Miles realized it would take time to complete all that needed to be done. With the assistance of prosperous local ranchers, bankers, civic leaders, and wealthy business owners, Quin and Miles were able to fast-track many of the red-tape procedures for the good of the community. The same construction company that reconfigured Miles's barn was selected to build dormitories and classroom buildings for the institute. To handle the additional motor traffic, the county agreed to widen and resurface existing roads to the college.

In the meantime, Quin and Ted saw to it that portable, modular prefab classrooms were set up on the Riverview property until the permanent structures were completed. Teachers flocked in from all over the state for interviews, hoping to be hired. Quin handled the consults. He gave special attention to applicants interested in teaching cultural mores to make certain the selected aspirant's ideology aligned with the viewpoints of the institute's founders.

The first ripple of students to enroll were temporarily housed with local residents or in motels paid for by anonymous benefactors— primarily Quin and Miles.

CHAPTER 8

ONE EVENING, AFTER A SUCCESSFUL pre-open house fundraiser for the institute, Ted Miles and Quin Luna sat beside the pool behind the main house. Under a brilliant array of glittering stars, they were mesmerized by the peace and quiet, interrupted only by the gentle, rhythmic pattern of the pool waterfalls.

Quin broke the spell when he blurted out, "Ted, I find it amazing how quickly we've been accepted into this community. Southern hospitality at its best, if you ask me."

Miles acknowledged his comment with a nod, thinking how glad he was to have cleaned up his ratty appearance for a more respectable image. "It probably didn't hurt that I ditched my derelict persona. Folks around these parts don't take kindly to bums and no-accounts."

Quin snickered and winked. "This ought to tickle your fancy, then. We just received an invitation to be the guests of a member for a week at some fancy new country club close by called Whispering Canyons."

Miles chuckled. "Who'd have ever thought?"

"Yep. He wants to show us around the place. Says they're on the lookout for outstanding folks from the surrounding communities to be put up for membership. He has the authority to shortcut the red tape since we're making such a grand contribution to the future prosperity of the Hill Country. What do you think? Want to give it a shot, just to see?"

"What the hell. Why not? Pillars of the community that we are," chimed in Miles.

ON THE SPUR OF THE MOMENT on Sunday morning, Liz and Bryce Lonagon jumped in their Lexus SUV and drove from The Circle M to Whispering Canyons. They went for no other reason than to unwind and reminisce over some of the McCall family nostalgia with her grandparents. Along the way, a notion popped into Bryce's head.

"How about we stay over for a week? We can clear out the cobwebs while we enjoy some of that Hill Country fresh air," Bryce suggested.

"A week sounds perfect. I'll call Tara and tell her we're on the road," Liz responded, then glanced over at her husband, who was chuckling in the background. "What's that all about? Something I said?"

"Naw, nothing like that. I just thought of something I used to do to my employees to keep them on their toes. Being that this is an unannounced visit, it would be the perfect opportunity for me to resurrect my old tactic."

With no advance notice, Bryce popped into the club office the morning after their arrival to make a cursory examination of the books. He was pleased to see that everything was in order. Checking over the membership roster, he felt the club should add a few more local members, which was allowed in the bylaws approved by the board of directors. As an incentive, the board had the option to reduce the initiation fee as well as the monthly dues.

A few days after the board approved the suggestion, the McCalls and Lonagons were having dinner in the club dining room when a charter member of the club brought two prospective guests over to introduce them. Ted Miles and Quin Luna didn't look the sort that played a lot of golf, but there were many social aspects of the club that members could enjoy. Liz studied Quin's face. There was something strangely familiar about him. She let it pass as a sign of being grossly overworked and having a vivid imagination. She smiled and shook hands with them both, as did Bryce, Trey, and Tara.

Out of earshot, as the guests walked away from the table, Trey commented, "Judging by the lack of calluses on their hands, neither of those fellas spent much time holding a golf club."

Bryce laughed it off. "They're probably tennis dudes, who, by the way, spend a hell of a lot of time in the bar after playing all those sets—*cha-ching*, money in the bank."

Liz made an observation. "By their actions and body language, my guess is those two have been acquaintances for a very long time. Strange though—Quin Luna struck me as someone I've run into before."

The next day, when Tara and Liz were talking at the cabin, Liz brought up the pair they met at dinner the previous night. She asked what her grandmother thought of them.

Tara was one of the best profilers Nemesis ever had. She replied, "Well, there's so little to go on. But if I were to take a stab in the dark, I'd say you are right on the money about them being longtime friends. Quin, the older one, seemed to be the alpha. Miles, the younger of the two, the beta. They were confident yet visibly uncomfortable in our presence, although it could have been the unfamiliar surroundings. And to Trey's point, they're probably not golfers."

Liz responded, "Thanks. I mean, well, I don't know why, but there's something about them that seems odd to me. I just can't put my finger on what. Another thing, you know I've always been good with facial recognition. Well, there's something seriously bugging me about Quin. Oh, look at me, rambling on. Chances are I'm still just wound up from work, searching for things that aren't there. Let's forget it for a while. Maybe it will go away while we check out some McCall clan history."

But it didn't go away. Not altogether, anyway. Especially since deep down, she believed Ari Moon was still alive. Liz saw Miles and Quin in passing a few more times during the week, and each time, it conjured up an anxious feeling. She was sure it was nothing but her imagination. She decided that the next week, when she got back to her office at The Circle M, she had run a check on them in the Warlock database to ease her curiosity.

THE PROSPECTS FROM COMFORT enjoyed being catered to during their week in Hill Country. On their drive back to Riverview Crest, Ted brought up their introduction to the McCalls and Lonagons.

"Hey, Quin. Did you get any funny vibes from Liz Lonagon when we met her at dinner? She kept staring at you. Gave me the friggin' heebie-jeebies. You don't think she recognized us, do you? What if she does a deep dive on our backgrounds?"

"No way she's made us. If she does check out our pasts, I've made sure our aliases have clean-as-a-whistle histories attached to them. To be on the safe side, I don't think it would be a good idea to join their ritzy club. I say we lie low and concentrate on getting this school business going. Chances are she'll forget all about us in a few weeks."

TO CHANGE THE SUBJECT and the mood, the Riverview Institute founders took a tour of the prospective campus. As was to be expected in a rural community, construction was slow but steady. Angel donors brought in additional construction crews from San Antonio to speed up the process. In the interim, more portable school rooms were set up to accommodate the growing number of students. Anxious locals applauded when Quin and Miles added an ROTC program, called the Military Training Corps (MTC), to the curriculum. Farmers and ranchers thought it fitting that colleges teach order and discipline to the youth of the country. *For the Riverview founders, it was a way to further influence a captive audience.*

AFTER AN INTERESTING WEEK IN the Hill Country, which was not as relaxing as she had intended, the first thing Liz did when she got back to The Circle M was contact Miranda in the cybercrime lab to have her run the names Quin Luna and Ted Miles through the Warlock program. It was silly, Liz knew, but she had to satisfy her curiosity. An hour later, Miranda rang her to say the AI program came up with nothing at all, not even an outstanding parking ticket. On a whim, Liz asked Miranda to dig up any photographs of the two men when they were younger. Miranda called back, saying there weren't any.

Odd, Liz thought. With all its capabilities, Warlock could not find a single old photo of either man. That being the case, she asked her lab boss to round up any recent photos the program could dredge up on the two men and meet her at one o'clock for lunch at the golf complex. It was pork tamale Monday at the snack bar, with homemade chili and Mexican rice—one of Liz's favorites. After lunch, the two ladies examined the pictures Miranda brought in a manilla envelope.

Unfortunately, there weren't many—less than a dozen. As the two studied the pictures, Liz had an idea and asked Miranda if Andy, the Nemesis sketch artist, was around. Unfortunately, Andy was gone for the day, but he promised to meet with them in the cyber lab at ten the next morning.

At ten sharp, the sketch artist walked into the lab with his book of interchangeable cellophane facial characteristics to lay over the photos. The three of them got busy. Exchanging facial characteristics one item at a time was tedious work. They were at it until dusk, but nothing moved the needle for Liz. She was frustrated and called it a day. Andy consoled her by saying that oftentimes, it was the next small tweak that did the trick.

ON A WHIM AND TO REFRESH HER MIND, Liz and Bryce joined Trey and Tara at Whispering Canyons the following weekend. Sensing there was something troubling Liz, Tara asked her how things were going at work.

Liz hesitated and sighed before she opened up. "Ever since I met that Quin Luna fella here at the club ... well, I can't get him out of my mind. I had Miranda check him out, and we got nothing at all—I mean zilch. We even brought in Andy, the Nemesis sketch artist, and so far, nada. Honestly, I'm at my wits' end because I know deep down I've seen that scoundrel somewhere before. I'd bet my life on it."

Tara made a sour face before commenting, "I know what you are going through. I can't tell you how many times Trey and I anguished over something we knew was right in front of us, but we just couldn't see it. Sometimes we got too close to see the whole picture. Maybe it's a good thing you and Bryce came back up here. A few days of peace and quiet might work wonders for you. The boys will be gone all day doing their guy things, leaving us girls free to do our own thing. If you need to talk, just let me know."

IN LIZ'S ABSENCE, MIRANDA KEPT a running investigation going on the suspects known to them as Quin Luna and Ted Miles. Although it did not appear the two had any prior experience in the educational system, their Riverview Institute had tremendous potential for success. In spite of the fact the school offered a limited curriculum, the student body encompassed individuals from dozens of countries. Nemesis, Miranda, and her colleagues had no way of knowing that the dramatic increase in the international student population and constant construction created a smoke screen to mask the arrival of human resources and equipment essential to Quin's ultimate objective. Guns, ammunition, and explosives were delivered disguised as farm implements and packed into the carriage house basement. No one knew that the institute's primary reason for offering an MTC program was to justify guns and ammo on the premises.

The whole thing was a colossal scam, camouflaged as an answer to everyone's prayers. Folks believed it was designed to turn around the country's young folks and teach them how to be productive in the world. Instead, it was no more than a factory that spit out clones programmed by the monsters who created them. Miles and Quin sat back and watched their machine gain momentum.

In the Nemesis cyber lab, Miranda, befuddled by the absence of basic info on Ted Miles and Quin Luna, was convinced all was not copacetic at Riverview Institute. When Liz returned, she found a note on her desk to call Miranda.

Liz listened while Miranda clued her in on what she suspected, which mirrored Liz's own misgivings. As a result, they decided to insert a couple of undercover agents as students at the institute to unearth the truth. Seth Collins and Becca Evans came to mind. They were the right demographic to blend into the college scene and the most in tune to deal with the attitudes of today's youth. If, by chance, Quin recognized them, it would confirm a notion Liz had rumbling about in her mind. Chiefly, that Quin had been at The Castle in Albania, escaped, and was most likely Ari Moon.

A WEEK LATER, SETH COLLINS and Becca Evans registered as students at Riverview Institute and enrolled in most of the same courses, but they found it odd that they were required to take cultural mores. After checking into their dorm rooms, Seth and Becca went for a casual tour of the expansive grounds. Walking back toward their dorms, they heard gunfire. It came from the firing range in a remote corner of the campus, far away from the majority of the population. They looked at each other, wondering if that was machine gun fire. Surely not, they decided. Firearms of that sort were illegal. They listened for a bit longer, but the gunfire had subsided.

They resumed their trek back to the dorms to change for dinner in the cafeteria. One of the easiest ways to find out all the scuttlebutt was at mealtime. New recruits jam-packed the cafeteria, so Seth and Becca shuffled along in line for their food. A slow-moving queue provided an excellent opportunity to pick up gossip.

In line two bodies back, Becca overheard a girl bitching about the assholes who ran the joint. She described how they'd made a promise to the student body that their doors would always be open if students had an issue. The girl had been trying to get an appointment with Quin Luna for over two weeks and swore the asshole put her on ignore. She had a legitimate complaint about the male professor teaching that compulsory cultural mores crap course. The guy promised her an A if she would stay after class for some extracurricular monkey business. The kinky jerk actually thought she was *that* desperate. She couldn't care less about his precious class.

Having overheard the girl's rant, Seth and Becca made it a point to sit with her after they all got their food. The girl hurried to a table in the back, and they followed. Becca explained that this was their first day at the institute and they were already concerned.

"I'm Emily Pressler," the girl started and then didn't hold back. "This place is more of an internment camp than a college. If you're not in accord with the almighty alliance, you might as well not be here at all.

"Members of the Military Training Corps pretty much run the student activities. Nothing happens on campus without their approval. If you don't like it, too friggin' bad. You can either suck it up or leave. When important visitors show up, the thugs simply lie low or put up a front by glad-handing the guests and praising the founders of the institute. I don't buy the bullshit they're teaching, but I need a diploma to get a job to support my daughter and myself. The lure of a free education brought me to Riverview Institute. Now I wish I hadn't taken the bait.

Finally, Emily stopped to take a breath.

"Thank you for being so candid, Emily," Seth said, making a mental note to see what Nemesis could do to help her situation. He got her phone number and wished her well. Seth and Becca left promptly. Their dinner was cold anyway. Famished, they stopped by the quad court for tacos, then went on to their respective dorm rooms. Aware that the quarters were probably bugged, Seth stopped short of the entrance to call Liz McCall on his mobile. He told her about their encounter with the girl at dinner. They had already hit pay dirt.

AS PART OF THEIR DAILY ROUTINE to stay svelte, Quin and Miles included a five-mile jog from the main house around the perimeter of the campus. The route gave them the most privacy from prying students. One day, quite by accident, they ran head-on into a couple strolling along the jogging path from the opposite direction. The boy and girl walked hand in hand like they did not have a care in the world. As the two pairs passed each other, they nodded their hellos and kept moving. A hundred yards down the path, Quin stopped with a curious expression on his face.

Miles stopped a few yards farther up, then jogged back. "What's up? You okay?"

"Yeah, I'm fine. Did you, by chance, get a good look at those two we just passed?"

"No, I wasn't paying attention. Why?"

Quin grimaced. "I have the strangest feeling that I've seen them before."

"Come on, man. Ever since that week at Whispering Canyons, you've become totally paranoid just because you think that lady might have recognized you," Miles chastised his partner.

"That lady just happens to be the head of Nemesis, in case you've forgotten," Quin fired back.

"I know, but it's obvious she didn't recognize you. Or they would have already been here looking for us."

"Maybe."

SETH AND BECCA CASUALLY WALKED back toward the campus. They'd gotten the close-up photo op they'd hoped for of the founders of the college. Thinking fast as they approached, Seth had faked a sneeze and activated a button video camera on his shirt to send back to Nemesis. Miranda would appreciate a video of the two persons of interest in motion. People tend to carry themselves with their own individual swagger. Seth was certain the eldest guy was Ari Moon. Hopefully, Liz and Miranda could confirm his identity from the video.

INSIDE THE MANOR HOUSE at Riverview Crest, Quin paced the floor, thinking about that big kid and his babe on the jogging path. Quin remembered him from somewhere. But where? Finally, he called his head of security to pull up the images of the couple from CCTV footage of the jogging path that morning. Then he had his security chief run a background check on the pair. Seth Collins and Becca Evans were recent arrivals, army veterans, and part of the government's GI Bill. Nothing suspicious in either one of their histories.

Still, it bothered Quin that they showed up so soon after the country club encounter at Whispering Canyons. He thought it was probably a coincidence. Just the same, he ordered his most dedicated recruits to surveil them. If nothing else, it would be real-life training for the young soldiers.

The amateur surveillance team assigned to follow them was pathetic. Seth and Becca picked up the tail immediately. The agents ran the amateurs in circles until, finally, one day, the novices weren't there anymore. Unfortunately, neither was the girl Seth and Becca had talked to that first night. Emily had been a good source of information until, all of a sudden, she was gone. No one at the institute knew where she went.

NOT LONG AFTER QUIN AND MILES opened Riverview Institute, they ventured farther west on a sightseeing tour of the countryside on back roads alongside the Guadalupe River. A few miles outside Hunt, Texas, they came across some boys' and girls' summer camps nestled against towering ancient cypress trees and clear streams of limestone-filtered spring water. Out of curiosity, Miles parked in front of the for sale sign. The couple who inherited the camp was not prepared to handle scores of rowdy youngsters for three one-month sessions. A single summer of screaming kids had been more than enough for the new owners, and they put the camp on the market. As they walked the property with the anxious sellers, it dawned on Miles and Quin that it would make a great cover for a clandestine indoctrination training facility. As soon as they arrived back at the camp meeting house, Quin made a cash offer that the relieved proprietors readily accepted.

Due to its worldwide reputation and popularity, they decided to keep the name Camp Topaz. Title to the property was discreetly transferred over to an acquisitions company, which was a subsidiary of a conglomerate overseeing a diverse number of corporations cunningly masked to hide any association with Quin or Ted. Counselors for the camp were handpicked from dissident students at Riverview Institute to ensure a proper month-long indoctrination of the young campers. Upgrade costs were recouped by substantial increases in pricing across the board. Elitist parents either understood or just did not care that prices were jacked up, just as long as they were free from their bratty kids for a month.

SETH PICKED UP ON THE ACRONYMS QUICKLY. Cadet officers in the MTC began referring to the YEP (Youth Enrichment Programs) facilities, which was unusual in that they had not alluded to it before. The more Seth and Becca found out how things were run at Riverview Institute, the more unsettled they became. Becca had trouble sleeping and was up periodically during the night, worrying. Most pressing was the disappearance of Emily Pressler. Emily had little money and no car. And she lived in the dorm, so she could walk where she needed to go on the grounds. Her suitemate refused to talk about the night Emily was taken kicking and screaming from her room. Prior to her disappearance, Emily spoke with her daughter and her grandparents every day. All of a sudden—nothing.

CHATTER ON CAMPUS ABOUT the missing Pressler girl suggested the authorities might soon be called in to investigate. When he found out, the commanding officer of the MTC was livid. He assumed the girl had been eliminated as he had ordered. Following a heated chat with First Lieutenant Johnson, the commander was assured the girl would be taken care of promptly.

The first lieutenant took the verbal bashing to heart and immediately jumped into his Jeep for the hour's drive from the college to Camp Topaz. Lieutenant Johnson previously disobeyed a direct order, hoping the girl would come around. Since she hadn't, he had no choice but to make sure Emily permanently disappeared and supply proof of such to his CO.

WHILE SHE WAS INCARCERATED in a cabin on the most remote pasture at the back of Camp Topaz, Emily's abductors administered designer drugs to open her mind to suggestion. The objective was to replace her old-world principles with a "new" world doctrine. But they couldn't break her—she didn't even bend.

Shortly thereafter, a Jeep came to a screeching halt outside. Emily fought through a clouded state of mind to listen to a shouting match in the next room between her three captors and their superior. The conversation quickly turned unpleasant as each one cast blame on the others. Then the front door slammed, and the Jeep roared away.

Early on in her captivity, Emily concluded that her kidnappers were not all that bright. Otherwise, they would've guessed that she was faking most of her enfeebled symptoms to appease them. They no longer restrained her and often left her alone for hours in what they thought was her twilight state. During those hours, she slowly used a dull dinner knife she had swiped to quietly pry up a three-foot-long one-by-two threshold board from the doorway to the bathroom, its protruding screw nails still in place.

Following the confrontation in the front room, one guard remained while the other went outside to cool off with the female coed recruit from Riverview he had brought along as a companion on the mission. The lone remaining guard burst through the door, looking for Emily on her bed. It was empty. He stopped in his tracks. As he stooped to search under the bed, Emily leaped from behind the door and swung her handmade weapon like a baseball bat. With all her might, she caught him square in the forehead, embedding several of the four-inch screw nails into his skull and piercing his brain.

The mortally wounded guard dropped like a stone before he could finish his final remark: "What the fu …"

SHE QUICKLY REACHED DOWN and jerked the nine-mil Beretta from the holster on his hip. Then she slipped two extra magazines from his belt into her pocket. In a full adrenaline rush, she waited on the couch, directly in front of the door, for the accomplices to come back from their breather outside.

As soon as they opened the door, they reached for their sidearms. But they were too late. Her desire to get revenge for what they had done to her took over, and Emily shot them dead. Then she dragged them all the way inside, closed the door, exchanged clothes with the deceased girl, and laid the female corpse under the covers of her bed.

Noticing the size of her feet, Emily thought for sure her shoes would fit. "Just like Cinderella," she mumbled. Emily closed and locked the door. Then, with a lighter she stole from the dead girl's jeans pocket, she set fire to the cabin. Using the smoke from the fire as cover, Emily hid in a thick grove of trees to wait and watch what unfolded.

ON HIS WAY BACK TO RIVERVIEW INSTITUTE, the first lieutenant received a call on his mobile from the MTC commander, ordering him to return to Camp Topaz to check out a cabin fire. By the time the bewildered first lieutenant reached the camp, the volunteer fire department had the fire contained. The cabin was reduced to smoke and ash, and the remains of three barbequed bodies were found inside. Two were in the main room, and another was in the bedroom. The first lieutenant had no idea one of his cadets had sneaked his twisted girlfriend out there to fool around. As far as he was concerned, his job was done—Emily Pressler was dead. He thought, *maybe this time, he'd get a pat on the back instead of a reprimand from his commander.*

AFTER SHE WAS SURE EVERYONE HAD GONE, Emily started her trek to the paved country road that led back to civilization. A trucker picked her up and dropped her in Kerrville. She had money in the wallet she lifted from the dead girl's purse—enough for food and a motel room for the night. As she got undressed in her single room, she thought about the phone number that nice guy and his girlfriend gave her at dinner one night at Riverview Institute. Emily dialed the number she had memorized. Half expecting it to be disconnected, she was surprised when the nice guy answered.

"Hi, this is Seth. To whom am I speaking, please?" he said.

She told him who she was and fervently divulged her ordeal at Camp Topaz, start to finish. He asked her to slow down and take a breath, then asked if it would be all right if he and Becca came to her motel for a chat. Emily was exhausted but agreed. Within the hour, the Nemesis agents had listened intently and recorded her story—every sordid detail. Seth was furious and immediately phoned Liz, putting the call on speaker so Emily could participate.

Afterward, Liz awkwardly calmed her own emotions enough to ask, "Emily, do you think the MTC crew has any idea that you survived the fire?"

"No, ma'am. I don't think they could. The bodies in the fire were burned to a crisp. Only way they could tell was if they took dental impressions. That takes time, right?"

Liz bounced her steepled hands against her lips before she continued. "Sweetheart, I'm going to ask you to do me a big favor. Will you come to The Circle M and meet with me and my Nemesis team? I could send a plane to Kerrville in the morning and have you at the ranch by lunch. Stay as long as you want. We can also make arrangements to have her daughter and grandparents brought here if you would like."

Emily looked at Seth and Becca, who were nodding yes.

"O … O … kay," Emily squeaked out. "Can Seth and Becca come to the ranch with me in the morning? I feel so much safer with them around."

Liz was all for it; Emily was more likely to unload her burden if she had friends in the room. "Sure, honey. That's no problem at all. I'll make the arrangements for tomorrow morning. Get a good night's sleep, young lady. You earned it."

Immediately after Liz hung up, she talked to the police about Emily and how the young woman dealt with the couple as they entered the cabin. The authorities looked at it as a clear case of self-defense or justifiable homicide. No charges were going to be brought against Emily, and she was free to travel to the ranch.

QUIN WAS IN HIS OFFICE LISTENING to the MTC first lieutenant's report on the fire at Camp Topaz. Miles moseyed in at the tail end in time to hear Quin ask the kid if he examined the scene closely or just took the word of the locals. A trickle of sweat formed on the cadet's brow. Quin guessed his answer was no. The young man began to stutter and run his words together in a pitiful defense of another irresponsible action. In a fit of rage, Quin unceremoniously dismissed the cadet and thought, *If this is what the world is coming to, God help us all.* In a couple of days, he would have Miles drive out to the site and sift through the rubble to see what he could dig up.

WHEN MILES ARRIVED AT THE CHARRED REMAINS of the cabin, someone in a hazmat suit was on their hands and knees, examining the three corpses. The stranger looked up as he approached and motioned for him to stop. Then the figure rose and walked gingerly over to Miles, took off the headgear, shook out a full mane of auburn hair, and calmly stared at him.

In a soft voice, a woman proclaimed, "Sorry for the stern warning, but I didn't want you to stir up a potential crime scene. I'm Martha Shaftner, medical examiner and forensic crime expert. People call me Marty."

She purposely left out what county she was from. Marty went on to add that she was asked to render her opinion on how the three poor souls died in the tragic incident.

Miles was caught completely by surprise, paying more attention to her looks than what she said. Even in her hazmat suit, Marty was stunning with her shoulder-length hair and blue-green eyes.

When he introduced himself to her, Miles almost forgot to use his alias, "I'm, ah, Mil … Ted Miles, but most folks call *me* Miles … Well, anyway, my cousin used to come to camp here, and I was just in the neighborhood, and you know how curiosity can get the best of you and … I guess I should just let you get back to it."

It had been ages since he had felt such a strong attraction to a woman, but he was totally smitten. Miles didn't want to leave, but he couldn't stay.

Before he left, Miles blurted out, "Any chance you are free? For dinner, that is?"

Marty gave him a look that said, "Where in the hell did that come from?"

Her reply puzzled him. "Why?" She let him dangle for a time. While he tried to find his voice to answer, Marty laughingly added, "Maybe. Here's my number. Give me a shout." She handed him a card with only her name and phone number printed on it, then went about her business.

CHAPTER 9

WHAT A BRILLIANT PIECE OF STRATEGY it was to send Marty Shaftner. Marty was one of Liz's fiercest agents and had been personally trained by Cassie Drakos, the bodyguard who kept Jefferson and Reanna McCall safe at their wedding in Barbados. Dr. Marty was cunning, tenacious, and ruthless. Plus, she had the skills to handle any social situation. Having been hit on by many hot-to-trot men since she was a teenager, she was nobody's fool. Marty was surprised Ted Miles showed up at Camp Topaz. Anyone from Riverview Institute would have sufficed. All she wanted to do was get her card to them, certain the card would pique their curiosity. They would be dying to know what she had found at the crime scene; she would tell them what they wanted to hear, not what she actually found.

During her stint in Army Intelligence, Marty was a forensic investigator before migrating to Nemesis. She knew what to look for and found some interesting evidence that corroborated Emily Pressler's account of what happened. She found blackened nail screws protruding from the skull of one of the males, which she carefully removed and bagged for evidence. The other two bodies were where Emily said they would be. She searched the area for nine-mil shell casings, then found and bagged them. Her experience suggested that whoever had Emily kidnapped would be back to the cabin to snoop around, but it would be a lost cause.

THE SECOND MILES GOT BACK to Riverview Institute, he made a beeline to Quin's office. He went straight to the wet bar and made himself a tall gin and tonic, took a long gulp, and then sat down on the sofa facing his partner.

Quin followed Miles around the room with his eyes before he said, "What's up with you?"

"I'll tell you what's up with me," Miles remarked and took another swig of his drink. "When I got out to Camp Topaz, there was already someone there in one of those hazmat suits sifting through the ashes of what used to be a cabin. I damn near lost it when she shed her hood. This woman was a vision of loveliness who absolutely took my breath away."

"Yeah, so what? It's not like you've never been around a beautiful woman. What did *you* find at the scene? Any idea who started the fire?"

Fumbling for a response, Miles decided his best play was to produce the card she had given him. Quin gazed at the card, raised his eyebrows, and gave him a quizzical look.

"It's her card, the lady doing the digging around. That's her number. She said to give her a call. She's some kind of crime scene phenom. I have no doubt that she'll give us all we need."

Wonderful, Quin thought, then shook his head. Another woman in his life to let him down.

MARTY SHAFTNER WAS FRESH OUT of the shower when her phone jingled on her glass-topped dressing table. She sat down on the swivel seat and looked at her phone vibrating in a semicircle. It was the man who did not seem to know his own name, the one she had met at the scene of the fire and knew would call her. She lit a cigarette, a habit she had picked up in the army and wished she hadn't. The good news was she was cutting way back. She took a long drag, slowly blowing out a plume of smoke just before she answered.

"Ah, Marty, this is Ted Miles from the scene of the fire at Camp Topaz earlier today. Anyway, I was wondering if we could meet for a drink and maybe dinner."

"Ted, how nice of you to call. I like a man who shows initiative. I'd love to meet you for a drink, but I'm afraid I have tentative plans for dinner. Sorry. Tell you what, how about we meet at the bar at La Cantera Resort around six this evening?"

"Awesome. See you then. Oh, and please call me Miles. Everyone does," Ted Miles replied in a voice he hoped didn't sound too eager.

DR. MARTY ORDERED A COSMO with Tito's vodka and a lemon twist. Miles went with a double Blanton's single-barrel bourbon, neat. They engaged in small talk for the first drink. By the third, they had moved on to what she had discovered at Camp Topaz. Miles was buzzed, and Marty faked it.

"My investigation turned up no evidence of foul play. Therefore, I concur with the local constabulary that the mishap occurred due to negligence on the part of the three victims and that drugs and alcohol were likely involved," Marty intentionally slurred to her companion.

Struggling to pay attention, Miles half heard her explanation. His head was spinning, and his eyes were blurred. No chance he could drive home. He reasoned she shouldn't either, so they took a suite at the hotel to sleep it off and maybe whatever.

By the time Marty got Miles to the room, he was wasted. She got him undressed and onto the king bed. She used her iPhone to film him in his birthday suit in hopes that Victoria or Eva might recognize something on his body that would identify him as the person they knew to be Miles Stewart. For props, she left a hint of her perfume on the pillow next to his and lipstick on a cigarette butt in an ashtray on the nightstand.

Then Marty turned out the lights, slipped out the door, and exited the hotel by a side entrance. She located her car in the lot and drove off.

WHEN HE PHONED LATER THAT DAY, she took his call on the first ring. Before Miles could utter a sound, Marty told him what a wonderful gentleman and lover he was and said she was sorry she had to leave before he woke. It was too bad, since she wanted so badly to give him that morning surprise he had gone on and on about. By the time she was done chatting, the stupid jerk thought he was the best lay in the land, but he hadn't a clue that nothing at all had transpired the night before.

"Oh my God, you were amazing. An eleven on a scale of one to ten. And you kept coming back for more! Unbelievable. Your stamina … I've never … it left me breathless." Marty laid it on thick as she paced the room, smoking and singing his praises. Before she could hit End, he asked her out to dinner. Again she begged off, saying she had a previous engagement for the evening but would love a raincheck. She heard the disappointment in his voice as he said good-bye.

He called back later. But he got no answer and was directed to leave a message, which he didn't. He phoned the following day, only to be turned down again because something came up; she was needed on a murder case—a triple homicide that would take her two or three days.

Miles was beside himself, trying to remember one blasted thing about this supposed fab night he spent with a devilish angel. It drove him mad, and he contemplated swearing off liquor for the rest of his life. How could he have been this Greek god in the sack and not remember at least one magical moment? *Maybe it was the bourbon, yeah,* he thought. *That was it. From now on, stick to clear booze—gin or vodka. That should do the trick. Please let there be a next time with Marty ...*"

MARTY STRUNG HIM ALONG FOR AS LONG as she dared. The next time he called, she agreed to meet him for dinner at a local steak house in an old relay station off the highway between Kerrville and San Antonio. Every element of the conversation was awkward for him at first, with her supposedly aware of what they did on their first date while he wondered and guessed. She made up all sorts of wicked stuff, and the dude bought it all. His imagination ran wild with anticipation of what would be forthcoming after dinner.

The mood was set, and the table cleared for dessert when Marty's phone buzzed. She frowned, excused herself from the table, and slipped outside quietly to take an important call. Two minutes later, she was back inside. There'd been a murder and suicide, and she was needed at the scene. As she raced toward the door, he asked about later. She just threw her hands in the air, indicating, "Who knows?"

When he heard her peel out of the parking lot with lights flashing and siren blaring, he knew it wouldn't be tonight. Marty had him hooked, without a doubt.

QUIN LUNA SAT IN HIS COMFY LEATHER CHAIR, sipping a brandy and listening to his favorite flamenco guitarist, the Spanish virtuoso Paco de Lucia, while he mulled over the latest set of circumstances that demanded his attention. As a rule, he did not tolerate incompetence. Already, he had demoted his MTC commander and his second-in-command. No sooner had he taken care of that matter than Ted Miles had lost his mind over some bitch doctor. What kind of idiots was he dealing with these days? Conveniently, Quin forgot his own blind obsession with Victoria and Eva, which plagued him to this day.

Nevertheless, something had to be done to bring his protégé back to reality. Things were getting out of hand. Quin decided to finagle a meeting with this Dr. Marty Shaftner to see what the attraction was for his lusting partner. He held her card in his hand, debating whether he should call her right now or not. He downed the rest of his drink, then immediately poured another. Halfway through his second brandy, he punched in her number.

Marty looked down at the caller's number and did not recognize it, so she ignored it. A few minutes later, a little ding signaled the caller had left a voice message.

IN THE VOICEMAIL, QUIN WONDERED if he might meet with her at her earliest convenience. Marty listened to the message twice to make sure her first take was accurate. All of it was crap, a smokescreen to meet her face-to-face, to size her up, and feel her out.

Her trap was set with the prey circling the bait.

FOLKS AT NEMESIS SAW IT AS a golden opportunity for Dr. Marty Shaftner to prove beyond a doubt that Quin Luna was Ari Moon. To embellish Marty's medical background, Warlock updated her profile to include her current case at Camp Topaz. Then Liz set Dr. Marty up in an office near La Cantera and a furnished casita a short drive down the hill from the resort hotel.

Midafternoon, Marty returned Quin's call to invite him to meet her at her office at ten the next morning. Then she gave him the business address and her cell number. He accepted the invite, saying he would be there at ten sharp and was looking forward to meeting her. In the meantime, Liz scanned a not-so-recent picture of Ari Moon, alongside a current picture of Quin Luna taken at Riverview Institute, for Marty to compare.

The man posing as Quin Luna was punctual for the midmorning meeting. When he entered her office, Marty had her back to him as she finished up some work on her computer and told him to please have a seat. Her long auburn hair reminded him of Victoria Novak, a pleasant memory that stirred old emotions. When Marty stood and turned to greet him, his jaw dropped while his eyes took in her captivating beauty.

She extended her hand and said, "Good day, Dean Luna. I'm Dr. Marty Shaftner. What can I do for you this fine morning?"

Quin took her hand and held it a second too long. She held his stare with a homed-in focus that never faltered.

At long last, he gained a modicum of composure and said, "I'm not exactly … sure."

Marty smiled at his awkwardness and ushered him to the sectional. All the while, she studied his features, comparing them in her mind to the picture of Ari Moon. As she took in his facial features and the shape of his ears, there was no doubt in her mind that Ari Moon and Quin Luna were one and the same person.

The disheveled man rambled on about the incident at Camp Topaz and then bluntly spouted, "Have the bodies at the camp been identified? Was it arson or accidental? Do you suspect any foul play?"

"Surely you are aware that I am prohibited by law from discussing cases with private citizens. But since it appears the three victims could be students at your fine school, I'll make an exception. Perhaps you could be of some assistance in identifying the deceased. At the scene, I determined the fire was not deliberately set but caused by smoldering ash, most likely from a marijuana cigarette left unattended. The drunk victims were overcome by smoke and perished in the flames. Those are my official findings." Marty dangled the bait, hoping he would bite.

HIS ATTENTION WAS ON HER and not on her words—and unprofessionally so. His eyes never left hers while she spoke. When she had finished, Quin sat there, dazed. Spellbound in her presence, he watched as she went to the bar and selected a bottle of eighteen-year-old single malt Macallan whiskey and two Waterford crystal glasses. Then she set them on the coffee table in front of him, next to a crystal ashtray, a humidor displaying expensive Cuban cigars, and her silver cigarette case.

This vision of loveliness poured two fingers of the golden liquid, neat, into the glasses, then opened the humidor to remove a cigar for Quin. She expertly snipped off the butt, lit it, took a drag, and playfully blew the smoke in his face before she handed the cigar to him. She lit a cigarette, undid a couple of buttons on her blouse, and slid in beside him with a lascivious grin on her face. Then …

She wasn't there. Neither were the drinks nor the smokes that had been burning in the crystal ashtray. The doctor was seated on the couch, fully dressed and not making suggestive advances toward him. All had been a grand hallucination.

Regaining a small amount of sanity, Quin couldn't recall whether Dr. Marty had answered his questions about the fire or not. Nor did he seem to care. He tried to put her out of his mind but couldn't. Somehow, he managed to thank the doctor for her time, offered to buy her a drink sometime, and slinked out of the office.

Marty closed and locked the office door behind the man, leaned back against it, and breathed a sigh of relief. *Oh, Miles will be so jealous now,* she thought. *Checkmate.*

SHOCK HUNG OVER THE CIRCLE M LIKE AN OMINOUS DARK CLOUD. No one at Nemesis headquarters was prepared for the tragic news that came down from Canada. Noah Bouchard and his wife, Greta, were killed in an automobile crash, a head-on collision, not far from their mountain retreat known as the Monastery. Liz Lonagon was devastated. Noah was not only a close friend and confidant, but he was also the creator of the Warlock programs, essential elements in AI cybercrime investigation for Nemesis. His advanced applications were the most cutting-edge innovations in existence and virtually undetectable.

Straight away, Liz sent Nemesis Canadian agents Tina Tremblay and Rose Conner to the Monastery to investigate the accident. Noah and Greta were family to the McCalls. It cut to the bone that they were gone. Liz wanted to get all the details of the mishap. If things didn't add up, she wanted to know.

WHILE THEY CONDUCTED THEIR INVESTIGATION, Tina and Rose moved into the Monastery. The elegant mountain fortress seemed so drab and dismal without the boisterous couple who brought so much love and joy to the place. Noah with his jokes and Greta with her stories, her raucous laughter constantly ricocheting off the walls. Now there was nothing but hollow echoes. The Canadian agents had stayed with Noah and Greta on numerous occasions in the past. Now they robotically migrated to the rooms Greta had designated for them back then. After unpacking a few things, Tina and Rose met downstairs in front of the massive fireplace to review the incident.

There wasn't any concrete evidence. Local scuttlebutt had it that Noah must have misjudged the distance he had to pass a slow-moving truck and met a semi head-on, scrunching their Mercedes into an accordion. The single eyewitness to the crash swore there was no driver in the semi's cab. However, they did see a man in a jumpsuit climb into a blue car and leave the scene. *And no one considered that the least bit suspicious?* Tina thought as she gave Rose a glance.

TINA AND ROSE SAW THE FATAL INCIDENT as a message to Nemesis— back off or pay the price. Nemesis was a huge headache for the illicit drug trade, mostly due to the negative propaganda barrage launched by its supercomputer, Warlock. It would be naïve to believe the cyber- crime world wasn't aware of it or Noah Bouchard, the genius behind Warlock. The wrong message had been sent to the wrong people.

Known for its tenacity, Nemesis pulled out all the stops to find and punish those responsible.

Brainstorming back at the Monastery, Rose pressed Tina. "So, how did they pull it off? Had to be professional. Too much timing and forethought not to be.

Rocking back and forth in her seat, Tina gazed off into the distance, freeing up her mind and searching her memory. Finally, she said, "Okay, here's how I see it. They did it using cell phones and a trail car. A member of the hit team called Noah and Greta and feigned some sort of emergency down the mountain that required their personal attention. As soon as the Bouchards turned onto the two-lane road from the Monastery, a spotter, via cell phone, alerted the driver of a semi parked a mile down the mountain to pull onto the highway. His job was to keep Noah from passing until the ascending semi was in position. As soon as they neared the halfway point, the truck holding up Noah slowed down on a straightaway and signaled for him to pass.

"When the Bouchard vehicle pulled out and was even with the semi, the driver in the descending semi matched speed with Noah until the poor man reached the point of no return. Then the trucker put the accelerator pedal to the floor to escape the head-on crash and hung poor Noah out to dry. The driver of the ascending truck, who was wearing a padded jumpsuit and crash helmet, waited until he saw Noah approaching in his lane. Then, at the last minute, he dived into a heavily cushioned space behind the cab. After the crash, he crawled out of his padded enclosure and made his way to the trail car, then off they went. And by the way, I didn't just come up with this scenario off the top of my head. I remembered reading about it in an actual case file years ago."

"But why would the drug goons wait until now to eliminate Noah? Surely there were plenty of prior opportunities and simpler ways to handle it," commented Rose.

"It might have something to do with the underworld rumor involving viral toxins developed by scientists formerly working for Suliman Kumar. After Suliman was killed during the massacre at The Castle, his lab staff in Qatar decided to explore the market for deadly pathogens on the dark web.

"Noah, via Warlock, intercepted numerous queries focused on one particular microorganism known as Muerte Lenta (slow death). Noah was resolute about tracking down and destroying the virus before it got into the wrong hands. Unfortunately, it looks like the underworld caught wind of it."

TINA AND ROSE SHARED their suspicions with Liz. Along with the grapevine gossip having to do with bioweapons, there were other extenuating circumstances to substantiate the theory that the collision was planned. The recording of a frantic emergency call to the Bouchards, a blue sedan seen conveniently parked on the side of the road, the specially outfitted reinforced sleeping compartment behind the seats of the damaged semi, and a man seen fleeing the scene in a blue car all added up to premeditated murder.

Liz agreed. There was too much corroborating evidence for it to have been happenstance. She instructed Tina and Rose to stick around the Monastery for a while and sniff around Banff for clues. On a hunch, Liz suggested they check out truck stops, motels, cafés, and hospital emergency rooms to see if anyone who looked out of place had been treated for injuries sustained in an automobile accident over the last several days. A few of the truckers remembered Rose from the Que Sera bar and volunteered to ask around.

Liz's intuition panned out, and one of Rose's regular customers came through with some useful info. There was this braggart in a local bar the night before the crash, a cocky dude going on about coming into some major bucks the next day. He was involved in a dangerous stunt and was having one last fling in case things didn't work out. Sloshed to the gills, the slightly built guy with the military haircut weaved out of the bar and crawled into the back seat of a dark-blue Buick in the parking lot. The fella was back in the bar a day or so later, bought rounds for the house, and hit on the ladies like he had really struck it rich. Rose's friend hadn't seen him since, but he remembered that the guy had a new ride when he left the bar. This one was a cherry-red Camaro. Not that the fool should have been driving anyway. He was so drunk he left his cell phone in a corner booth.

TREY MCCALL WAS BOTH HEARTBROKEN and majorly pissed off at what happened to Noah and Greta. In response to the catastrophic event in West Canada, Liz and Bryce flew to Whispering Canyons so they could console Trey and Tara on their loss and Liz could seek advice from Trey. As her predecessor at Nemesis, her grandfather had a world of experience dealing with underworld thugs. Liz wanted to pick his brain, so she didn't miss anything.

Having given it considerable thought over the past few days, Trey already had a course of action in mind when Liz approached him. "Why don't you blindside the bastards who ordered the Bouchard murders and set up the duo running Riverview Institute as patsies to draw out the culprits?" he said. "Here's how. Program Warlock will use Riverview Institute's IP address to send a message out on the dark web congratulating the drug lords responsible for taking out Noah Bouchard on a job well done. Coming out of nowhere like, that ought to stir things up."

And did it ever. Anxious to muzzle the unwanted attention, the drug lords launched their own investigation into the founders of the institute. At the same time, Dr. Marty Shaftner pitted Miles and Quin against each other for her affection. A budding chain reaction was in the making. Neither the cartel, Quin, nor Miles was aware that Warlock monitored their every move via the internet, cleverly concealed bugs, and spy cam devices. Unrest prevailed, and there was no better place to observe Trey's plan in action than at Whispering Canyons with the man himself.

QUIN LUNA AND TED MILES WERE so distracted by irate drug lords and Dr. Marty Shaftner that they missed the warning signs of impending rebellion aimed at the MTC over the missing student. A growing countermovement swept the campus, which the management passed off as nothing more than growing pains.

They figured if they ignored it, it would go away. Not so in this case. The names of the three students who died in the fire at the girl's camp were released. A large group of students thought it highly suspicious that the female, identified as Emily Pressler (a ruse set up by the authorities to protect her), would willingly go out all the way out to Camp Topaz with two male MTC cadets—an organization she vehemently detested.

THANKS TO NEMESIS POSTS on the internet about the turmoil at Riverview Institute, interested parties in the civilian community demanded answers. Overnight, they took a closer look at what really went on at Riverview Institute—from the narrow curriculum to the biased selection of instructors. Folks had second thoughts about the MTC program and what it actually provided to the student body. Suddenly, the grand plan for a model sect presided over by its two masterminds was in dire straits. All the signs were there, and minor skirmishes cropped up on campus until a violent encounter finally erupted. During the fray, one of the loose-cannon militant MTC cadets gunned down an angry student who dishonored him and his cause. The cadet swore he was only obeying the tenet drilled into him during training—*defend the honor of the corps.*

With local police dispatched to the institute and due to arrive any second, Quin and Miles managed to put their differences about Dr. Marty aside long enough to hide their most sensitive documents in the carriage house bunker.

"What a shitstorm," Quin remarked as he stared outside. "Never saw this coming. You?"

Shaking his head in disgust, Miles answered, "Not really. At least not until those idiots kidnapped that girl and the fire happened at Camp Topaz. Man, what a fucking mess this turned out to be. What in the hell were we thinking, letting the MTC run amok? Too wrapped up in our own shit to notice what was going on, I guess. And now we are so *screwed.*"

TO SUSTAIN THE MOMENTUM, Liz pumped out malicious propaganda on social media from the confiscated notebooks she and Bryce found on their honeymoon. Inside the files was more than enough credible material to keep the pharmaceutical investigators busy putting out fires of their own while they sought revenge on the Riverview cofounders.

OVERNIGHT, THERE WAS A NEW FACE in Comfort, Texas—a German by the name of Rolf Gehring. Rolf was known in the pharmaceutical sphere as a fixer, one who confronts the problem and takes care of it. He milled around the town square, watching, listening, and scribbling an occasional note in his booklet.

Comfort was a small community surrounded by towns like Fredericksburg, Kerrville, and New Braunfels, which were made up of rural and retired folks largely of German heritage. So Rolf blended in nicely. Settling in a small bed-and-breakfast just off the square, he posed as a freelance journalist looking to do a story on Riverview Institute. He told his interviewees he was intrigued by the concept of operating a free college in a world where educational costs had skyrocketed. It was a safe cover, and people openly expressed to him their opinions about Riverview. Not all had high praise for the institution; those were the ones he pressed for more information—the ones who would give him leads he could pursue. One of those leads turned out to be a doctor, a female medical examiner, who recently worked a suspicious fire at a girl's camp where three of the college's students perished. Gehring wanted to find out more details about that fire, so he made an appointment with Dr. Marty Shaftner.

Like most men who met Marty for the first time, Rolf was stunned by her natural beauty. He focused on the art on the wall to distract himself from her allure. Dr. Shaftner asked him how she could help him. Gehring gave her his cover story about doing a piece on the college but was sidetracked when he learned about the fire involving the three students. His investigative reporter's cover unraveled quickly as he became more adamant about the mishap.

She repeated that the case was closed. The bodies had been identified and the names of the students had been announced. There was nothing left to talk about.

Rolf frowned, then asked, "So, what were those three kids doing out there alone at the camp? Wasn't the camp shut down? Was there something else going on out there we should know about?"

Marty was not particularly fond of reporters. This one had gotten under her skin quicker than most. "Let me make this perfectly clear, Mr. Gehring. We found no evidence whatsoever to substantiate what you are inferring," she replied curtly.

He was about to blow a gasket but caught himself. "Seems I ruffled your pretty little feathers, ay, Doc? Guess I touched on a sore subject."

With that, he dropped a card with his phone number on her desk and made his exit without saying another word. But his actions and reactions revealed all she needed to know. Rolf was no more a reporter than she was an astronaut. Marty always recorded her meetings as a precaution. She had the guy on audio and video, a copy of which she sent off to Liz lickety-split. Within the hour, Marty was staring down at the file of Rolf Gehring, mob mercenary and renowned assassin.

"Oh boy, this is going to be fun," Marty said to no one there as she licked her lips in anticipation.

LIZ ASSIGNED SETH COLLINS and Becca Evans to keep twenty-four-hour surveillance on Rolf, who she assumed would shadow Dr. Marty Shaftner's every move. Using Warlock, Nemesis also monitored all of

Rolf's communications for clues about the identities of those calling the shots.

Liz's tactic called for Marty to lead her bird dog on a series of wild-goose chases and provide misleading information by means of a bug he had not so stealthily planted in her office. Liz laughed to herself, thinking, *It never ceases to amaze me how overconfident cocky mercs tend to be.*

ROLF SAW NO RHYME OR REASON to the places the stupid bitch doctor visited in the Hill Country. Berry farms, boutiques, and novelty gift shops were not Rolf's cup of tea. If she kept this up, he would have to resort to a more sinister approach. It would be a shame to mess up such a pretty face, but his bosses were getting impatient for answers. The media barrage was taking its toll.

Unknown to Rolf, Nemesis agents picked up an urgent message sent to him from overseas telling him to cut to the chase—either get the answers they needed from the doctor or waste her.

Liz alerted Marty. "Heads up, girl. Rolf has his orders to take you out. You know what to do. Any questions?"

Before she hung up, Marty asked, "Dead or alive?"

"Alive if possible. Use your discretion."

The predetermined site Marty selected for her showdown with Rolf was off the beaten path—a dilapidated old barn out in the country. The German merc followed her out to the godforsaken wreck of a building. When she parked and went inside, he made up his mind—this was it. She was history. She was kneeling, facing away from him, as he sneaked up behind her.

As Rolf reached into his coat for his gun, she said, "Hello, Mr. Gehring. Welcome to the party."

He was so startled that he hesitated long enough for her to sweep his feet out from under him with a lightning-swift whip kick. His gun fell to the floor, and she kicked it away as he jumped to his feet. He was smiling ear to ear as he prepared to tear her apart with his bare hands. Like all Nemesis agents, Marty was a master of Krav Maga, something Rolf might have wished he had known before he rushed her.

Marty easily dodged his advance, giving him a little something to remember her by as she slammed her elbow full force into his back, knocking the wind out of him. She cautioned him to stay down, but he didn't listen. After he regained his breath, he grabbed a rusty old pitchfork off the dirt floor with the intention of skewering her like appetizer shrimp.

She toyed with him until he lunged at her. Grasping the shaft of the pitchfork with both hands, Marty went with his forward motion, swirled him around, and flipped him like a pancake. His chest landed on the tines of the pitchfork, and the weight of his body pushed the sharp points through his torso and out his back. The look of surprise was transfixed on his face in a horrific death mask. Marty was disappointed. She thought the notorious fixer would have put up a more respectable fight.

Having barely broken a sweat, she went outside to call Liz with her report that Rolf Gehring was no more. Her description of the brief scuffle and grisly demise of the subject elicited a brief *hmm* from the chief of Nemesis and a fervent warning to be on the lookout for replacements in the near future.

According to messages commandeered by Warlock off the dark web shortly thereafter, the criminal element who employed Rolf were baffled and wondered where in the hell their hitman had gone. There was little chance they would ever find him since Dr. Marty arranged for Rolf to be placed in cold storage at the morgue as a John Doe until further notice. Now that Rolf Gehring was permanently out of the picture, Liz focused on Ari Moon and Miles Stewart.

FOR THE TIME BEING, MILES STEWART sat on the porch of the main house at Riverview Crest, gazing out at a cluster of buildings and the mass of disgruntled humanity negotiating the maze around them. He pictured the openness of it all when he had first set eyes on it, trying to come to grips with why he agreed to the transformation in the first place. He could have been at peace out here without a single care, with a brand-new identity and more money than he would have ever needed to live out his days as a forgotten man. But no. He jeopardized all that. And for what? A partnership with an obsessed bigot pitching another pipe-dream scam. Where would all this bullshit lead? Was there a way out at all? Or would he go down with a man who was anything but the mentor he claimed to be? Prospects didn't look all that great at the moment.

IN HIS OFFICE, ARI MOON was oblivious to the outside world, fixated on saving his precious movement and the illusion he could possess the unattainable woman he desired. Ari couldn't see it. No longer did he possess the power or influence to make things happen, and he would soon be the forgotten man in it all. Oh, there were still a few who carried his torch—the ones who had nothing better to believe in. Most of his previous followers deserted him and moved on to the next wackadoodle crusade.

THE CYBERCRIME TEAM AT NEMESIS watched as problems compounded for the felonious administrators of Riverview Institute. The clash at the school between students and the MTC that resulted in one fatality remained under investigation by local and federal authorities. Biased curriculum and staffing issues were under intense scrutiny from the community and the state. Finally, there was serious concern as to why the college rented off-campus facilities for extracurricular activities when they had an abundance of undeveloped property available on-site.

Liz bet it wouldn't be long before new mercenaries came to Texas to check on their missing fixer. And within the week, a renegade drug bigwig sent a team of five men down to the Hill Country from Chicago. *Why would you send thugs from Illinois to Texas to investigate anything?* she wondered. *They'll stand out like a sore thumb. What a dumbass.*

He was, and they did. A grade-schooler could have tailed the quintet that arrived all cowboyed up like department store mannequins. It didn't take long before the whole of Kendall County knew that a bunch of Yankees were in town asking questions about some German dude who disappeared a while back. Folks around Comfort didn't know or care whether the dude was still there or not.

Word about the strangers and their inquiries eventually got to Ari Moon and Miles Stewart. They were puzzled at first, then they put two and two together: underworld big shots sent someone to check them out, and something must have happened to the guy before he got to them at the institute. With small towns being such gossip mills and all, they thought it was funny that they had never heard about it. They told each other that whoever the drug kingpins had selected for the first go-round must have skipped out or met with foul play and that the new guys must be reinforcements.

When nothing turned up after a week, the Midwest hoods got bored and decided to speed up the process. In an attempt to get answers, two of the punks threatened and slapped around a couple of elderly citizens. That may have worked in Chicago, but it did not sit well with the locals in Comfort. On their way back to their digs, the two brave souls met some real cowboys—Army Rangers and Nemesis agents fresh from the fighting in Afghanistan. They beat the living shit out of the gutless bastards and easily got them to cough up the name of the guy who'd sent them. After being dropped off on the doorstep of where they were staying, the hoodlums threw their belongings into suitcases and tripped over each other on their way out the door, leaving tire marks on the pavement as they burned rubber to the airport.

THE DRUG EXECUTIVE RESPONSIBLE for dispatching the five men to Texas was president of Worthington Pharmaceuticals Research and Manufacturing, located near Oak Brook, a suburb of Chicago. Liz found frequent references to Lew Worthington in her evidence files and had the Warlock program work up a detailed file on him, starting with the day he was born.

Things were about to get nasty for Lew Worthington, who was pacing around his lavish office and wondering what was going on with his boys down in Comfort. Their last report said they were being stonewalled and were about *to change tactics. So what did they do? he wondered.* Did it work? Where in the hell are they now? He had been assured that the guys were top-of-the-line mercenaries, war veterans, battle tested, and street smart—all that bullshit the guy he hired them from promised. Shit, it cost him a fortune in advance. Now, nobody returned his calls, messages, or emails.

It got worse. His secretary burst into the office, frantic about something on the internet relating to him. Lew had just started to read the allegations being leveled at him on social media when his secretary flipped on the TV. ABC was airing the story. He attempted to watch the TV while he finished reading the posts, but his head was spinning, and his concentration was shot. He managed to glance up at the TV screen in time to catch nefarious individuals' names being connected to his. Ice-cold fear overcame him as he slouched in his leather chair. Names of crime bosses, known felons, porn stars, and pedophiles scrolled across the video display. According to ABC, there were pictures and flash drives to back up the accusations. Most were too vile to be shown on air.

Years back, Lew found it exciting and seductively naughty to indulge in gross perversities. In fact, most in his twisted realm participated. Now that it was out in the open, he realized it had been nothing more than an exercise in depravity. His phones buzzed, rang, beeped, and chimed. His voicemail was full, and his wife had called ten times. He was so *done*. As he hastily made for the exit, Lew instructed his secretary to inform everyone he would be unavailable until further notice.

What to do? On his way home, he racked his brain to no avail. When he pulled into his driveway at home, his wife flipped him off as she left for the airport with her yoga instructor. After he pulled into the garage, Lew noticed his golf clubs scattered on the floor, with all the shafts snapped in two. And when he went inside, he was greeted with a huge "Fuck You" spray-painted on the wall in the kitchen.

He staggered over to the breakfast nook and sat down to gather his thoughts. No way would he stay at the house. Too many folks knew where he lived. *Where could I go to get away from all this crap?*

he wondered. Well, he did have a small place at a lake not too far away where he kept a boat. Nobody else knew about it, aside from a few hookers he had entertained there. Not even his wife.

With no other real options, Lew changed into a pair of cargo shorts, a Hula Grill tee shirt, and some Crocs. Then he grabbed a handful of tee shirts and cargo shorts out of his dresser drawer, along with his favorite pair of sneakers from the closet, and tossed them into a duffle bag. He donned a pair of Maui Jim sunglasses and a Chicago Cubs baseball cap, jumped in the car, and drove to the lake.

His first two days in self-exile went by without incident, which allowed Lew to let down his guard. He thought maybe he had slipped away from the assholes who had doxed him and was home free. Feeling frisky on the third day, he took his Boston Whaler, dubbed *Destiny*, out for a run. The last anyone saw of Lew, he was captaining his boat out of the marina and heading for the far side of the lake.

A couple of days later, lake security found a splintered fragment of the stern with the *De* of the boat's name bobbing up and down near the shore—with a Chicago Cubs baseball cap beside it. Lew was not the first corrupt exec to pay dearly for a depraved lifestyle. Nor would he be the last.

One by one, Lew's cohorts disappeared off the grid, thanks to Nemesis, Liz's blistering media campaign, and karma. Although that retribution was singularly satisfying to Nemesis, more enlightening was the confirmation of those who'd actually financed the corruption behind the scenes—international and domestic billionaires and influential political dynasties. It didn't matter what level of exploitation and corruption they were at. To save themselves, criminals were willing to give up the ones above them on the ladder. Nemesis believed that if enough of the pompous elites felt the sting of justice, it might just wake up the narcissists to what little power they actually wielded.

MEANWHILE, IN TEXAS AND UNDER INVESTIGATION for numerous felonies, Ari Moon and Miles Stewart, on the advice of counsel, replied, "No comment," to every question. Search warrants and subpoenas kept their lawyers at bay while everything they owned and every document found was scrutinized. Predictably, the two suspects circled the wagons.

Ari realized he and Miles weren't going to walk away this time; they were done. He decided to come clean about everything in the hopes of getting a reduced sentence, which meant he would have to throw his partner under the bus. When Miles heard what Ari did, he went ballistic.

Unfortunately, there was little he could do about it except paint himself in the best light possible as a victim under the spell of a mind-bending manipulator. Ari had one observer present while he was being questioned—Dr. Marty Shaftner. He thought she was there for moral support. She wasn't. When the interrogators finished with him, she asked if she might have a private moment with the accused.

They were escorted to an empty cell and given five minutes. Ari was all smiles as the steel door closed behind him and Marty. He started to speak, but she hushed him and ever so slowly undid the top button of her blouse and temptingly uttered, "So, this is what you wanted so badly... Well, I just wanted to give you a little something to remember me by." She stepped closer as if to embrace him. But instead, Marty whirled around and kicked him in the groin with all her might.

He dropped straight to the floor, grabbing his crotch and screaming in pain.

"That ought to give you a rough idea of my contempt for you. Have a lovely time in prison, lover boy. Ciao," she said with a smile and a one-finger salute.

He was crying like a baby when she knocked on the door to leave the cell.

Dr. Marty apologized to the guards as she squeezed past them into the hall. "Sorry, fellas. He threatened me with bodily harm. I had no recourse but to defend myself."

After he saw Ari squirming on the floor, one guard said to the other, "No wonder she had us switch off the video feed before they entered the cell."

THE CRIMINAL PROCEEDINGS for the founders of Riverview Institute took place at the courthouse in San Antonio. Miles and Ari were arraigned separately on the same day and in different courtrooms.

At his arraignment, which was rushed through the court system, Ari pleaded not guilty to a massive array of felony charges, including attempted murder and kidnapping at the top of the list. He was denied bail and remanded to jail until his trial date.

In a nifty maneuver, Miles's attorney arranged a plea bargain with the DA at the Kendall County District Attorney's office in Boerne, Texas, on charges his client unwittingly aided and abetted felonious activities. His lawyer convinced the DA that Miles had been a pawn, skillfully manipulated by his mentor. As evidence of Ari's charismatic powers of persuasion, the lawyer cited the multitude of Nobilis Familia followers who had fallen under Ari Moon's spell. Miles agreed to fully cooperate with the authorities and throw himself on the mercy of the court. In accordance with his plea, Miles was given a court date to appear for sentencing, placed under house arrest, and made to wear an ankle bracelet tracking device until his sentencing.

Ari couldn't believe what had happened. The pupil just schooled the teacher. The irony of it all irked him to no end. Here poor old Ari sat, rotting in a jail cell, contemplating his bleak future, counting down the days until his trial, reading worn-out paperbacks with torn covers and earmarked pages, and forcing down meals that tasted like cardboard. In contrast, Miles lived the life of Riley at Riverview Crest with all the comforts of home—watching cable TV, eating home-cooked meals, sunning by the pool with an afternoon cocktail … and … there was nothing Ari could do about it.

At long last, the day of the trial arrived. At the insistence of the prosecutors, Ari Moon was perp-walked into the courtroom in shackles. From the beginning, Liz McCall and her agents watched the court proceedings with great interest. She was impressed by the theatrics the DA exhibited early on to portray Ari Moon as a hardened criminal, all designed to leave a lasting first impression on the jury. Even with that and all the incriminating evidence against the defendant, a conviction was no slam dunk. It became apparent from the opening statements and the number of witnesses scheduled from each side that this trial was going to take months to complete. Liz sat patiently through Ari's lengthy trial. In light of the army of witnesses and mountains of evidence, the proceedings did indeed drag on for months.

Fortunately, the jury deliberated for only a couple of hours before they found Ari guilty on all charges and recommended the judge sentence him to consecutive life terms in a federal prison with no chance of parole.

WITH ARI'S TRIAL BEHIND HER, LIZ TURNED her attention to Miles Stewart, curious as to how she could entice him to move over to her side. Miles knew where all the skeletons were buried and who put them there. The FBI and several other initialed agencies owed Liz a favor or two for her behind-the-scenes help in solving some high-profile cases for them in the past. Now would be an excellent time for her to call one in.

With all the evidence he had on scores of nefarious big shots who ran the show for the criminal underground, Miles Stewart could actually tie them to unspeakable offenses they'd personally carried out or authorized. It was not an everyday occurrence in the crime-fighting realm, and Liz wondered if there was a way to tap that source to everyone's benefit. Perhaps the feds could share the responsibility of keeping Miles out of harm's way with Nemesis—like joint protective custody for a material witness. When approached with the idea, the feds bought in after the powers that be determined it would save money on manpower. But the judge who presided over Miles Stewart's case signed off on it in hopes that Miles could help thin the herd of empowered morally bankrupt imbeciles.

IN THE INTERIM, MILES WAS SECRETLY transferred to The Circle M while an agreement was pieced together. From a picture window in his quarters adjacent to the main house at the ranch, Miles took in an amazing array of projects that blended into a kaleidoscope of colors and functions. Temporarily mesmerized, Miles barely heard the gentle knock on his door.

"Excuse me, Mr. Stewart. My name is Jasper. I'm an agent-in-training for Nemesis. Liz Lonagon wondered if you could join her and a pair of federal agents in half an hour in the library of the main house."

Snapping out of his trance, Miles smiled and answered. "But of course. I'll just change and be there in a jiffy."

Much to the chagrin of elitists scrambling to keep their prima donna lifestyles intact, Miles agreed to the witness protection program partnership in the library at The Circle M and sang like a canary.

First, he opened up to the feds, then in greater detail to Liz and her crew, whom he trusted more. Rumors circulated on the dark web about a $5 million proof-of-death bounty placed on Miles's life. As a precautionary measure, he went under the knife to alter his appearance. Once his scars from surgery healed, Miles took up residence in Las Cruces, New Mexico, with a new name and a new life. Early on in the alliance, the feds brandished an air of superiority. Liz didn't have the time or patience for such nonsense, and she let the feds know that Miles was too important a witness to screw around playing the DC power game of whose is bigger.

FOLLOWING HIS CONVICTION, ARI MOON took up residence at the federal corrections institute at Three Rivers south of San Antonio to serve out his sentences. Wisely, he was placed in a wing with other nonviolent prisoners, away from the general prison population, where he would have been fair game for a hit. In his more sophisticated confines, Ari met a man who, for a price, could get things done on the outside. Ari resented being in there for the rest of his life while Miles wasn't. Revenge dominated his thoughts. Perhaps Big Louie De Luca could be of assistance.

During Louie's colorful history, he had run numbers and a protection racket for the mob in South Chicago until he crossed paths with a young upstart from Texas who wanted his position. They clashed off and on. Then, one night, the police showed up at Big Louie's door. His competition had been found dead in his home in Dallas, and Louie was their prime suspect. Whisked off to Texas and indicted by a grand jury, Louie was convicted purely on circumstantial evidence—at least, that was *his* story. So here he was in the joint at Three Rivers, serving five to ninety-nine for solicitation of capital murder.

Always looking for an angle, Louie groomed a naïve guard on his cell block to do favors for him on the inside while Louie's people reciprocated in kind for the guard on the outside—the good, old prison barter system, pure and simple. In the end, Louie had so much dirt on the guard that he owned the guy. All of which played into what happened next between Big Louie and Ari Moon.

Thoroughly pissed off and festering in his jail cell, Ari would have given the rest of what he had in the world to have Miles Stewart whacked. To that end, Louie intrigued Ari. The newbie inmate paid close attention to his surroundings and the way Louie conducted business. One day, Ari worked up the gumption and asked Big Louie what it would cost to do him a favor on the outside.

MEANWHILE, THANKS TO THE NEMESIS FOUNDATION, the new staff of instructors who took over at Riverview Institute made good on their promise to provide a low-cost, quality college education for students who chose to remain at Riverview. They offered a versatile curriculum that encouraged critical thinking. The MTC was disbanded. Instead, the school provided classes in self-defense overseen by retired martial arts instructors from Nemesis HQ at The Circle M. Camp Topaz returned to a summer camp for kids, managed under the umbrella of the Nemesis Foundation. Finally, Emily Pressler, with a full-ride scholarship awarded to her by Liz and the Nemesis Foundation Board and wearing a smile as big as Texas, was first in line to enroll when the institute reopened.

CHAPTER 10

ONE STATE WEST, IN LAS CRUCES, NEW MEXICO, Miles Stewart assumed the role of manager at a local hardware store using the alias Marcus Ward. Located at the foot of the Organ Mountains and along the banks of the Rio Grande, Las Cruces was rich in Hispanic heritage, offering a laid-back, easy-going lifestyle. Miles's new life fit the norm—uncomplicated, nine-to-five, and cold beers after work with his coworkers at the Out of the Way bar. Two of his fellow workers—a cashier at the hardware store and an assistant manager—were undercover Nemesis agents Liz assigned to watch over him.

Miles, aka Marcus Ward, made good on his promises to Nemesis and the feds. He provided them with serious dirt on members of corrupt political families and confirmed the participation of unscrupulous billionaire fanatics in merciless atrocities to topple governments and stifle the global population. So far, his intel had been spot on. So much so that it ruffled quite a few feathers in the criminal world's hierarchy, a situation Liz learned about through chatter that

Warlock intercepted on the dark web. Evidently, Ari Moon wasn't the only person who wanted to dispose of Miles. There was a queue of like-minded folks who pressured law enforcement to reveal Miles's whereabouts.

Liz could not have been happier. Her ploy to use Ari's former partner in crime to lure in the big fish panned out. In order to avoid raising suspicion, she made it a challenge for the unsuspecting horde to acquire the location.

THE FIRST SERIOUS NIBBLE AT THE BAIT came from an established political dynasty. Anxious to cover up a relative's careless behavior at a place known as The Castle in Albania, *their* people made subtle inquiries about Miles and where he might be but came up empty.

When Nemesis pushed the envelope and flooded the internet with compromising documentation that exposed their relative, the family called in some IOUs from old friends in their party. Reliable sources in DC corroborated the accuracy of the evidence and singled out Miles Stewart as the only possible source for such damaging material. If Miles was silenced, the family could claim plausible deniability. It was exactly the conclusion Liz and her colleagues had expected.

Adhering to her plan, Liz and her Nemesis squad steered a team of would-be assassins down a rabbit hole, chasing false clues and fake sightings of Miles Stewart. They followed up leads all over East Texas and into Louisiana until everything finally came to a head in Mississippi. A reliable underworld source confirmed that a Miles Stewart had recently paid cash to rent a bungalow on an isolated stretch of beach near Biloxi.

What a break! Big mistake for our mark to use his real name instead of an alias, thought the leader of the hit team. As it turned out, it wasn't a mistake, and it wasn't *the* Miles Stewart. Instead, it was a Nemesis agent named Curt Chesterfield, a head-to-toe dead ringer for Miles whom Liz had stationed there two days before as a decoy.

The scene was set. Over the next few days, it played out. Pretending to fish from the bank of a lagoon behind a nearby grove of trees, the hatchet team surveilled their target's bungalow. Curt busily checked out his digs and settled in while Nemesis agents watched the watchers from inside a telephone company repair van at the end of the cul-de-sac.

After three days, the killers made their move. At four a.m., two hit men dressed in all black approached the bungalow—one from the front, the other from the rear. Unaware they were being watched, they moved slowly in the dark until they reached the front and back doors, then expertly picked the locks. At almost the same instant they reached for their weapons to attach silencers and chamber a round, Nemesis agents converged on them and captured them without a shot fired.

It came as no surprise to Nemesis. The hit men were inexorably linked to the nefarious family. Months of data and recorded communications between the hired killers and their employers left no doubt as to who arranged the contract. Although genuinely pleased with the outcome, due to the family's influence, Liz wasn't convinced the government would prosecute the guilty party.

A short time later, whether by coincidence, karma, or an elaborate cover-up, the politically shielded relative who instigated the hunt for Miles was found dead in a single-car accident beneath the American Legion Memorial Bridge on Martha's Vineyard. He was the only occupant found in the car, which was resting on the bottom of Sengekontacket Pond. There were no indications of foul play, no marks whatsoever on the body, no witnesses, and no suspects.

THE SECOND INDIVIDUAL TO CIRCLE the chum should have considered the fate of the foolish aristocrat in DC who meddled where he didn't belong. But litigious billionaire Wayne Bianco, head of a Chicago lobby firm, was far too busy building his empire to be bothered. Accustomed to being the center of controversy, Wayne was thick skinned. In the past, most of the allegations leveled at him were fabricated insinuations he could easily refute. But not today.

On a gloomy Chicago day, with massive thunderstorms predicted until midnight, a more serious black cloud loomed on the horizon for the cocky wise guy. That morning, Liz's cyber crew began to covertly circulate bits of ruinous information about Wayne on the web, with the promise of more to follow. The problem for Wayne was that this time, it was all true. When he read the posts, the volatile lobbyist went ballistic. *How in bloody hell did they find out? I'm done for if the big bosses buy it.*

Immediately, he summoned Don Brinkley, or DB, his head facilitator, and ordered him to take care of whoever or whatever was responsible for this crap getting out. When DB hesitated, his boss threw another tantrum. "Get it done! And make it permanent! That's an order from Louie De Luca!" Wayne lied.

Something about Wayne's abrupt overreaction gave DB second thoughts, which he quickly dismissed when he heard that the mandate came down from Big Louie.

Without hesitation, DB enjoined his contacts in the media to sort out who provided the evidence that was spewing out about his employer. Efforts stalled until the name Miles Stewart surfaced. The fixer knew exactly who *that* guy was. Miles's reputation at The Castle was legendary. Wayne Bianco was totally screwed as long as the Albanian fortress facilitator was alive.

DB RECALLED MILES FROM his only time at The Castle and several other less provocative gatherings his boss attended. Miles was the expeditor for Ari Moon, just as Don Brinkley was for Wayne Bianco. Miles was likable enough but probably not as sincere as he put on. He was nobody's fool, and neither were the people keeping Miles out of sight. It was going to take careful planning to pull off Wayne's orders.

WITH THE LURE OF A GENEROUS REWARD, DB put out feelers and a description of Miles on the underground grapevine. A waitress and small-time mob informant at Rocky's on the Beach in Biloxi, Mississippi, responded. From the description DB provided, she was certain it was the guy who owned a bungalow on the water, down the beach from where she worked. The man was a regular at her eatery and a spitting image of the man DB described. On the chance she was right, Wayne's taskmaster made a special trip to Mississippi to surveil Rocky's.

Bingo! Late evening, around sevenish, on the second day, the man in question drove up in a dark-blue Lexus and parked two cars down from DB on the sandy parking lot in front of Rocky's. DB watched the man climb the steps up to the restaurant before he exited his car. The guy could be Miles Stewart with a few subtle surgical alterations. DB walked in just as Miles's doppelgänger slid up to the bar and entered a conversation with folks who were obviously friends of his. Casually, DB drifted to the other side of the bar with a good view of the action and ordered a Tito's on the rocks.

After cocktails, the mark and his friends went upstairs for dinner. DB nursed his drink at the bar while he watched and waited. He had no idea that the man he was following was an undercover agent named

Curt Chesterfield working for Liz Lonagon. As soon as the dinner party upstairs broke up, the assassin paid his tab and went outside to wait in his car. Five minutes later, Curt and his friends walked outside, said their good-byes, and started toward their cars.

DB watched as one of the women—a drop-dead gorgeous auburn-haired beauty—peeled off to join Curt. *Nice going, my man,* thought DB enviously, having no way of knowing that Dr. Marty Shaftner was the backup Liz had sent to Biloxi for Curt.

There was enough traffic on the beach highway for DB to squeeze in two cars behind Curt and Marty. As an experienced agent, Curt spotted a white car following him from the restaurant, recognized the shadowing maneuver it employed right away, and decided to toy with his pursuer. First chance he got on a straightaway, Curt floored the Lexus and whipped around four cars before he veered back into his lane in front of an oncoming vehicle. DB was caught by surprise and boxed in, with long lines of traffic on both sides of the road.

Certain he had lost them, DB was cursing up a storm when he saw the blue Lexus pull out of a gas station just ahead. *What a stroke of luck,* the assassin thought.

Looking in his rearview mirror, Curt had to laugh as he led the way to the beach condo.

A few minutes later, the blue Lexus pulled into the circular drive in front of a bungalow. Don Brinkley parked out of sight in a dark, secluded spot and silently slipped over to a copse of trees facing the beach cottage, with the sound of waves gently washing up to the shore in the bay behind him. Kneeling, he took out his infrared camera with a telephoto lens to scan the exterior of the beach house and determine the most promising kill zone. The plantation shades in the bedroom were half open, and he took the opportunity to snap a few photos of its interior. He continued a slow, sweeping scan of the bungalow, stopping occasionally to click off a pic or two.

Inside the house, the man and woman paraded hand in hand into the bedroom. Stripped to his boxers, the man turned down the bed and climbed in while the woman went into the bathroom. Several minutes later, she came out in a nightshirt, switched off the lights—saving for a night-light—and joined him under the sheets for a make-believe love session. Afterward, the woman lit up a smoke.

Their interested onlooker established the bedroom as his kill zone when he noted that the couple left the shades cracked open and the night-light was bright enough for him to zero in on them with the night scope he had removed from his camera case. The warm glow of a cigarette showing through the gap in the shades solidified his decision.

FOR THE NEXT SEVERAL DAYS, Curt and Marty gave their bird dog an expensive tour of all the hot spots and eateries in the Biloxi area. By the end of the week, the Chicago facilitator was convinced Curt was Miles Stewart. Unaware Nemesis was on to him, DB phoned his boss to advise him the mission was a go. In that Nemesis monitored all calls coming in and out of Wayne Bianco's office, Warlock intercepted DB's call, recorded it, then sent it on to Liz Lonagon, who kept her agents in Biloxi up to date. With DB's exemplary kill-shot record as an army sniper, Nemesis was fully aware it wasn't dealing with just any assassin.

NOW THAT HE WAS POSITIVE he had the man and the location, DB only had to lay low until the right moment. He knew from his reconnaissance that there was enough light escaping through the shutters for him to make out the shape of their bodies. All he had to do was wait until they were stationary. *This'll be a piece of cake. Too bad about the dame. She is so beautiful. What a shame to have to kill her. Collateral damage,* he mouthed to himself. He hated that term.

He snickered and thought of the bonus Wayne would surely give him when he got back to Chicago. For now, he hadn't a care in the world until he had his victims in his sights. Unfortunately, DB had no idea Liz's team had him in *their* sights while they waited and listened.

DB decided to put his plan in motion on Friday night. He went back to his hotel to ready his weapon of choice, an MK12 Special Purpose Rife—one of the lightest, most accurate sniper rifles in the world under a thousand yards. To reduce the rifle's report to a whisper, he attached a custom-designed suppressor. He wasn't going to miss from the grove of trees where he had set up his hide.

Friday night rolled around, and Curt took Marty to dinner at the Beau Rivage. This time, DB didn't follow but remained in his car, catty-cornered from their bungalow. After twenty minutes, he left the car, stayed in the shadows, and carried his rifle, with an extra magazine, into the grove of trees bordering the shoreline to settle into his hide. Nemesis agents in the background watched it all. They'd fingered him as soon as DB arrived at the Gulfport-Biloxi International Airport from Chicago and tailed him in his white Malibu since DB left the rental car lot.

Shortly after ten, the blue Lexus pulled into the drive. Curt and Marty got out of the car in hysterics, pretending to be tipsy from a bit too much wine, and staggered inside. Impatient with uncooperative buttons, they simply ripped off their clothes and dived under the covers to vociferously pretend to make love. Nemesis agents took it all in. DB smiled as he watched the nightly ritual unfold through his rifle scope.

As soon as cigarettes were lit, he fired back-to-back rounds into the heads of the stationary shapes. Both went down with direct hits. Confident he had accomplished his mission, DB flung the rifle into the lagoon behind him and casually strolled out of the trees as though he had just relieved himself. The look on his face was priceless when he walked straight into armed Nemesis agents standing there waiting for him.

The would-be assassin gained his composure long enough to say, "You're too late. Killed 'em both stone dead. Perfect head shots."

The agents didn't respond. They just frisked him, then cuffed him and carted him away. Another agent waded out onto the shallow shelf in the water to retrieve the rifle. DB couldn't figure out why no one was upset by what he had just done.

INSIDE THE BUNGALOW, THE SUPPOSED VICTIMS were on their knees by the far wall, putting out small fires caused by the lit cigarettes that had flown out of the mouths of mannequins when they lost their heads.

Marty looked at her partner and the headless dummies. "I think you're right, Curt. Cigarette smoking can definitely be hazardous to your health," the doctor uttered with a guttural laugh. Then Marty kissed him for real.

DURING THE TWO-AND-A-HALF HOURS since DB was apprehended coming out of the grove of trees, nobody had said a word to him. They had him dead to rights, but at least he had completed his mission.

After another hour in a dismal gray room with no windows, the door swung open. A woman and an older gentleman walked in with stern, no-nonsense expressions on their faces. They sat across from him on metal chairs at a metal table bolted to the concrete floor.

They stared at each other. No one said a word for what seemed an eternity, until DB finally blurted out, "Okay, what the fuck gives here? Nobody's read me my rights or nothing. That's against the law, ya know. I could just get up and walk out of here right now if I wanted." He made a move to get up and leave.

Liz said harshly, "Sit down! You're not going anywhere for a very long time. We're not with law enforcement, so we don't have to abide by constraints like Miranda rights and such. You, sir, are at our mercy until we decide you are not."

"Who the fuck are you people? What gives you the right to hold me against my will?"

Trey McCall answered, "Who we are is none of your concern. What you should be worried about is your immediate future. From where we sit, it doesn't look particularly promising for you."

Before the prisoner spoke again, Trey reminded him of what he'd said when he was apprehended. Then he played it for him on tape as a refresher.

DB hung his head, and the blood drained from his face. Then, slowly, the prisoner raised his head and said, "I'm *not* going to take the fall for this murder wrap. What do you want to know?"

"Everything you do."

"That's gonna take a while, my friend. Been with Wayne Bianco a long time—too long, the more I think about it. That SOB is a stone-hearted freak. Ain't nobody in his company can stand the *mother*. I don't think he has a friend in the world. I'd be shocked if he did. He treats people like shit. If he didn't pay so big, no one would touch him. Ask anybody who knows him."

DB took a breath. "Everything he's into is illegal—drugs, prostitution, gambling, smuggling, human trafficking, you name it. I'll tell you all I know and even testify against the scumbag. That's how much I hate that clown."

Nemesis personnel recorded the entire session. Tara and Miranda would have a field day back in the cybercrime lab, feeding all the data supplied by DB to Warlock to be analyzed and organized.

LIZ IMAGINED WAYNE BIANCO alone at his desk reading the *Chicago Times*, engrossed in a front-page story about the assassination of a man believed to be the notorious Miles Stewart and his lovely companion inside a beach house in Biloxi, Mississippi. There was no doubt in Liz's mind that Wayne Bianco was riding high, basking in his glory without a single concern about the fate of his accomplice. To him, men like Don Brinkley were expendable.

As part of her elaborate scheme, Liz made sure to include pictures in the headline news article of coroner assistants wheeling two body bags out of the house and into an ambulance. She envisioned Wayne leaning back in his office chair with a Cheshire cat grin on his face while he gloated about how easily he had pulled a fast one over on his anonymous adversary.

BY REASON OF DON BRINKLEY'S DISCLOSURES, the authorities had probable cause to conduct a personal and private search of Wayne Bianco's dealings. Liz and Trey accompanied the feds when they marched into the lobbyist's Chicago office with search and arrest warrants in hand, including one for solicitation of murder for hire.

Wayne's fate was sealed. Headlines about him in papers around the world were brutal but not nearly as unkind as the photo and video evidence that surfaced on the internet and in social media. After his arraignment on multiple charges, including murder for hire, an unsympathetic judge denied him bail and remanded the accused to jail. Naked, alone, locked down in solitary confinement in maximum security, and under twenty-four-hour guard, Wayne Bianco somehow took his own life.

ARI MOON READ THE NEWSPAPER ACCOUNTS about his former partner's execution in Biloxi, thrilled that the man met such a fitting end. Sitting on his bunk in his cell, he mused about Miles, who never saw what hit him. He smirked, relieved he would never have to deal with Miles again.

Then it occurred to him that there was no proof of death. His gusto turned to anguish. Where were the pictures of the bodies? There weren't any. Only body bags carted out of the house to the meat wagon.

Ari had to find Big Louie, and fast.

BIG LOUIE WAS ECSTATIC AND BESIDE HIMSELF that he still had sway in his old hometown. When Ari located him in the rec room, Louie was bloviating about the old days with his crew. That is until he saw the expression on Ari's face. The Chicago crime boss stopped mid-sentence to listen to Ari and agreed with his assessment: "No bodies, no proof."

For Louie to save face and remove all doubt, he had to find out if Miles was dead or alive. Fortunately, Louie's cabal had eyes and ears pretty much everywhere.

By means of the underground grapevine, Louie received a coded message, and Ari's suspicions were confirmed. The body bags in Biloxi contained two headless mannequins. Moreover, a high-profile criminal had been placed in witness protection in Las Cruces, New Mexico, at the time of Miles's disappearance. After applying some unfriendly persuasion on the informants, the mob obtained the alias of the man and his place of employment.

WARLOCK PICKED UP ON A TRIGGERED reference and traced all inquiries mentioning Miles coming out of Chicago to Texas. The simple cipher used in the communications, which the Warlock AI program decrypted, implicated a federal agent in collusion with an inmate at Three Rivers Federal Penitentiary in Texas. Liz debated whether or not to expose the participants. Thanks to some heady advice from her grandfather Trey McCall, she remained patient to see how deep into the cesspool the corruption sank.

TOP GUNS IN THE MOB were perplexed by all the negative crap plaguing them on the web and the internet. Someone was onto their game—a player who played by gangster rules—and the criminals were ill-prepared to combat it. *They* were supposed to be the ones to mold public opinion, not the other way around. This new tactic handcuffed the crime establishment, who, like everyone else, could no longer trust what they heard, saw, or read in the media. Tech-savvy crime bosses were forced to communicate via coded written correspondence.

Incarcerated mob boss, Louie De Luca, was old school and had never trusted modern-day communication channels anyway. A dinosaur of sorts, he preferred to communicate by snail mail. He was wise to the fact that his letters would be censored before they went out and the replies censored as they came in. Every week since he had arrived at Three Rivers, Louie sent letters back to the family in Illinois to establish a pattern and a code—one that Nemesis had already broken. After years of scrutinizing De Luca family correspondence, the prison censors grew lax and haphazardly scanned the documents—or so Louie thought. In fact, with the cooperation of the personnel at Three Rivers, the letters were thoroughly scrutinized, decoded, copied, and filed by Nemesis.

Outgoing letters were addressed to a house in the suburbs of Chicago owned by a Patricia De Luca, Louie's aunt and only living relative. On Wednesday nights, she would hand over the letters to Louie's boys when they came over to sample her exquisite Italian cuisine—lasagna, her specialty. Aunt Pat mailed back typewritten responses with apologies that her Parkinson's made her handwriting a thing of the past.

When Louie found out that the new generation of criminal bigwigs had to go retro to keep in touch, he sighed, shook his head, then burst out laughing. *How about that? Whiz kids got schooled. Gotta love it,* he thought and settled down to the business at hand.

While discussing the questionable demise of Miles Stewart, Louie related an interesting take from his boys in Illinois.

"Contrary to the popular perception that Miles and his lady were killed, a couple of old-timers in my gang are convinced Miles is in protective custody in New Mexico. Seems they witnessed the same scam worked to perfection on the South Side of Chicago during Prohibition. They claim the other sightings are a deflection, nothing more than smoke and mirrors. One old fella reckons a heavy-duty crew is behind it all, spreading all that negative shit about us on the internet. The old fart's money's on Nemesis," Louie offered, hoping to get a rise out of his friend.

Instead of a rise, Ari lowered his head and sulked. "Could be the old boy is right. Those bastards at Nemesis have their tentacles into everything. Question is, What in the hell are we going to do about it?"

"I've got some IT brainiacs working on a solution. So far, they're stumped. According to them, some cyber genius masterfully cloaked the IP address that's sending all the propaganda to the web. My guys aren't sure if *anyone* can break the encryption to sabotage the program."

TOO BAD LIZ HADN'T HEARD THE EXCHANGE between Ari and Louie. She would have beamed with pride and passed it on to Levon Vargas. The son of Jorge and Sidney Vargas, Levon was part of the extended McCall family at The Circle M and the new Nemesis computer whiz kid. Mentored by the late Noah Bouchard, Levon was technically leaps and bounds ahead of the corrupt cybercrime organizations. Innovations incorporated by Levon took Noah Bouchard's creation to the next level. Enhanced AI Warlock could invisibly retrieve and send information, which was completely untraceable, and could alter data to fit whatever narrative necessary. Destined to own the internet, much like the media did for so long, the situation changed drastically in Nemesis's favor. Thanks to Levon, Liz held the upper hand. She suspected that whoever was responsible for the murder of Noah Bouchard and his wife, Greta, was also involved in the hunt for Miles Stewart. Perhaps Warlock could sort it out.

BIG LOUIE GLANCED OVER at his friend Ari. "What's with the frown?"

"Nothing much. Just thinking. Wondering, really. You think your crew out in New Mexico can locate this Marcus Ward, who is supposedly Miles Stewart?"

"Hope so. They're new to me, but they come highly recommended. With Don Brinkley in custody, they're the best I could round up on the spur of the moment."

Louie De Luca would not be able to resist playing the big man in charge to impress his fellow inmates and fortify his precious prison reputation. Ari exploited De Luca's arrogance to shift the blame for the collision that killed Noah and Greta Bouchard to Louie.

THANKS TO WARLOCK, NEMESIS PICKED up the trigger name Marcus Ward from chatter between two parties in Las Cruces, New Mexico—allegedly on a mission to take out Miles Stewart. Louie's hires were unaware they were being electronically surveilled and haphazardly used email or text to communicate with their cohorts. Nemesis gathered up every word and informed its agents in Las Cruces to be on the lookout for a pair of two-person teams sent to take out Miles Stewart.

Due to Warlock, Liz was already ahead of Ari and Louie at Three Rivers. While the mob hit teams searched for Ari Moon's long-time accomplice in New Mexico, Liz relocated Miles to Flagstaff, Arizona. Then she replaced him in Las Cruces with his doppelgänger, Curt Chesterfield.

For a week, Nemesis agents watched two hit teams shadow their target to establish Curt's patterns. Liz's agents kept them in sight the whole time, waiting for the right moment to step in and apprehend the hired killers. Every single day, Curt visited a dilapidated farmhouse on the outskirts of town to suggest he had something of value hidden there. It was a routine Liz counted on to get the gangsters' attention and stimulate not only their curiosity but also their greed. Kill the mark and steal his stash—a two-for-one special. The trap was set.

WHILE NEMESIS AGENTS BACK AT THE TEXAS headquarters monitored the Miles Stewart situation, Trey McCall returned as well to help Liz out and get in some quality golf time. Novél Vargas, the young star on the LPGA, wanted to step up her game but was too shy to ask Trey for help. Her mother, Sidney Baker Vargas, the primary attorney for the McCall family, asked her boss if he had time to work with Novél to help her over the hump in her golf career. Trey was more than willing to analyze Novél's game. Besides, it was a relaxing way for him to escape the crime-solving rat race for a while.

A notion came to Trey's mind. Ben Hogan once said LPGA Hall of Fame member Mickey Wright had the finest golf swing he had ever seen. Period. If Ben Hogan thought so highly of Mickey Wright, perhaps Novél should model her action after Wright's. With that in mind, Trey searched through all the films he could find of Wright's swing back in the 1960s, when she dominated women's golf. He found there were quite a few similarities between Hogan's and Wright's swings. They were too obvious for him to ignore. Trey jotted down the common denominators of the two swings and then arranged for Novél and Jefferson to join him in the morning so he could share what he had discovered.

The three professionals gathered on the practice ground for what turned out to be an enlightening day for Novél Vargas. They sat on one of the wooden benches at the back of the range, facing a large viewing screen on the far wall of the teaching facility. Trey started a side-by-side video presentation of Hogan's and Wright's swings face on, then from behind, stopping at different stages of their swings to point out striking similarities.

Next, Trey had Hogan, Wright, Jefferson, and Novél on the screen—face on and from behind—to compare swing positions. As a teacher, Trey was always hands-on with his protégés, not one to use much video. But when the elder McCall compared Hogan and Wright videos from back in the day to those of Jefferson and Novél today, he saw ways to help them become more consistent. To Jefferson, Trey pointed out the footwork both legendary players blended into the motion of their swing. It was a light bulb moment for his son, who hustled to the far corner of the range to test it out.

Trey put the Mickey Wright video back on, side by side with Ben Hogan's, and asked Novél to watch it several times, then tell him what she saw that was different from how she swung the club. Several things popped up, like takeaway, balance, tempo, rotation, and clearing the left side.

Trey was impressed. "Very observant, Novél, but a little overcritical on your part. Most of those things you already do very well."

She smiled.

Trey continued. "Note how both legends waggle the club and have movement in their lower body in preparation for taking the club back. They both widen their stance and square up by setting the back foot prior to the start of the backswing. The arc of their backswings is wide and full as they turn behind the ball, then set the club at the top. Both clear the left side as the right side fires on the downswing. I would like to see you pay more attention to the waggle and movement you use to get your swing started. Under pressure, you tend to vary your rhythm because you lack motion at the start. Be conscientious of your right hand during takeaway. Don't jerk the club back. Instead, drag the right back on a wider arc. Work on the waggle, lower body movement, and the takeaway. Once you get the feel of it, you'll be amazed how relaxed and powerful your golf swing will become."

LIZ THOUGHT HOW WONDERFUL IT WAS to have such a versatile, generous man for a grandfather. One who made time for everyone in the extended McCall family. Here he was, back in her office after sharing his expertise at the driving range. At the moment, he was going on about the old days before Warlock and how the world sped up so much with the computer generation, the internet, and social media. Trey missed the old days, like most older folks, she supposed.

"Grandpa, how did it all get so crazy? I mean, we're losing ground. Even with Warlock's new AI additions and a crack team of agents, the criminal element grows faster than we can bring them to justice," Liz commented in a shaky voice, in need of bolstering.

"Two reasons, my dear. Greed and corruption abound in our societies, more so today than ever. Until folks understand that they are being used to further the aspirations of the wicked, we'll continue to fight a losing battle. For generations, predatory families established their dominance over the populace, relying on lies and exploitation to create wealth and perpetuate dynasties.

"Be mindful that Nemesis is a godsend to the downtrodden, a beacon of light to combat the darkness. You have a huge responsibility to fight the evil in humankind and rein in the madness. Remember what your great-grandfather whispered in your ear. 'You are the one we have all been waiting for.' He saw your integrity, which makes you able to rock the very soul of our enemies."

Misty-eyed, Liz kissed him on the cheek. "Thank you, Grandpa. I needed that. You always seem to know the right things to say."

LONGING TO SHARE MORE MEMORIES with his lovely wife, Tara, Trey took the Nemesis Cessna Citation jet back to Whispering Canyons. Late one morning at the McCall cabin, when she came to tidy up, their housekeeper found Trey and Tara in bed together, hand in hand, smiling and staring blankly into each other's soul. There was no sign of a struggle or foul play. By the grace of God, they had passed peacefully during the night.

The news of Trey's and Tara's passing shocked many. Thanks to them, Nemesis's justice had been felt in every corner of the world. Condolence letters and comments on social media poured into The Circle M by the thousands. At the wake held at Nemesis headquarters, Liz and her team vowed to continue the mission Mac McCall adopted when he founded the cybercrime-fighting giant. She promised to implement the same disciplines Trey and Tara had established to ensure actions had consequences.

Davis McCall was devastated by the loss of his grandparents. Trey and Tara had been his confidants when he felt he couldn't share things with his parents. Trey not only taught him to play golf, he and Tara shared the Nemesis legacy and the McCall involvement in it with their grandson.

At long length, his grandfather had explained to Davis how his own reckless behavior as a young man cost him dearly and precipitated his shift in priorities from golf to Nemesis in order to preserve the family estate. Over the years, with Tara by his side, Trey had grown to embrace the massive role Nemesis played in getting retribution for the underdog. Davis had clung to every word.

FOOLISHLY, MOB ENTERPRISES celebrated the deaths of Trey and Tara McCall on social media. It was a seriously poor decision on their part, since Liz McCall Lonagon took it personally. With all the resources available to Warlock, she continued her game-changer media attacks on the underworld elite.

BACK IN PRISON, IF AND WHEN LOUIE FOUND OUT Ari was using him as a scapegoat for the Bouchard murders, Ari would pay with his life. Before that happened, Ari had to escape.

Ari came up with an idea. Given that Louie owned one of the guards in their cell block and still ran his Chicago operation on the outside, it just might work. One Sunday afternoon, when the prison was filled with visitors, they put their plan into action. A member of Louie's gang, who closely resembled Ari, dressed in jeans, sweatshirt, sneakers, sunglasses, and a ball cap, then came to the prison to see an old friend. With the crooked jailor standing guard, Ari and the visitor quickly exchanged clothes in adjoining stalls in the visitors' men's room. When visiting hours were over, Ari calmly walked out of the gates impersonating the visitor—sunglasses, ball cap, and all.

Louie's men drove Ari across the border into Mexico, where he had established substantial bank accounts up and down the Mexican east coast. For his part in the escape, Big Louie received $2 million in cash, deposited into a secret offshore account. The breakout went undiscovered until the next day. By then, Ari Moon was long gone, cruising along the Gulf of Mexico.

HIS FIRST STOP WAS IN TAMPICO, where one of Ari Moon's fondest acquaintances had retired to a beautiful plantation villa. Years earlier, Ari bankrolled Carlos Morales on the man's first entrepreneurial venture—a tequila distillery. Carlos made a fortune and never forgot who took a chance on him.

When Ari showed up on his doorstep at the villa, the old man greeted him with open arms. Fully aware that his friend was on the run, he paid it no mind—they were amigos, and Carlos owed him. A comfortable cabana near the pool provided cover while Ari Moon altered his appearance and retrieved a large sum of money from a bank account he had established years before under another name. His host, Carlos Morales, did a considerable amount of business at that very same bank.

Juan Pesaro, the bank president, was elated to see his wealthiest client and barely glanced at Ari when they were introduced. Ari took no offence, happy to remain in the background for the moment.

Motioning Ari over, Carlos stated his business. "Nice to see you as well, Juan. I hate to be a bother, but we need a favor. My amigo here has a small problem. He would like to retrieve some items from a safe deposit box he set up in your bank many years ago. But his key and identification were stolen in a recent burglary. Is there any way you can be of assistance?"

"As long as you can vouch for him, I see no problem at all," replied the banker, relieved to have such a simple task to delegate since, at times, Carlos could be a handful to deal with. "Follow me to the vault, and we'll take care of this straight away."

The bank president handed Ari off to his assistant while he and Carlos retreated for a drink in his office. Ari had the box number and its location in the vault tucked away in his memory. As soon as the barred inner vault was opened, Ari pranced straight over to box 229. When he produced contents from inside that confirmed his identity, the assistant excused himself.

Methodically, Ari cleaned out the box and pocketed the money and IDs. He put the nine-mil Beretta handgun, the box of ammo, and the remaining papers in a valise Carlos lent him. The bank president looked at Ari quizzically as they left, as if he was trying to figure out where he had seen Carlos's friend before today. Ari noticed but acted natural and thanked the man in Spanish for his assistance.

When they got back to the villa, Ari excused himself to put his spoils away in his quarters—but mainly to count his money. *I have $500,000 US and some change. One bank down, two more to go.* He remained at the villa long enough to let his hair and beard grow out a bit before he left for his next destination.

ON THE OUTSKIRTS OF VERACRUZ, Ari, now known as Felix Montoya, chose a modest oceanside hotel on the Gulf of Mexico. For a few days, as if on vacation, he sunned on the beach, indulged in exotic drinks, and windsurfed with the locals. Then, early one afternoon, he sauntered casually into the Banco Azteca in the town center of Veracruz and emptied his bank account and safe deposit box. To reinforce his cover, Felix remained at the seaside hotel for several more days, laughing it up on the beach with his new buds, before he loaded up his car and headed farther south, to Mérida.

THE JOURNEY TO MÉRIDA was a scenic fourteen-hour drive along the coastline of the Gulf of Mexico. Felix chopped it up into a three-day journey and was slated to arrive on Thursday, the slowest day at Banco Azteca, where he had scheduled an eleven a.m. appointment with the bank president, Javier Pinero. Along the way, Felix stopped to refuel, eat, and catch a few winks in mom-and-pop motels.

Precisely at eleven o'clock on Thursday, Felix Montoya strolled into the bank and informed a knock-out attractive secretary that he had an appointment with Señor Pinero.

After a brief meeting in the president's office, the two men shook hands. Pinero thanked Felix for his business and directed him to the bank's customer service officer to close out Señor Montoya's account and retrieve his safe deposit box from the vault.

Exhausted yet grateful that Mérida was his final stop, Felix drove back to his unassuming motel and took a four-hour nap, dreaming of his future on the Yucatán Peninsula. When he woke up, he dumped his loot out on the bed and counted it—twice.

INSIDE A MONTH, SEÑOR MONTOYA gathered together in excess of $3.5 million US, enough to set up residence and establish headquarters on the Yucatán Peninsula at an abandoned henequen plantation southeast of Mérida—a property he had surreptitiously purchased sixteen years prior and maintained remotely in case he needed an ultra-secret hideout someday. Utilizing bona fides he had recouped in Mérida, Ari abandoned his Montoya alias for good and adopted Alberto Magus, the magician. Since he believed in making a lasting first impression, Magus ditched his rental car and instead chose to arrive at his auspicious homecoming by helicopter.

LA BUENA VIDA, THE NAME MAGUS GAVE to the abandoned plantation, was surrounded by the Yucatán rainforest; even from the air, it was almost impossible to find until one was right on top of it—an ideal private location for Magus to establish his blueprint for worldwide supremacy. Kai Camal, a full-blooded Mayan, had been the estate custodian ever since he had purchased the plantation for his employer, Magus. As overseer for La Buena Vida, Kai managed an eclectic workforce of men and women with military training and experience, creative builders and artistic construction workers, cyber-savvy experts, and scientists and researchers, as well as rural folk with domestic and agricultural skills. A decade and a half earlier, Magus sent Kai an architectural plan to build a world-class tourist destination. Updates and additions arrived at odd intervals through the years, enough to keep the Mayan and his crews busy building Magus's dream.

Several miles north of the original plantation house, in an area referred to as The Preserve, dormitories, classrooms, and medical facilities equipped with research laboratories stood ready. A half-mile away perched the airstrip where Magus was due to land, a nine-thousand-foot runway built to accommodate the largest aircraft of the day. Near the end of the strip sat three helipads and a massive hangar.

On the way over from Mérida, Magus had his chopper pilot take him for a treetop gander at the La Buena Vida property. He was astounded by the extensive changes to the grounds subsequent to his initial visit to the plantation. He was delighted to see that a considerable number of his pet projects were finished or in the final stages of completion. *Most impressive,* he thought.

KAI CAMAL WAITED ANXIOUSLY NEAR the helipads to finally meet the man in person. He expected to greet an elderly gentleman—feeble, with pale skin and little or no hair. When the helicopter touched down and the rotor blades shut down, the man who energetically exited the Bell 206 JetRanger was nowhere near what his caretaker pictured. Alberto Magus had a head full of close-cropped dark-brown hair, a matching beard, blue eyes, and an even tan on a physique without a hint of frailty. He flashed an engaging smile with brilliant white teeth. The two men shook hands and made their way to the main house in Kai's Jeep.

Along the way, Kai glanced over at the man. "Ah, welcome home, sir. We at La Buena Vida are honored by your presence. If I may ask, how do you wish us to address you?"

"I prefer to dispense with formalities. To simplify things, just call me Magus."

WHILE HE UNPACKED UPSTAIRS in his colossal quarters, Magus studied the solid new construction with attention to detail. He was awestruck by the polished burnt mahogany wood floors, the thirty-foot ceiling, ten-foot triple-ply windows, dark wood paneling on the walls, and louvered plantation shutters. Behind louvered pocket doors, a luxurious master bathroom featured travertine floors and native rock walls. Brushed brass fixtures adorned the sinks, spa, and walk-in shower. And a huge retractable skylight let in rays of bright sunlight and soothing moonlight.

Outside on his second-story balcony, Magus studied the breathtaking view of the rainforest. The density of the growth below was astounding. Drifting up from the jungle, sounds of birds and chattering spider monkeys lifted his already soaring spirits. Surprisingly, he could barely make out the newly finished structures or the airstrip where he had landed. Best of all, there weren't any nagging neighbors to ruin the mood—only the beauty of nature in the raw.

Settled in for the moment, Magus descended to the foyer on a magnificent spiral staircase of ebony-gloss-stained bamboo polished to a brilliant, radiant shine.

The plantation custodian acknowledged Magus's presence with a brief bow of his head, then asked meekly, "If I may, sir. I'm curious as to your first impressions."

Magus looked around him before he answered. "Too early to tell. Although there is evidence that you and your crew have been quite busy." Magus abruptly changed the subject. "By the way, before I forget. Did you receive the package I had sent here from Qatar, labeled 'Medical Supplies—handle with care'"?

"Indeed, sir. As soon as it arrived, we put it in a cold storage containment room at the clinic, as you directed."

Confused by and a bit annoyed at the sudden change of topic, Kai digressed. "As far as the *plantation* goes, we all hoped to have everything finished by the time you returned, but you surprised us with the timing of your visit. Rest assured, the final touches on the offices, living quarters, and labs will be completed by month's end. Generators, water and air purifiers, and electrical components for the escape tunnel from the plantation house to the secure bunker are being installed as we speak. The spa and health club at the La Buena Vida Hotel, along with the casino, will be ready by the end of the month as well. Would you care to take a spin around the grounds to see our progress?"

"Yes, yes, I would," Magus mumbled absentmindedly. Anxious to view what all Kai had accomplished, Magus followed the plantation custodian to the Jeep.

The guided tour was impressive. Magus listened with great interest as Kai filled him in. "La Vida Gran condominiums, with their own health club and spa for VIP guests, are under construction a mile west of the airport. Additional guest accommodations will be available in clustered three-bedroom, three-bath bungalows sprinkled around the club and spa. Acting as the agent for the plantation, I convinced our local government officials that a world-class hotel, spa, and casino would not only enhance their personal bottom line but create positive PR for the area.

"Several miles to the east of the airstrip is our designated wildlife preserve surrounded by a twelve-foot-high electrified fence—off-limits to anyone but staff with armed rangers on patrol to discourage trespassers. Sir, you'll be pleased to know our government officials were so impressed with the conservation aspect of that project, as well as the generous donation we provided to them, they unanimously approved the plans for The Preserve—which, as you know, is much more than an animal refuge."

MAGUS THOUGHT, *How nice it must have been to operate with what amounted to an unlimited budget.* Twenty-five million dollars US had been wired from one of Magus's Cayman Islands accounts to Kai's account, arranged by a crooked officer in a bank near Ticul, Mexico, and another $25 million set aside in reserve. Magus chuckled to himself and thought, *Money was always the international catalyst that got things done.*

It was Magus's vision to use The Preserve as cover for a specialized training and indoctrination camp. Under Kai's supervision, it became the most secure area on the property. Barracks, classrooms, firing ranges, and obstacle courses stood ready for raw recruits. It was similar in most aspects to other military training facilities, with the exception of four multilevel structures remotely situated at the edge of dense jungle and marshland.

The secluded complex known as the infirmary was outfitted to conduct scientific experiments, perfect bioweapons, and devise techniques for transmission of deadly, infectious pathogens. The basement of the infirmary building was equipped with soundproofed interrogation rooms, a sealed-off lockup area with barred prison cells, and solitary confinement holds lined up on opposite sides of the hallway. The noise level from below was kept to a whisper.

Delighted with the headway, Magus had Kai drive them back to the plantation house. Both men were on a mission, although it was far from the same one. Each saw the other as expendable.

CHAPTER 11

A MONTH EARLIER, WHILE NURSING a cerveza across the street from his bank in Tampico, Miguel Angel Mendoza watched as an old acquaintance of his, Ari Moon, presently known as Alberto Magus, walked out of the bank with Carlos Morales, the tequila magnate. At the time, Miguel didn't think much about it. Later, aware that Ari Moon was an escaped convict from Texas, curiosity got the better of Mendoza. He phoned a mob associate of his in San Antonio to report the sighting of the former prisoner from Three Rivers.

A Warlock program picked up on the reference to Ari and Three Rivers, then recorded and forwarded the conversation to Nemesis. Moments later, Liz Lonagon was listening to the Mendoza conversation. Trusting her intuition, she sent Rich Martel and Sam Smithwick down south to investigate the chance encounter.

WHILE LIZ WAITED FOR REPORTS from Mexico, she met with her younger brother in her office. Through the years, Liz and Bryce had been his biggest fans and watched him grow as a golfer and a man. As often as their schedules allowed, they were in his gallery to cheer him on. Big sis admired his swagger; Bryce was impressed with his talent. After setting the record for the most tournament victories in a junior golf career, during which he won events at every level, Davis McCall continued to improve and was fresh off another individual win in his senior year of high school—his third one of the season. Given his talent level, everyone figured the young man would follow in his father's and grandfather's footsteps in the world of professional golf.

Davis had other ideas. The talent was there, but he didn't really want to travel down that path.

"Sis, I've got something to run by you," he started. "Although, I'm not sure how you'll take it." Then he added, "Grandpa Trey planted the seed a long time ago. Just sayin'. Plus, Levon and I talked a bit and … well …"

Liz gave him a funny look. "Go for it."

Davis blurted out, "When I get old enough, I want to join Nemesis."

The shock on his sister's face told him this was not going to be an easy conversation. *"Seriously?* What about your golf? You've worked so hard. Why would you want to throw all that away? What about a pro career? Are you sure you've given this enough thought? Or is it just a whim?"

The youngster sighed and took a breath. "It's not just a whim. It's been in the back of my mind for a long time. Like with you, Nemesis is in my blood. As an agent, I can still get my fill of golf playing in amateur events."

"Have you spoken to our father about this yet? Or did you just spring it on me, hoping I would broach the subject with him?" she questioned.

Davis gave her his best devilish smile. "Well, I was kind of hoping ..."

"You little monster. What in the world are we going to do with you?" She laughed and shooed him toward the door. "Okay, I'll talk to Dad about it. I know how you are when you sink your teeth into something. You don't let go. It's the McCall way."

THE NEXT AFTERNOON, WHEN DAVIS, Jefferson, and Novél Vargas were at The Circle M practice range, Jefferson casually mentioned he'd had an interesting conversation with Liz.

"So, I hear you want to be a crime fighter and pass on the Tour. Did I hear that correctly?" Jefferson asked Davis.

"Yes, sir. It's really what I want to do," his son replied.

Jefferson winked at Novél, then came back with, "And you think three professional golfers in one family is enough—and four is too many?"

"Well, I don't know about that, but I can still make a name for myself in golf as an amateur like Bobby Jones," Davis replied respectfully.

His father had to give him that one. "Son, if you want to join Nemesis when you turn twenty-one, I'm not going to stand in your way. You have my blessing. But I want you to promise me that you'll keep golf an important part of your life. Through the years, Trey and I taught you some valuable keys. Don't let them go to waste."

Davis smiled and gave his father a huge hug. "Absolutely, I'll never lose respect for the game, and I promise to keep our secrets tucked away, safe and sound."

Jefferson rushed home from the practice ground to enlighten Reanna about his chat with Davis. "You'll never guess what your son confided in me this afternoon."

"Hmm. Let's see. He wants to join Nemesis. Am I close?" Reanna replied coyly.

"I ... what? He told you?"

"No, I've suspected as much for quite a while. Ever since he started hanging out with Levon Vargas. A mother knows."

All Jefferson could do was shake his head in awe of the woman's intuition.

AFTER HIS TALK WITH THEIR FATHER, Davis found Liz to thank her for breaking the ice. She hugged him tight. "You are welcome. But next time, it's on you to spring stuff like that on Dad. Oh, by the way, I'm tickled to death that you and Levon have teamed up. Both of you are brilliant, and your skills complement each other. I find that very intriguing—something I might like to explore in earnest further down the road. "

Even though he was too young to join Nemesis, Davis wasn't too young to learn about it. Liz encouraged her brother to sit in on classes while he familiarized himself with the different branches of the cyber-crime-fighting giant. She spurred him on to continue the Krav Maga training he had begun at the age of five—and to tap the genius of his pal Levon Vargas and the potential of Warlock.

DURING A RARE MOMENT OF SOLITUDE, Liz relaxed on her office couch, contemplating an issue that she just couldn't shake. What was the best way to take Nemesis to the next level of cybercrime investigation? She tilted her head back, closed her eyes, and drifted off to sleep. Then the answer came to her. It had been there all along, cloistered in the wizardry of Levon Vargas.

If Levon could develop a stealth program to transmit misinformation directly from the actual IP addresses of the twisted freaks who lurked in the deepest, dankest shadows of the underworld and controlled the game, Nemesis could totally fuck up their world.

When Liz proposed her idea to Levon, his eyes lit up. He placed his chin on top of his steepled fingertips and cracked a viciously wicked smile. Wasting no time, Levon gathered a diversified team of Nemesis cyber experts to tackle their monumental task. While they collaborated in the cybercrime lab, Liz focused on her agents in Mexico.

RICH MARTEL AND SAM SMITHWICK arrived in Tampico at nine in the morning on a commercial flight from Dallas. Warlock provided them with background info and a downtown office location for Miguel Angel Mendoza, Ari Moon's old acquaintance. After enduring the usual hassle of renting a car in a foreign country, they finally got on their way. Flush with Aztec and Franciscan history, Tampico boasted a variety of eye-catching architecture and landscapes on the seventeen-mile drive into downtown.

Along the way, Sam Smithwick glanced over the file of Miguel's colorful history. "Wow, this fella is something else. He has his dirty little fingers into about every illegal activity you can imagine. The fact that he is still alive speaks to his cunning. As shifty as Miguel is, we best keep on our toes."

Much to their surprise, Miguel was cordial but guarded. "I'm sorry you two traveled so far for so little information. As to your inquiry about Ari Moon, yes, on occasion, he and I did business in the past. However, I found him to be unreliable, and I severed our ties. Imagine my surprise when I saw Ari walk out of the bank where

I do business here in Tampico. Strange because he was supposed to be in prison in Texas.

"Perhaps you should direct your attention to the man he was with. His name is Carlos Morales, an entrepreneur who has made a fortune in the tequila business. Supposedly, he and Ari are close friends. Carlos lives in a beautiful villa on his plantation, not far from the coast, only twenty minutes away. As a courtesy, it would be my pleasure to call Señor Morales to set up a meeting with you two. That's all I have. I wish you luck. Now, if there's nothing else, please excuse me. I have a busy day."

With a strained smile painted on his face, Rich replied flatly, "Very well, then. Thanks for your time. Oh, that call to Señor Morales would be much appreciated."

On their drive to the villa, Sam commented, "Well, at least it wasn't a total dead end. Hopefully, Carlos Morales will be more forthcoming."

"He certainly couldn't be any less."

CARLOS MORALES WAS AMIABLE and quite taken with Sam's beauty. When he greeted them at the door, his eyes drank her in—top to bottom. Their host quickly gathered his composure and led them out to a patio that overlooked a massive infinity pool framed by the Gulf of Mexico in the background. They placed their drink orders, made their selections from a buffet of salads, fruits, and gulf seafood delicacies, and took their seats around a stylishly set glass-topped table.

Carlos addressed them in flawless English. "Rumor has it you two are here to ask about my old friend Ari Moon."

"Yes, sir, we are. It is our understanding the man stayed with you for a while after his jailbreak in Texas." It was all conjecture on Rich's part—an educated guess.

Carlos thought for a second, then responded, "Yes, he did, although I can't imagine how you found out. At the time, I wasn't aware he was an escaped prisoner, only that he'd lent me money in the past to get started in my business, which has made me a very wealthy man. When I found out about his escape, it was too late. And I did owe him a favor. That obligation has been met. Ari is what you would call complex, to say the least. Let's just say our ideologies are on opposite sides of the spectrum. That being the case, I'll assist you in any way I can."

"Excellent!" Sam exclaimed. "Our boss believes Ari is in Mexico to rebuild a force of disciples dedicated to him and his creed. It's something he has attempted on several occasions and failed. We hoped you might know where he planned to set up his base of operation."

"I don't know anything about that, but I do know his next two stops from here were Veracruz, then Mérida. He mentioned those two places in a phone call I overheard him make to a man called Kai. I hope that will be of some help to you. My old friend has changed, and not for the better. I wish you luck in your quest," declared the distinguished multimillionaire.

Rich thanked him and asked one more question. "Sir, do you have any idea why he would single out those two destinations?"

Morales smiled. "Judging from his primary objective while here, I'd say he has bank accounts in those towns. I can think of no other reason."

HALF AN HOUR LATER, RICH AND SAM motored down the coast highway on their way to Veracruz. Sam called Liz to report in and ask if Warlock could check banks in Veracruz and Mérida for unusually large cash withdrawals.

A beautiful sunset rocked the azure sky with radiant hues of pastel

colors as the Nemesis agents arrived in Veracruz. It was too late to
check out banks, so they found a lovely hotel downtown and reserved
a suite for the night. After which, Rich phoned Liz to see if Warlock
had any luck with its search for possible banks. There were two, and
one happened to be across the public square from their hotel.

They unpacked and changed for dinner. It was a lovely night for a
stroll, with a gentle breeze wafting across the plaza. The sky was clear
and bright, with a full moon to help them navigate their outing. The
fragrance of plumeria filled the air, and crickets chirped, joining in
symphony with Mexican tree frogs and cicadas to accompany the
festive music drifting out of restaurants and cantinas. One could hardly
imagine a more romantic setting.

After breakfast the next morning, Rich and Sam meandered across
the plaza to the bank. In an earlier wake-up call, Liz had informed
them that Warlock had discovered a large withdrawal made by a bank
customer named Felix Montoya. It was worth a visit to the bank's president to see if he remembered the man and the transaction.

Posing as investigators checking on possible fraud on behalf of a
well-respected international insurance firm in London, the Nemesis
agents were ushered into the bank official's office.

Although he had done nothing wrong, the bank president was
unnerved by their visit, breaking into a cold sweat, most likely due to a
case of imaginary guilt. Reassured he was not suspected of any wrong-
doing, the president relaxed and admitted he had personally dealt with
Felix Montoya when the gentleman cleaned out his account. And that
was the extent of the president's involvement. He recalled that Montoya
said very little. He had simply closed his account and emptied his safe
deposit box. Then the man promptly left with the contents of the box
in addition to $1.2 million US dollars.

SINCE IT WAS, AT BEST, a fourteen-hour road trip to Mérida, Sam and Rich chose to spend one more delightful night in Veracruz to soak up the native ambiance. With the warm afterglow of an amorous evening fresh in their minds the next morning, the couple enjoyed a continental breakfast and left the hotel shortly thereafter.

Halfway to their destination, Sam spotted an oceanfront hotel in a spectacular setting alongside a restaurant that overlooked the water.

"Rich?"

"I know, I see it. Should we?"

She giggled and excitedly rubbed her hands together. "Of course we should. Why not?"

They rented a lovely casita on the beach and dined on fresh seafood partnered with outstanding local wines on the restaurant's patio. After dinner, they strolled hand in hand back to their casita, playfully dodging the incoming tide as it rolled up onto the beach. They stopped to embrace and were about to kiss when Sam's cell phone buzzed in her purse.

"Mother Liz here. Are you lovebirds okay? Warlock's GPS has you two somewhere between Veracruz and Mérida. I'm guessing on a moonlit beach. Am I close?"

Sam had to laugh. "Of course, and I must say, your timing is frightening. Please tell me this is Nemesis business and not a chaperone fetish you've developed."

"Best not give me any ideas. No, dear. This is purely business. Warlock came up with the name of the bank in Mérida, where Felix Montoya made his most recent withdrawal—Banco Azteca in the center of town. Thought you ought to know straight away. Sorry if I intruded on a moment."

She had, but it was of no consequence. By the time Sam and Rich reached the beach house, all was forgiven and soon forgotten. The pair of young agents resumed their journey midmorning with smiles on their faces and the night before fresh in their minds. The drive along the coast was stunning, including row upon row of aqua-hued waves crashing against rugged rock outcroppings and spraying a salty mist up to the road. Farther out, blue whales put on a show as they breached the surface of the gulf.

ETA at the bank—two p.m.

AHEAD IN MÉRIDA, the Banco Azteca president was forewarned of their visit in what he took to be an official text. Generated by Warlock, it read: *Be advised: Two agents from the Bunco Division of the International Independent Insurance Alliance are en route to investigate a suspected fraud at your bank involving one Felix Montoya. Your cooperation in this matter would be greatly appreciated.*

When the bank official read the text, his heart raced, and sweat dripped off his brow. There was no such agency, but the bank president didn't know that. He could ill afford to open his books to anybody. Maybe he had misread the text. When he looked down at his phone to reread it, the message was gone.

Anxious to make a good impression, the bank exec greeted Rich and Sam at the front door with open arms. "Welcome. Please come into my office and have a seat," he said nervously. "My name is Javier Pinero. How may I be of assistance this afternoon?"

The agents looked quizzically at each other before Rich answered. "Señor Pinero, we are here in a quasi-official capacity. A gentleman by the name of Felix Montoya made a highly suspicious withdrawal from your bank. Are you familiar with that transaction?"

"But of course. Although Señor Montoya had been a customer for years, it was the first time I'd met him in person. He dealt primarily with my assistant, Kai, who happened to be absent that day. I simply stepped in. Señor Montoya was distraught over a domestic dispute at home and needed the cash to smooth things over; he did, however, promise to replenish the account when the dust cleared. All was above board, I assure you. And, oh yes, he did ask for directions to Ticul, if that's any help."

AFTER THANKING THE BANKER FOR HIS TIME, Rich and Sam sat in their car outside the bank while Rich checked his GPS to see how far it was to Ticul.

"An hour and a half drive. Sam, what do ya ..." he began, but he stopped mid-sentence when he glanced over at her. She had her head down, busily typing a text to Liz with a request about how she wanted them to proceed. A few seconds later, Sam received a reply.

"Okay, Liz wants us to drive to Ticul and settle in. She's booked us a suite at Hacienda San Jose. Her gut instinct suggests that Ari, most likely under another assumed name, is in the general vicinity of Ticul. There are lots of ancient Mayan ruins sprinkled about the area. The boss suggests we pose as curious lost culture buffs, there to scope out the ruins. I get this feeling we may be in Ticul for a while."

FARTHER SOUTHEAST AND JUST A FORTY-MINUTE drive inland from Ticul, Magus took the Jeep for a ride around the plantation alone, mostly to marvel at the extent of improvements his caretaker and talented crew had fashioned. It was comforting to know Kai Camal was his key agent and most devoted disciple. He would have had second thoughts had he known the truth. While an employee of Banco Azteca, Kai befriended bank officers in Mérida and Ticul. Due to the vast amount of money coming to their banks from Magus's accounts in the Cayman Islands, Kai easily convinced the unsuspecting executives to join in a few shady undertakings that turned a healthy profit. And now Kai owned them.

Magus was unaware that shortly after his right-hand man purchased the henequen plantation for his boss, Kai negotiated a deal for himself with the Mexican government for 20 percent of the mineral rights on the property—a transaction that required an extremely large sum of money to pay off government officials under the table. Since then, oil and gas were discovered on the land, as well as a number of other valuable elements and minerals—uranium and copper among them. Geologists speculated the plantation could be sitting on tons of lithium ore as well. All totaled a virtual bonanza of wealth. Potentially, Kai's contract was worth billions.

To date, Kai had relied solely on monies Magus sent him from Cayman Islands accounts to rebuild the plantation, train an army of mercenaries, and grease the palms of greedy government adminis-trators. Kai took it upon himself to establish an elite personal secu-rity force to guard Magus and himself. Anyone posing a problem to their domain was quickly and permanently disposed of by the special security guerilla teams. Word spread quickly—the plantation and its owners were hands off, or else.

Back in his office from his solo excursion, Magus realized how weary he had grown after so many campaigns. This was likely his final opportunity to make a success of his beloved movement. Everything and almost everyone was expendable when it came to achieving his goal. The exception was Kai Camal, whom Magus mistakenly envisioned as his successor. Kai feigned his loyalty—unwilling to jeopardize the flow of money he discreetly siphoned off of Magus.

RECRUITING FOR MAGUS'S MOVEMENT, Nuevo Mañana (New Tomorrow), amplified from a trickle to a flood in the spring and summer months. Nuevo Mañana recruiters focused on transients and starry-eyed, naïve youth who vacationed around Cancún and the Mayan ruins in the Yucatán. Vetting stations were set up to sift through the masses for the fifty most desirable subjects. Magus was not interested only in the naïve. He wanted disillusioned adults as well to serve as spirited role models for the younger crowd.

Sam and Rich observed the bait-and-switch recruiting program in progress at the Mayan ruins in Chichén Itzá. They moved in close enough to listen as a recruiter made his pitch to young college students about a wonderful opportunity to be a part of a revolutionary movement. A few of the brighter college kids lost interest quickly and moved on; the rest stayed to listen. That in itself disturbed the two Nemesis agents. By the end of the presentation, a mixture of young men and women, about a dozen, remained along with Sam and Rich.

Rich leaned over and whispered in Sam's ear, "How about we hang here with this dude and act interested? This sounds like something Ari Moon would conjure up."

Sam just nodded, her eyes glued to the recruiter as he went on and on about the glorious, rebellious life of a crusader. The Robin Hood and his Merry Men crap couldn't be further from the truth. The guy showed off for the hot babe, who seemed to really dig what he was spouting out and hung on his every word. Rich picked up on what she was doing and joined in, as if mesmerized by the recruiter's message. It was getting close to dark when the rep pointed the college crowd over to the vetting station near the exit. Then he turned to face the older duo.

"Well, are you two ready for a major life change?" he asked, ignoring Rich and staring intently into Sam's beautiful eyes.

She looked away, faking embarrassment, shrugged, and mumbled, "I don't know. Maybe." Rich shuffled his feet, stared at the ground, and didn't say a word.

"Well, I'll be back here tomorrow if you want to ask me any questions. Why don't y'all sleep on it. Nuevo Mañana can change your life for the better, forever," the recruiter echoed before he slinked away.

On the way back to their hotel in Ticul, Rich asked, "So, Sam. What do you think? Did we fool him or not?"

"Oh, we fooled him all right. An Academy Award performance if there ever was one." Sam couldn't wait to tell Liz.

Rich wondered if Nuevo Mañana would actually recruit the two of them, given how much older they were than the target demographic. He was almost old enough to be the young recruits' father, and Sam their mother. Why would Nuevo Mañana be interested in them? He knew they'd have to run that by Liz and the think tank at Nemesis. He and Sam had plenty to sort through on the two-and-a-half-hour drive back to the Hacienda.

It was late when they got Liz on the phone. The head of Nemesis couldn't believe what she heard. There was no doubt in her mind that Alberto Magus was Ari Moon and had a new center of operations recruiting followers for something called Nuevo Mañana on the Yucatán Peninsula. By chance, her agents had run into one of the fabulists and played him—even got a meet set up with him for the following day.

Liz took a stab at an answer to their question as to why they would be asked to join. "My guess is they are looking for mentors, like life coaches, for their younger converts. You said you both acted down and out, disgruntled, uncertain, fed up with the status quo in the world. People in that state of mind are easy to turn into role models. Just maybe they're looking at you two for that reason. What do you think?"

Rich came back with a quick reply, "Yeah, could be. Although, I think the guy has his eye on Sam for other reasons. Boy, is he in for a rude awakening if he tries anything. After we listen to the guy's spiel tomorrow, do you want us to sign up with Nuevo Mañana?"

"Absolutely, but don't seem too anxious. Hem and haw around like you're not sure. Make him convince you to join. Give him the feeling that he put one over on you. That's what we want," Liz responded excitedly.

THERE WASN'T A CLOUD IN THE SKY the next morning when Rich and Sam approached the Mayan ruins at Chichén Itzá. The temperature had already climbed up near ninety degrees, with just a hint of a breeze that did little to cool the air. They dressed appropriately for the heat in shorts, an open-collar polo for him, and a halter top for her. They were sockless with open-toed sandals, and both wore Maui Jim aviator shades to cut the glare. Each donned a Panama hat. Hers was cocked to one side, fashionable and sexy. Sam saw the Nuevo Mañana recruiter before he spotted her and gave Rich a nudge with her elbow.

When the recruiter recognized them coming toward him, he cracked a smile. Confident that his clever rhetoric from the previous day lured them back, he remarked, "Hey, you two. So glad you showed up."

Rich said, "To tell you the truth, I'm not sure why we came back. I mean, we both have had it with the establishment. That's a given. But we're not sure if we know what to do about it. To go out on some glorified crusade with a bunch of smart-ass punk kids isn't our idea of the life change we are looking for. We did our share of rioting and demonstrating back in our day. Protesting useless wars and insane political rhetoric isn't what we want for the rest of our lives. We want to settle somewhere away from the hustle and bustle of cities, traffic, and neighbors who report your every frigging move if it doesn't fit their ideology."

The Nuevo Mañana agent stared intently at Sam as he spoke to Rich. "Hey, man. I get that. Been in your shoes. Does the little lady feel the same way?"

Sam was ready to respond as soon as she heard the derogatory term' *little lady*. "Damn straight I do. I'm sick and tired of listening to the dimwits of the world tell me how to think and act. Screw them. Hell, 90 percent of them haven't done jack shit in their lives. They get brave on the internet and think they can run the world online. It's all bullshit, man, and I'm fed up."

In an attempt to regroup, the agent changed subjects. "Wow, okay. So, hmm, ah, listen. My name is Jerry, by the way. And your names are?"

They'd decided earlier to use their real first names if asked.

"I'm Richie but go by Rich, and her name is Samantha. Sam for short."

Jerry responded, "Sam and Rich, a pleasure to meet you both. Perhaps I can clarify a few misconceptions you two seem to have about us. In the first place, we would not expect you to go back out into the world on a crusade for our cause. If you pass our background check, your new home would be a five-diamond hotel, spa, and casino with your choice of a grand suite or a three-bedroom bungalow. Your sole responsibility would be to counsel our young recruits to guide and reassure them. It's as simple as that. You'll have run of the place and report directly to Kai or our supreme leader. All I'll need is for you two to fill out this form with your personal information and a contact number here in Mexico to get the ball rolling."

Rich took the forms from Jerry, handed one to Sam, and looked his over. She did the same. After a brief private discussion, Sam handed the forms back to Jerry, who looked crestfallen. He was sure he'd snared them.

"I don't understand. Is there something on the forms you don't understand?" Jerry asked with a groan.

"No," Sam whimpered. "It's a big step and, well, we're not sure …"

"Tell you what. Why don't you take the forms back with you and look them over. I'll give you my number, and you call me if you have any questions. I can meet you anywhere at any time. We can meet here again if you want. You tell me," Jerry exclaimed in desperation.

Sam glanced over at Rich, who sort of nodded, then she replied, "I guess it wouldn't hurt to think on it some more. You know, sort it out in our minds and all. Okay, give us the forms and your number. We'll be in touch."

Jerry fumbled for a pen, jotted down his phone number, and handed the forms back to Sam.

As soon as they got back to Ticul, Sam was on the phone with Liz—filling her in on the meeting with Jerry, what was said, and how it ended. Liz was ecstatic with the couple's performance and immediately had Warlock create an appropriate criminal history for them that would make Magus and his sidekick, Kai, salivate to bring the couple on board. Their rap sheet, which tied them to all sorts of anarchistic underground organizations, was littered with arrests, incarcerations, riots, and major demonstrations—all aimed at the establishment.

Rich and Sam let Jerry stew for a couple of days before she called him on her cell to tell him they'd thought it over and decided to join. They agreed to meet him at the Chichén Itzá ruins at ten o'clock the next morning to give him the forms they'd filled out. Jerry immediately had his boss, Kai, trace the number and begin a deep search of the owner's personal history prior to the meet. They learned Sam Smithwick had an extensive record for civil disturbance, accompanied by numerous arrests and jail time. Her known associates included a Richie Martel, the son of Maisey Martel, a Canadian madam and operative for the western province mob. Rumor had it Richie's father was none other than the late Lucky Richards. Rich had his share of scrapes with the law as well. Kai told Jerry to do whatever it took to bring the two veteran activists into Nuevo Mañana. The couple's experience would bring instant credibility to the program.

As soon as Sam answered her phone and Kai mentioned his name and the nature of his call, Warlock traced Kai's number, then recorded the dialogue. Now that Nemesis knew the location of Nuevo Mañana headquarters, it could keep track of Alberto Magus and his movement.

JERRY WAS RELIEVED WHEN HE SAW the couple moving toward him at Chichén Itzá. "Hey, you two. Thanks for the call. I wasn't sure you'd show, but I certainly am glad you did," said Jerry, trying to hold in his true emotions. He was aware his fate depended on Sam and Rich. If he didn't land these two, he would have to high-tail it out of the country or face Kai's wrath in the infirmary's dungeon.

As she spoke, Sam handed Jerry their application forms. "Like Rich told you at our last meeting, we are no strangers to fighting for what we believe in. Speaking of that, we added a caveat to your form. If we find we are being used or misled in any way by your esteemed leaders, we walk away. That must be understood and made perfectly clear, or it's no deal. We need latitude from your leaders to work with adolescents who oftentimes decide to fly off course on a whim. Rich and I are very good at what we do. Just leave us alone to do it. That is all we ask."

Jerry gleaned two things about Sam from what she said. First, she was no candy-ass. Second, she had the moxie to force him to make an uncomfortable decision far above his station in Nuevo Mañana. He had no choice. Kai ordered him to do whatever it took to entice them to join. He hoped Kai understood. Unless Jerry agreed to that caveat, the deal was off.

"Wow, okay. Sam, what you are asking for is most unusual. However, considering your and Rich's considerable experience as activists, we'll honor your request."

On the way to the ruins, Rich predicted the man would fold. Pleased that his prediction came true, he added, "Thanks, Jerry. Sam and I look forward to working inside Nuevo Mañana. Your cause is just. Rest assured, we can be of service in persuading the uncertain trainees to see the light. When and where do we meet with your esteemed leader to discuss and iron out the details?"

Jerry became evasive. "I, ah, well. How about I call you this evening with that info?"

The Nemesis agents nodded. Over her shoulder on the way to their car, Sam taunted, "Jerry, don't make it too late. Tonight could be our last night to get wild and nasty before we move in at the plantation."

The activist turned bright red with an image of the lovers passionately locked together, indelibly implanted in his brain. "Oh, yeah, okay, got it, ten-four that," was all he could manage as he watched them disappear around a corner.

In the car, Rich laughed his ass off at Sam's final comment to Jerry. He could barely talk between outbreaks of hilarity. "Did you see the dude's face? And his response to your comment about getting wild and nasty was priceless."

"YOU DID WHAT?" SCREAMED KAI CAMAL at his top recruiter, Jerry Ling. "I can't frigging believe you are that damn stupid. You let them pretty much write their own ticket to join Nuevo Mañana. Who in the hell gave you permission to do that?"

The man sitting behind the massive desk in his office on the top floor of Hotel La Buena Vida answered, "You did, Kai. I heard you in this very office after we found out our American couple was so well credentialed. You told Jerry to do whatever it took." Magus continued, "Given the circumstances, I believe he made the right decision."

Kai's temper flared, then subsided. This was neither the time nor the place to quarrel with the self-anointed supreme leader. He was embarrassed to have been chastised by his boss in front of an underling, but it was done and, for now, best forgotten. Rich and Sam were the perfect role models to motivate the trainees. It was a no-brainer to bring the couple on board. Jerry breathed a sigh of relief. Magus was pleased with the decision and instructed Jerry to set up a meeting with Rich and Sam at the plantation.

TUESDAY, AT TEN IN THE MORNING, Rich and Sam were shown into an ornate office on the top floor of the La Buena Vida Hotel. Magus rose from his chair behind his massive desk to properly greet his prospective new mentors. He gave Rich a cursory handshake and pat on the back, then turned his attention to Sam. After a lengthy once-over, Magus took her hand and kissed it. Lost in her gaze, he held on for a moment longer than he intended. She noticed and gave him a dazzling smile to acknowledge his kind gesture.

He smiled and took his seat behind the desk while his guests took theirs in two chairs facing him. "Welcome to the plantation, the La Buena Vida Resort, and last but not least, the Nuevo Mañana movement to make the world a better place," said the man they were now positive was Ari Moon. "Before we get into the particulars, I would like for my assistant, Kai Camal, to give you a tour of our hotel, spa, and options for housing—as well as our training facility several miles east of the hotel.

"We have gone to great lengths to make this a world-class property. The Hotel La Buena Vida and Spa can comfortably accommodate up to one hundred guests at one time. These elite guests—sympathetic to our cause—are invited and endorsed by advocates of our crusade. No doubt you'll find that our training facility is one of the finest in the world—well-staffed and equipped to handle three ninety-day sessions with a thirty-day break between each training period to recruit."

Without further ado, he pushed a button on his desk. Seconds later, Kai Camal entered the office and escorted them outside. On the west side of the driveway, he had parked a six-passenger golf cart to show them around the plantation complex while he sized up Rich and Sam.

The hotel and its surrounding accommodations were indeed special, with well-groomed lawns and a dazzling array of flora that gave the place a world-class feel. The bungalows were tastefully decorated and included all the amenities one could imagine. During their tour, Sam mentioned to Rich under her breath that she preferred the bungalows to the hotel. He nodded his agreement.

For the ride over to the training facility, they boarded a Land Rover. The Preserve was where they'd be spending most of their time. The Nuevo Mañana movement leader was right about how well equipped it was with everything they would need to turn out enthusiastic ambassadors to spread their message. Rich and Sam managed to stay indifferent toward the experimental labs, interrogation chambers, and dungeon-like cubicles that dominated the basement of the outermost building.

Neither of the Nemesis agents gave him a hint of disapproval. Sam even commented on how efficient it was to have alternative methods of persuasion for stubborn subjects reluctant to support the party line. Kai smiled. After they were shown the rest of the grounds, they headed back for lunch with the supreme leader at the hotel, followed by a lengthy session in Magus's office to explain the doctrine of Nuevo Mañana in detail.

RICH AND SAM WERE NOT IMPRESSED as the man bloviated about his mission and the importance of his cause to salvage a lost civilization, as well as the planet. It was all Rich and Sam could do to stomach the garbage he spewed. To show him they had been paying attention, they asked him a few irrelevant questions when he finished. Satisfied they understood the program, Magus asked his soon-to-be new staff members when they could assume their responsibilities.

Rich didn't recall the man asking them if they were ready to sign on. Magus took it for granted they would. *Interesting,* thought the undercover agent. Ignoring the oversight, Rich said, "By week's end, if that suits you. We need a little time to settle things and wrap our heads around what we are getting into again, but that should be enough time for us to sort it all."

"Good, that's great. Alrighty then, we'll make preparations for your lodging here and any other issues you might have. Just give us a call if you think of anything else. Great to have you as part of our program. I suspect it will be most beneficial to your net worth. Off, you two. See you in a few days," the militant leader gushed, obviously overjoyed at the new additions to his staff.

ON THE WAY BACK TO TICUL, Rich and Sam made small talk about this and that—nothing of importance. They lived in a cyber world where people used every means possible to eavesdrop on their targets. The Nemesis duo suspected Kai bugged their car while they were at the plantation and their hotel room in Ticul while they were gone. So when they got back to the hotel, they bypassed their suite and went for a walk out in the open.

Sam asked her boyfriend, "So, what do you make of our visit to the plantation?"

"Honestly, it was pretty much what I expected. Magus's bullshit is a bit much. He thinks he has all the answers. Kai is in it for the money. So is Jerry. We need to be extra careful for a while until they trust us enough to let down their guard. I think your prediction of us being here in Yucatán for a long while was well founded," Rich replied. Then he questioned, "So what's your take?"

"My *take?* I'd like to take Magus and his goons out in the middle of the jungle and let nature dispose of them. I can't believe these kids are falling for the crap Jerry the barker dishes out, but they are—hook, line, and sinker. Makes you wonder how it all got this upside down. Hopefully, we can turn some of the fence-riders around before they ruin their lives forever.

"Good news is that the big fish of Nuevo Mañana have only one of our cell phone numbers, so we can use the other to communicate with Liz, *alias Mother,* back in Texas. If we stay patient and placid, with only a little luck, we put these folks in a place where they can do no more harm," Sam remarked in a disciplined tone.

Rich nodded and grinned. His partner was a black belt in multiple martial arts, including Krav Maga, all of which were about emotional control and focus. After seeing her in action, Rich was thankful he wouldn't be on the receiving end of her lightning-quick moves. The couple continued to stroll, circled the plaza, and went upstairs to their suite.

CHAPTER 12

COMPUTER GENIUS LEVON VARGAS was in his element, operating in his two favorite theaters—cyber science and criminal psychoses. Working out of the Nemesis headquarters in Texas with Nemesis's leading profiler, Miranda Dossier, Levon had developed Merlin, the most highly sophisticated AI cybercrime-fighting program to date. Merlin was equipped with undetectable multifunctional capabilities. One of the most useful tools was the data drop function that enabled the Nemesis cybercrime team to covertly engage IP addresses belonging to radical enterprises throughout the world.

From years of experience and exhaustive research, Miranda found that criminal masterminds tended to be vulnerable to paranoid ideation—a type of reaction characterized by persistent thoughts of suspicion and mistrust. With Merlin's assistance, Levon intended to introduce confusion and doubt into the psyche of the vain overlords, who believed they were invincible and in control. Bogus data Merlin released over the web via the dark web dwellers' IP addresses created a growing sense of skepticism toward the authors.

Once the scheme was in full swing, it didn't take long for the criminal element to feel the repercussions. Everything was thrown off kilter. Where could the privileged go to get the real story? Nowhere. Who could they trust? Nobody. What could they do to combat it? Nothing.

International wheeler-dealer elites fumed. Former allies disappeared, along with trusted staff members. Stocks fell, product lines were discontinued, and wealthy investors sold out and moved their money elsewhere. Levon was amazed at how rapidly the rats jumped ship. But this was only phase one. Thanks to Liz and Nemesis, grander plans were in store for the corrupt cabal.

FARTHER SOUTH, AT LA BUENA VIDA on the Yucatán Peninsula, Magus unveiled a two-fold strategy of his own.

His first objective, an undertaking as old as the hills for the flimflam artist, was purely financial. With his silver-tongued rhetoric, he once more planned to seduce a captive audience of fat cat tools at the resort into pledging support for his latest altruistic cause. This time, it was the Nuevo Mañana movement for the restoration of the Mayan culture.

The second and more significant objective centered around revenge and presented Magus with more of a challenge in that he had to entice the participation of two primary individuals in the Nemesis organization—Liz Lonagon and her husband, Bryce. Lonagon Golf Course Design and Development was in the final stages of negotiations with representatives of La Buena Vida to tackle a monumental task. Preliminary discussions called for an elite eighteen-hole golf course community meant to wind through marshland and an ancient primitive jungle, skirted by luxurious single-family homes and cluster pods of guest casitas. Behind the scenes, Magus saw to it that the Lonagon firm won the bid for the project. Not only did he feel the Texas group could do the best job, he personally wanted to get Bryce Lonagon on the property.

Due mostly to the lay of the land, construction would be costly and time-consuming. Magus could afford to be patient if what he foresaw for the venture came to fruition. A one-of-a-kind championship golf course development associated with the existing five-diamond amenities of La Buena Vida Resort was a license to steal. Word of mouth and social media would bolster the plantation's exposure and appeal. He poured money into his dream at a furious rate, leaving no stone unturned. This was his last chance for success, and he was not going to cut any corners to get there. *Best of all*, thought Magus, *Bryce Lonagon would be on-site to supervise.*

Kai Camal worried that his boss overestimated the return on his investment. After all, they were in a relatively remote area of the Yucatán Peninsula, not exactly a cozy drive to the neighborhood country club.

"That's the point," Magus explained to Kai. "We want our resort to be a destination property where people come to spend a week, a month, maybe more, to soak up all the amenities and the subliminal spin. With our target demographic away from the comforts of home, in a fresh new environment, we have the ideal setting for separating them from their money. I expect memberships and associated revenues to generate enough income to not only recoup our investment but fund our precious movement in perpetuity."

To date, Magus had not seen or talked to Bryce face-to-face at La Buena Vida. Best to keep it that way, he decided, especially if wifey came along. With the recent enhancements to his appearance, chances were the Lonagons wouldn't recognize him from their dinner run-in years earlier. Still, there was no reason to take the risk. Kai could handle the Lonagon deal while Magus was conveniently away, supposedly in Europe on a promotional tour for the resort.

The idea of having the Lonagons as captives on the plantation property made his heart race. *Imagine*, Magus thought, *Liz Lonagon detained in the basement of horrors at The Preserve Infirmary to endure endless hours of pain and torture supervised by the head of viral research and development, Dr. Anton Pucci. Only to then be infected with one of Dr. Pucci's insidious pathogens and released out into the world to contaminate everyone Liz came in contact with—how delicious.* What just punishment that would be for the anguish she and her family had caused him over his lifetime.

FAR FROM THE DELUSIONAL MADMAN in Yucatán, the first casualty of Levon's Merlin program surfaced. Sonny Fairchild, of the Massachusetts Fairchilds, received a series of disturbing emails. At first, he thought they were pranks and ignored them. His chosen profession, as a bought and paid-for lawyer for the ruling class, allowed for a certain amount of harassment from unhappy adversaries—even clients. When more vexing emails arrived on the horizon, Sonny wondered, *Why would they be messing with me?* Innuendos and accusations were too close to the truth. *How and where did they get their evidence, and from whom?* Before he summoned Peggy, his shapely private secretary, he did some soul-searching.

On occasion, when Peggy accompanied him on the road, after a few too many drinks, they would hook up. Nothing serious—just a romp in the hay. *Wait, Peggy? Couldn't be … or …* Now he wasn't so sure. Come to think of it, Peggy had been acting strangely lately. Or did he just imagine it? Had he told anybody else about him and Peggy? No. *Yes!*

Oh shit, he thought. He'd bragged about it to his buddies at the bar he frequented. The ones who'd bet him he couldn't get into the iron maiden's pants. They'd all tried and failed. It felt macho to one-up them. She was good friends with a couple of them. *What if … My God, the woman knows everything about me and my underworld ties, the backroom deals, the bribes. Every fucking thing.* If any of that got out, he was a dead man.

Judging by the emails, it already had. He was on his own, with no one he could trust to help him. Without a word, Sonny sneaked out of his office.

WHEN PEGGY COULDN'T RAISE HIM on the intercom, she searched his office, then followed the instructions she found in a note slipped under the door. The note read:

> *Peggy, Just a heads-up. Your boss is in serious trouble. The threats he received by email are real. When he disappears, wait forty-eight hours, then call the cops. Erase the emails and burn this note in the interim. Tell the cops nothing. After they clear you, leave town, change your name, and use the money in this envelope to set up a new life for yourself somewhere far away.*
>
> *Good luck,*
>
> *A Friend*

Pressured by the authorities for answers, Peggy kept her statement brief. "No, officers, I have no idea where Sonny went. One minute, he was here. The next, he was gone. It's not like him to be away this long without notifying me. Sorry, that's all I've got."

When she was no longer a person of interest in her boss's disappearance, Peggy bought a plane ticket to the West Coast and took up residence under an alias, far, far away from Boston. The whereabouts of Sonny Fairchild remained an unsolved mystery. Without even a thread of circumstantial evidence, the general consensus among the authorities was that Sonny's handlers from the abyss were to blame, and they left it at that.

CONGRESSMAN CHANDLER DEAN was Merlin's next victim. A sitting US senator, Dean was a career politician with no worthwhile accomplishments to his credit. He rode the fence about as well as anybody in Washington ever had. Dean enjoyed his celebrity as chairman of several obscure committees that were a drain on the taxpayer and contributed exactly zilch to the well-being of anyone but himself. Recently, he had been targeted by an array of malicious emails pointing out his lackluster performance in Congress. Instead of his adversaries and constituents—the usual culprits in such slander—this time, the criticisms came from his peers. Never in his forty-two years in federal government had he been so maligned.

When Dean confronted his fellow senators, none of them seemed to know what he was talking about. To a person, they denied sending anything derogatory to him in an email. He took their denials as the old DC shuffle to get rid of him. To substantiate his accusations, he checked his server to make copies of the emails in question.

They were gone.

This infuriated the tenured senator. In retaliation, he made threats in the press that he was going to expose the guilty parties. As a result, he made some serious enemies within the most powerful DC factions.

Because of his perceived stature, Dean was given a warning. He chose to ignore the threat and called a press conference for the next afternoon at three. By three-thirty, it was clear the senator was not going to show. Odd that he didn't send a note or an aide to explain his absence. Baffled authorities earmarked it as another mysterious unsolved case. Word on the street was that the autocracy was responsible.

HOLLYWOOD, CALIFORNIA, WAS THE SETTING for the third Merlin-arranged travesty. An out-of-work cinema star from the past by the name of Randy Spears had played opposite some of the greatest leading men in movie history. She had been quite the looker back in her day and was still a beautiful lady. In the prime of her career, she had even had top billing in a handful of films. Randy was a proud woman with high standards who never slept with a studio exec she didn't marry. Her talent and work ethic carried her through. Now she struggled to get the fame she craved, which made her easy prey for bogus causes.

Thanks to the all-powerful draw of nostalgia and the cinema stations that showed reruns of her classic movies, the name Randy Spears still carried weight with an adoring public. One questionable charity bearing the name of a power-crazed family in the States took gross advantage of Randy's popularity to generate donations to their cause.

When it became known that less than 4 percent of the donations went to the charity, the general public went ballistic. Randy Spears became the scapegoat for the exposed family, all of whom slithered away unscathed. The negative feedback brought about by the scandal destroyed Randy, who locked herself away inside her Beverly Hills mansion until she disappeared one day. The bogus foundation was implicated. However, no evidence survived to prove its involvement.

ONLY LIZ AND HER TEAM KNEW what really happened to the victims. In each case, the blindsided party had valuable information to trade for their freedom. Names, addresses, phone numbers, and associates of individuals complicit in shadow governance around the world headed the list. Instead of a witness protection program, Nemesis took things to a much more secure level.

A decade and a half earlier, as a token of his appreciation for saving his life, a well-heeled associate gifted Nemesis a private island in the Caribbean Sea off the coast of Central America. It was a magnanimous gesture in that Isla Paraíso came with a walled resort village the previous owner had built for himself and his friends to vacation in. Over the years, Nemesis expanded and technically upgraded the island oasis.

Liz increased the height of the wall to ten feet and added a guard gate. Nemesis-trained security patrolled the property twenty-four hours a day. Levon Vargas added high-tech security throughout. His innovations, which were tailored to accommodate Warlock AI systems, gave Liz another branch office for Nemesis—this time with a captive audience. Borrowed from the pages of Liz's favorite novel by Ayn Rand, Paraíso boasted a community of disappeared residents. Only this time, they consisted of Nemesis's most valued expert witnesses and confidential informants.

Sonny Fairchild, Chandler Dean, and Randy Spears became its newest inhabitants.

CHAPTER 13

LESS THAN FIVE HUNDRED MILES northeast of Isla Paraíso, Rich and Sam settled into their bungalow at La Buena Vida. Their first group of inductees showed up on Monday morning. By the time the new recruits were issued their uniforms, assigned their quarters, and required to sit through an orientation by Kai, it was time for evening mess in the cafeteria.

At the conclusion of the mess, stern instructors passed out handbooks to the trainees and new staff members, then called attention to the notice on the front: all recruits were expected to have the material memorized by the end of the second week of training. If a person of authority asked, they must be able to recite the tenets of the movement in detail. Sam guessed the first tenet summed up the whole of the rest. It read, *Whatever any Nuevo Mañana member orders a recruit to do, the plebe must obey.*

Rich and Sam thumbed through their manuals, astounded at the plagiarized content stolen from past unsuccessful regimes that promised a world without care or responsibility. They pretended to go along with the program and even nodded to Kai when they noticed him staring their way. After dinner, the recruits were ordered to their rooms and instructed to be on the parade ground in sweats and athletic sneakers at five thirty a.m. sharp.

KAI INVITED RICH AND SAM to accompany him in the Land Rover to the infirmary building to inspect their recently completed office space on the second floor. His and her work spaces sat catty-cornered from each other. Across the room, copiers, scanners, and fax machines lined up along the far wall. Brand-new laptop computers, along with iPads and iPhones, were plugged in and charging at their respective desks. The flooring was more suited to a dojo than an office—a firm rubberized surface, which was easy on the feet and muffled the sounds in the room. All windows were reinforced with steel mesh and iron bars.

Odd, thought Rich, since they were two floors up.

They were about to leave when a weasely slip of a man crept into their office to introduce himself as Dr. Anton Pucci. His voice cracked slightly when he announced he was the head of research in the labs below, which he referred to as his inner sanctum.

Rich introduced Sam and himself and shook the man's clammy hand. Sam nodded shyly and looked away. Dr. Pucci offered to show them around his domain if they had time in the morning. Sam explained that tomorrow was the first day of training for the recruits, and therefore, she and Rich were tied up all day. Maybe they could visit at a later date. Pucci shrugged and abruptly took his leave to scurry back to his cubbyhole below.

Kai observed the exchange, interested primarily in Rich and

Sam's interaction with the scientist. When he perceived nothing out of the ordinary, the second-in-command of Nuevo Mañana let out an extended exhale. The off-putting doctor was crucial to the success of Nuevo Mañana. Pucci had come to the plantation out of greed and ego from a North Korea laboratory, where he was reputed to have extensive knowledge of biochemical weapons, including lethal infectious diseases, hallucinogens, and truth serum drugs. It was essential that the recently recruited couple, Rich and Sam, be able to work hand in hand with the doctor to bend the minds of the reluctant recruits. Convinced that was the case for the moment, Kai loaded his passengers in the Land Rover and dropped them back at their quarters.

AT THE END OF A STRESSFUL DAY, Rich and Sam were worn out and in need of a shower to wash the dirt and dust off, but more so to discuss what had transpired. Rich figured everything they did and said at the plantation was videoed and recorded to be scrutinized and evaluated by their superiors. The safest place to have a conversation was in the shower, where the sound of the water drowned out their voices.

Sam whispered in Rich's ear, "What a shit show! How about that ridiculous orientation speech Magus delivered to those reprobates he calls cadets? And Dr. Pucci, a throwback poster boy for bent doctors from the Second World War. It would make a terrific comedy if these idiots weren't deadly serious."

Rich smiled, nodded, and kissed her passionately, as if she had just propositioned him—a convincing act for anyone who might be watching. Who knew how long they would have to keep up their façade before Magus fully accepted them and allowed the couple to venture off the plantation on their own.

MAGUS AND KAI ENJOYED the shower scene as the couple soaped each other down. But they were disappointed when the steam from the shower fogged the lens of the miniature video camera, making lipreading futile while water pelting down from the showerhead distorted the audio so much it was impossible to understand what they said. Nonetheless, it aroused latent emotions of heated interactions Magus had experienced in the past with two of the most erotic vixens he had ever encountered.

What were their names? He searched his memory. They were … right on the tip of his tongue. *Eva and Victoria! How could I forget those gorgeous faces and their magnificent bodies? What memories. I wonder what those two are up to nowadays.*

Magus would have been shocked to learn Eva and Victoria were on Nemesis's Isla Paraíso, cowriting mystery novels under the pseudonyms Jane and Joan Lovejoy. Their novels landed on *The New York Times* Best Seller list, with each keeping readers on the edge of their seats, wondering what mayhem the protagonist, Condor, would stir up next. If Magus only knew who they patterned Condor after, no doubt he would have been flattered.

Unable to rid his mind of past affairs, Magus wondered if he could create new memories to ease his sudden urges. As Kai reached for the office door's knob to leave, the potentate of the plantation requested that his second-in-command rustle up two pretty little recruits to satisfy the leader's needs and well-being. The expression of disgust and disdain reflected on Kai's face escaped Magus's notice, as he had already turned his back in dismissal.

AT FIVE THIRTY A.M., THE NEW RECRUITS, less two females, met on the parade grounds for calisthenics, followed by a five-mile run before breakfast. The pathetic group of out-of-shape juveniles struggled through even the simplest exercises. Fewer than half of the forty-eight finished the run. Most staggered along the route in various stages of collapse. Kai faced a next-to-impossible task. He had eighty-nine days to whip this bunch of degenerates into soldiers fit to champion the Nuevo Mañana cause.

Rich and Sam watched the farcical display from the sidelines of the parade grounds and shook their heads in disgust. On the opposite side, flanked by Britany and Sloane—the two female recruits who'd kept Magus company for the night—Kai and Magus observed the train wreck from the viewing stands. Much to the disdain of an already distraught mass of inept recruits, the leaders' only recourse was to soup up boot camp and hope to make magic happen.

As a buffer, Magus designated Rich and Sam as his HR advocates to address any grievances the recruits might have. As soon as Kai established his next-level boot camp, the line was out the door, with kids complaining about everything under the sun, from the lack of safe places to discrimination and bullying by their drill instructors. The new grievance counselors explained there was nothing they could do. Whiners should have read the fine print before they signed the agreement with Nuevo Mañana.

Sam suggested the complainants button their traps and toughen up. Boot camp was a walk in the park compared to Pucci's playground. Rich concurred. The line to HR shrunk to a trickle after word got out about the basement and what took place down there. Neophytes subjected to electroshock treatments to soften their resolve were never the same afterward. After Pucci and his assistants got through with a bright, outgoing girl sent to the lab for insubordination, the poor thing was a stammering introvert, unable to make eye contact or carry on a halfway intelligent conversation. Britany and Sloane, Magus's paramours, were friends with the victim and took the lesson to heart.

Pleasantly surprised at how willing his female companions were to please him, Magus settled into his role. He imagined himself a true Mayan ruler with his concubines standing faithfully by his side and his loyal subjects bowing at his feet, hanging on his every word as gospel. Kai took Magus's escalating delusion as a major flaw—something he could use to his advantage in the future.

LIZ WAITED PATIENTLY TO HEAR from her two spies inside Nuevo Mañana. She knew it would take time for Magus and his crowd to trust her undercover agents. Still, that didn't ease the sense of helplessness she experienced in the meantime. Finally, she received a text from Rich's cell phone addressed to *Mother,* saying all was going well on their extended holiday. Not to worry—the natives were friendly and thankful for their help in the village. An innocent message that, if intercepted somehow by Kai, wouldn't raise any red flags.

When Liz decoded the message, it read, "We are in solid with the enemy and have some limited opportunity to communicate with headquarters."

"Thank God," Liz remarked out loud and sighed in relief. She responded by text, wished them well, and thanked them for touching base. Just as she signed off, there was a knock on her office door.

Davis McCall was there to pay his sister an unscheduled visit. She had picked up on her brother's infatuation with computer science and the role the boy's mentor, Levon Vargas, played in the Nemesis cybercrime program. While Levon refined the Merlin disinformation database in the Nemesis labs in Texas, her brother noted every move. It had not been quite a month since Levon relocated back to his lab at the Monastery in Canada to complete the project. Liz sensed that Davis was bored.

"So, what brings my not-so-little brother to see me this fine morning?" Liz remarked as she gazed up at him from her desk.

He met her gaze. "It seems like you've had a lot on your mind lately. I just stopped by to chat and tell you I moved up another belt in my Krav Maga training. That and I've had several conversations with Levon Vargas about Merlin. He kind of asked if I would like to come to the Monastery to witness the final touches he's adding to the enhanced Merlin program. So, what do you think? Can I go? Please," Davis pleaded in his most convincing manner.

Toying with him to get a rise, Liz replied, "I don't know. That's such a long way. And you have your training and studies here to think about. What about your promise to keep working on your golf game? There is so much for you to do here. Let me think about it."

"But, sis. Really? You know how keen I am to learn how our cyber-crime tools work. And now, with Merlin in the picture … there's so much I can glean, and I do so miss him and his sense of humor. Think of it as an educational field trip to expand my expertise."

She cocked her head and played him for a reaction. "I don't think so. Not right now. He's busy with an ongoing mission we have in Mexico, and I don't want him distracted."

"*Distracted*, really? After all the time and hard work I've put in to join Nemesis, you're telling me I'm nothing but a distraction. Seriously! Maybe I'll scrap the idea and move on to something else," Davis said as he turned on his heels to leave.

Before he took a step, Liz said behind his back, "Well, if you decide to do that, please let me know. I'd hate to waste the time and jet fuel to fly someone all the way to Canada, especially if they're leaving the company."

In a raised voice, Davis uttered, "If that's the way you f ... Wait a minute, what did you just say? Then I can really go? No shit? You're not jacking with me? You're serious?"

"Yes, you can go, and no, I'm not jacking with you. But let me clue you in on something, little brother. I don't take kindly to idle threats. Best keep that in mind for the future. And watch that language, buddy." She reprimanded him in a scolding, motherly tone.

Davis lowered his head shamefully. "Yes, ma'am. I'm sorry. It won't happen again, promise. You know how much I love you and Nemesis, right?"

"I do," she said. "That's one reason I want you to go and meet with Levon. Besides, my intuition tells me you two are *the future of Nemesis*."

AS THE HELICOPTER APPROACHED the Monastery, just as his grandfather did decades before, Davis panicked and hunkered down thinking the helicopter was going to crash into the mountainside.

Levon Vargas was there to greet him in the hangar with a huge smile and a bear hug. He was anxious to show Davis Merlin's expanded capabilities—the newest program he had created to further thwart the criminal element.

But first, perched in front of a blazing fire in the great room, Levon shared, "You know, Davis, we were blessed to grow in an environment in Texas where we were given the opportunity and support to excel. Here at the Monastery, Noah and Greta Bouchard provided the same type of inspirational atmosphere for me. Noah mentored me, and Greta encouraged my creativity. Not a day goes by that I don't think about them. In memory of Noah and Greta, I've redoubled my efforts to find the fiend who ordered their execution. More and more, the evidence points to one man, but knowing and proving are two different animals."

For security reasons, Levon would not reveal the man's name to Davis, who'd already figured out it was Ari Moon—aka Alberto Magus.

FOLLOWING A MARVELOUS MEAL that the chef prepared for them, Davis and Levon sat in front of the fire and talked into the wee hours of the morning about Nemesis, from its beginning until the present. The next morning, bright and early, they were back at it again. Davis drank in the history as fast as Levon could pour it out. Midday, they broke for lunch, after which Levon took his friend down into the bowels of the Monastery to see Warlock up close and personal. What would be an eye-opening experience for anyone was magnified for Davis, being that he had heard so much about the megacomputer since he was a wee child. Levon explained the huge machine's multifunctional capabilities the best he could in layman's terms. His guest followed the litany of jargon, mesmerized by what he heard.

At the conclusion of the tutorial, Levon looked over at his young friend and asked, "Any questions?"

"About a million is all," Davis remarked, dumbfounded. "I mean, how did you learn to arrange mind-blowingly complex sequences of zeros and ones to expand Warlock's capabilities?"

"First of all, Noah Bouchard came up with the concept and initial programs for Warlock. Plus, I had the benefit of his expertise and innovation to study before I began. I grasped the way he presented things. It all fell into place for me—it was my calling, just like when you decided to make Nemesis yours. I think we're born to our passions. Same with your sister and you, my friend."

"I get that. But I genuinely want to learn and understand the cyber side of Nemesis," Davis said reservedly. "Can you possibly break it down to the basics to give me a better idea?"

"Sure, let me think on it a bit, and we can give it a go later when I show you what I came up with for the Merlin program. Right now, I'd like to show you around the place and formally introduce you to the staff. They're wonderful people, and this property is really quite extraordinary."

Levon was right on all counts. The personnel were outstanding, and the property itself was charming, with a colorful history of previous residents. Plus, the cool weather was delightful. Davis was in no hurry to go back to Texas, where it was blazing hot. Instead, he was more interested in spreading his wings in the cybersphere among the Canadian Rockies with Levon.

MEANWHILE, IN A NOT-SO-SUBTLE WAY, Davis inquired of Levon, "So, what's Banff like? I mean, I kinda heard it was, you know, like a classic place for sightseeing. One day, do you think we could maybe check it out?"

"Yeah, I get your drift. It does get a bit claustrophobic up here. I don't notice it so much because I'm used to it. To your point, I think we should check it out tomorrow first thing. We'll take in the sights and grab a bite to eat at one of my favorite hangouts. This time of year, I think the sightseeing should be pretty good." Levon grinned and tousled Davis's thick head of blond hair.

AS PROMISED, THEIR FINAL STOP IN BANFF was Levon's favorite spot—a friendly bar called Que Sera, which Rose Conner purchased years earlier after she and her partner, Tina Tremblay, retired from Nemesis. Levon introduced Rose to Davis, wondering what his reaction would be once he found she had been an agent for his mom's organization. Davis stared at her for quite a long while, trying to figure out where he had seen her before. She wasn't busy, so she came out from behind the bar to sit and chat with the two younger men. Rose caught young McCall peering at her as she lit a cigarette. It wasn't a goo-goo-eyed fixation of an admirer. It was more of an *I know you from somewhere* look.

As Rose blew out a plume of smoke, she giggled and asked, "Okay, Davis. What's up with the eagle-eyed stare?"

"What?" Davis froze and looked away, mumbling, "I'm not. Well, I guess I was staring. This isn't a pickup line, I swear. But, don't I know you from somewhere?"

The ex-agent laughed. "Well, I'd be flattered if it were. It's been a while since a good-looking young man tried to pick me up. Back in my prime, I'd be mighty tempted to take you up on the offer. I'm betting since your last name is McCall that you know what Nemesis is."

Davis's head swiveled over to look at Levon, who was doing an excellent job of holding back his laughter. The young McCall was cornered and not sure what to say. "I've heard of it, but that's about it."

"Really?"

"Yes, ma'am."

"Hmm. How about Warlock?"

"Nope. 'Cept for, like, in witchcraft or the old-time western movie is all."

Levon couldn't take it anymore and burst out laughing. Instantly, Davis knew he was the brunt of a joke but didn't get it.

"Well done, young man, and believable at that," Rose announced as she stood, walked over to Davis, and gave him a huge hug. "You have seen me before. Most likely in a picture or two from the old days of Nemesis. You see, while I was an agent for Nemesis, I had the honor of working with a lot of your kin and many of the agents you know. When I retired from fighting cybercrime, I came back to Banff and bought the Que Sera, where I used to work tending bar. Your friend Levon called to see if we could wind you up a bit and see what shook out. Nothing did. No doubt you're going to be a fine asset for Nemesis one day."

The fact that Rose and Levon had taken the trouble to test him gave Davis a sense of belonging, and it felt pretty damn good when he passed. They visited for a while longer, and Rose shared her favorite observations of her tenure at Nemesis.

"Tina and I made quite a team back in the day—undercover work was our specialty. I'll spare you the raunchy details. Let's just say we were the best in the world at it. Yessir, we tangled with some of the most notorious criminals of the day. Lucky Richards and his scribes were our primary nemeses and gave us a run for our money, but we took down some of their finest. Didn't hurt that we had karma on our side and the likes of Mac and Trey McCall to back us up."

Davis thought back to an evening sitting in the library at Whispering Canyons with his grandfather shortly before Trey and Tara passed away. As clear as if it were yesterday, Davis could hear his late grandpa say, "You know, Davis. I had some mighty fine agents at Nemesis through the years, but none as gutsy as those gals of mine up in Banff. Yep, those two were tougher than nails. Tina Tremblay and Rose Conner. Wish I'd had a dozen just like 'em."

And now Davis was face-to-face with one of them.

Rose bought them lunch and slipped a note into Davis's hand on his way out the door. On the drive back to the Monastery, Levon asked him what she wrote on the note. Davis replied that it was private—for his eyes only. Levon laughed and let it go. Davis had already memorized the message he'd quickly glanced at while getting into the car; it was her private number if he ever got in trouble and needed help.

DIRE, LAME, CATASTROPHIC, PATHETIC—pick a word. They all applied to the graduating class from the first training session at The Preserve. At least, that's how Sam and Rich summed it up. Without exception, the grads were grossly under-trained militarily and barely schooled in the basics of salesmanship—definitely too green to promote a cause as worldly as Nuevo Mañana. Forty recruits out of the fifty who enlisted were deployed to hot spots all over the globe to recruit bodies for the second session.

Of the ten recruits who were not deployed, the Nemesis agents already knew two of them were Magus's courtesans. That left eight. Sam and Rich gathered from the resort grapevine that three of them died in the infirmary, while, unbeknownst to Kai and Magus, the other five were confined in the dungeon, undergoing experimental procedures cooked up by Dr. Pucci.

Based on mixed messages conveyed from the top over time, it didn't take a genius to figure out that each of the three bigwigs at La Buena Vida—Magus, Kai, and Dr. Pucci—functioned independently of the other two. When they were proceeding in such a slipshod manner, there was no possible way that the dreams the leaders at The Preserve promoted could ever succeed. Rich and Sam recognized the disconnect within the triumvirate as their greatest weakness—one Nemesis could exploit to turn them against one another.

AFTER A THIRTY-DAY BREAK, the second wave of enlistees descended on the plantation to spend ninety days under the rigid training program set up by Kai Camal. Again, most of the newbies were out of condition. Although there seemed to be more fit cadets than in the first class of recruits, few were prepared for the grueling boot camp ahead of them. As before, many lined up outside the HR office to voice their complaints. Rich and Sam told them exactly the same thing they'd told the first group of recruits—they should have looked more carefully at what they signed. Now they would have to either suck it up and face the consequences or play human voodoo doll in the research lab.

WATCHING DR. PUCCI USE MALCONTENTS as test subjects with little or no concern for their well-being turned Kai's stomach. Three recruits from the first session died under the *doctor's* care and supervision. A man completely unfamiliar with the truth, Pucci fabricated an outlandish tale that the individuals in question had escaped from the dungeon lab and wandered into the jungle, never to be seen again. With a straight face and a sinister grin, the baseless doctor stated emphatically to Kai that his people were scientists doing research, not common jailers. Anton Pucci's lack of empathy was as repulsive as the man himself.

There was no doubt that the missing recruits ended up in the jungle, but it was not of their own accord. No bodies were recovered. What with the abundance of carnivorous predators like crocodiles and anaconda, that was predictable. Kai was in a quandary. As time went by, it became painfully apparent that Dr. Pucci was a PR nightmare for La Buena Vida. Unfortunately, due to his glorified reputation in the field of microbial mutations, Pucci was deemed essential to the success of

Nuevo Mañana. Until Pucci came up with a suitable biotoxin weapon, Kai was forced to supply the mad scientist with test subjects.

NEMESIS AGENTS SETH COLLINS and Becca Evans joined the ranks of new recruits as backup for Liz's two agents already in place. Posing as disgruntled radicals, long-standing undercover operatives, Seth and Becca spouted hatred for the pigs who enslaved the little people of the world with their outdated policies. Familiar with Ari Moon, aka Magus, they had been instrumental in foiling the man's sinister plans at his castle in Albania and the Riverview Institute.

On the outside chance Magus might recognize the two, they significantly modified their appearances. By the time Becca and Seth showed up, they looked like worn-out hippies from the sixties, perfect for their assignment in Magus's jungle plantation lair. Seth had long, graying hair tied in a ponytail, John Lennon-style dark glasses, a tie-dyed shirt, faded holey jeans, and Jesus sandals. Becca's silver-streaked hair cascaded down to her waist, and aviator shades shielded her eyes. A tie-dyed crop top, bell-bottom flower child jeans, and leather moccasins filled out her guise. When they arrived with all the other trainees, Rich and Sam barely recognized them and probably never would have if Liz hadn't told them what to look for. Seth and Becca knew the doctrine of the cult from their past experience and were surprised that Magus hadn't bothered to change things up.

Just as well. It made their mission simpler.

As Kai Camal reviewed the new recruits at orientation, he stopped in front of Seth and Becca, looked them up and down, and thought, *Nothing but a couple of glorified hippies*. Shaking his head in disgust, he turned on his heels and focused on possibilities to come. Once Kai's barbaric training program for the newcomers was underway, there would be a bevy of lovely females begging to become one of Magus's harlots. Just the thought of it brought a smile to his face since he got his pick of the rejects before he sent the rest to Dr. Death. As his sense of power grew, so did Kai's sense of entitlement.

On their way out of the orientation, Magus introduced his HR duo to the newest older recruits.

"Seth and Becca, I would like you to meet Rich and Sam, who handle our complaint department." Then he turned to Rich and Sam and said, "Having read their resumes, I've decided our new disciples will work out of your department as mentors to the young recruits."

Rich and Sam nodded their approval, then Rich added, "Awesome. Sam and I welcome you both, and please note our door is always open."

Seth thanked them for the opportunity to guide the young social warriors on their quest for a better world. As soon as Seth closed out his thoughts, Kai Camal moved in behind Rich and whispered in his ear. Magus had forgotten to introduce the very distinguished Dr. Anton Pucci, who was livid at the omission. *Could it have been an intentional oversight?"* Kai wondered.

Rich snickered and wickedly winked at the little fraud.

IT WAS WIDELY KNOWN AT THE PLANTATION that the diminutive rodent craved attention and constant praise for his accomplishments in the field of scientific experimentation. But for what accomplishments in what field of experimentation? Even with the help of Warlock, Nemesis could not find one shred of evidence in any medical journal or publication that Dr. Pucci contributed anything to his specialty.

Pucci held himself in high regard, and the idea of playing lead doctor to the one and only Alberto Magus, a descendant of the ancient Mayan ruling class, made him feel giddy inside. What he truly enjoyed was the godlike power he wielded over the populace of the plantation, except for the two HR gurus. They seemed to have figured him for the phony he was—something he would love to discuss privately with them in his dungeon.

Actually, none of the diplomas displayed in Pucci's office were real. He had made it partway through medical school in Havana, until his world collapsed when he was experimenting with drugs—hallucinogens mostly, and not on himself but on others—without their permission. Caught up in experimenting on humans, the would-be doctor fled Cuba for South America, where he gained notoriety as a brilliant researcher and peddler of dangerous substances.

Pucci adopted the art of being seen and photographed in the right places with the right people. Everyone just assumed he belonged and was the renowned doctor he pretended to be. When all he truly possessed was a mediocre knowledge of medicine and some twisted ideas he played with in his labs, using human beings as guinea pigs. So far, in his dungeon at La Buena Vida Preserve, none of his experiments had panned out, leaving a great many of his patients as fodder for the animal population in the surrounding jungle. His arrogance betrayed him. It was no surprise that he became the brunt of ridicule and disdain from the staff at La Buena Vida.

RICH AND SAM STUCK AROUND after the orientation to welcome Seth and Becca to the faculty. As strangers do to feel each other out, the two couples were making small talk, and for some reason, Dr. Pucci's name popped up.

Barely within earshot of Dr. Pucci, Seth inquired, "So, what's with the good doctor? Clue us in. What's he like to work with and all?"

Sam answered, "We don't really know yet. We've only had one class of cadets come through so far, and they kept us busy. As far as I know, the man keeps to himself down in his labs. Rich and I haven't had much contact with the good doctor."

Becca groaned and chimed in. "I guess we'll all find out soon enough. He's walking over here right now."

"Did I hear someone over here mention my name? No doubt you have heard of me. Well, no matter. Allow me to welcome, you newbies, to the new world order. The four of you look as if you've fought this social battle for a long time. Let me guess. Beginning, like, at Woodstock in August 1969, for crying out loud." He chuckled at his own remarks. "Hey, guys, I'm only kidding. Always trying to bring a little joy into the world. That's me, Dr. Christmas. Once you get to know me, I'm really a barrel of laughs. You'll see."

With that, the cocky little prick doctor turned on his heel, walked over to the pontiff of the plantation, and put his arm around the man as they strolled out of the room, chatting. Seth Collins caught part of the conversation as they passed him. Pucci mentioned something about two Asian virologists, a Dr. Wong and a Dr. Wu, he had just brought to the plantation for a consult. Magus seemed keenly interested.

Once they got out of earshot, Rich asked Seth why he had a worried look. What Seth told him sent shivers down Rich's spine. Dr. Wong and Dr. Wu were two of the most knowledgeable research scientists on lethal toxins and pathogens in the world.

WITH THE EXCEPTION OF THE CHAMPIONSHIP golf course development, La Buena Vida Hotel, Spa, and Casino was fully operational and running at full capacity. The five-diamond resort proved to be an ideal setting where the elite of the world could congregate and contemplate the future of mankind and the planet. Magus catered to the whims of the self-anointed aristocracy just like he had years ago at his castle in Albania. Nothing was out of bounds—every perversion was provided for by the management, and everything was filmed and recorded by hidden devices. It still amazed Magus how the most powerful individuals could be so naïve in an environment they perceived as a haven.

AS FAR AS THE GOLF COURSE PROJECT was concerned, Bryce Lonagon and his team moved at the speed the terrain and weather allowed. Currently, they were ahead of schedule, which pleased Alberto Magus, Kai Camal, and Dr. Anton Pucci.

Dr. Pucci proposed, "Once the golf development is done, I suggest we arrange for Bryce to be kidnapped and held for ransom. My prediction is Chairperson Liz Lonagon will be on the next flight to Yucatán with the ransom money. At that point, we drug her and make her a resident of my underground laboratory."

Kai half-heartedly listened to Pucci's lamebrained plan before he rolled his eyes at the pathetically amateurish proposal, which was destined to fail.

Before he could voice his opinion, Magus chimed in. "I like it. Of course, we'll deny any knowledge of the kidnappings and blame it on the locals."

Kai watched and listened as the two maniacs contrived an insane scheme that he would have to carry out. At that moment, he fully understood that he was expendable. Neither Magus nor Pucci was interested in anyone's welfare, other than their own.

Instantly gaining his composure when Magus asked if he liked the plan, Kai replied, "Yes, I believe we could benefit from such an action. And if I might add that prior to implementation, we maintain a positive relationship with Bryce Lonagon in order to avoid being considered as serious suspects by the authorities."

Both men looked at Kai in a different light. His observation was right on. Magus commented, "Well said there, my friend. I think you've added the final piece to the puzzle."

"How long do you think all of this will take? I'm a patient man, but I have my limits," responded the rogue doctor.

Kai glared at the spitting image of Napoleon. "Now, now, Dr. Pucci. Some things just can't be rushed. You, of all people, should realize that. I'm sure our esteemed leader sees it that way as well."

"I most certainly do. This is a golden opportunity to eliminate our most ardent foe. We cannot afford to give away our hand due to impatience," replied Magus, backing up his second-in-command.

The piercing look that Dr. Pucci gave Kai Camal left nothing to the imagination as to how he felt about the Mayan. "As you wish, my lord" was all Pucci could manage without losing it entirely. The faux researcher knew that he must somehow remove this foul disgrace of a human being from the face of the earth to preserve the world for those who were more suitable to rule—like himself. He imagined the Mayan struggling to escape the tightening clutches of a giant anaconda before the man was swallowed whole, kicking and screaming—a fitting end indeed. With that image in his mind, Dr. Pucci excused himself from the office and rushed over to his dungeon lab to mull over the possibilities of making it happen.

Score a point for Kai Camal.

KAI AND MAGUS REMAINED in the office, going over contingencies. The hotel complex was raking in cash—more than enough to offer the Lonagon firm a sizeable incentive bonus if they could finish the golf course in record time. With the number of available workers and heavy machinery already on the premises, Kai saw it as a real possibility. Magus was elated at the idea and foresaw an additional flood of riches showering down on them with revenues generated by the golf course and development.

DR. PUCCI WAS FUMING when he got to his lab from Magus's office. He summoned Dr. Wu and Dr. Wong in for a spur-of-the-moment chat. "Tell me, gentlemen, how far along are you with the toxic pathogen project we discussed?"

"Truth is, sir, we've slowed to a crawl. Not enough female subjects available," Dr. Wu reluctantly responded.

"Are you fucking kid ... What if I supply you with as many females as you need? Then how long do you estimate it would take to develop the pathogen?" Pucci shrieked.

"Depends," Dr. Wong added.

"Depends on what, may I ask?"

"On the number of females who carry the mutant host cells necessary to create the virus. But you should know that, Dr. Pucci. How far along are *you* in *your* research?" Dr. Wong inquired curiously, troubled by a sinking feeling over their colleague's lack of qualifications.

"That is completely beside the point. Magus and I brought you two on board to do a job, and we expect you to do it. Is that clear?"

"Crystal," Dr. Wu growled through clenched teeth. "A question or two, Doctor, if you don't mind. Just to clarify a few things, in your research, have you found the host cell can self-correct a replicated mistake? And have you determined why we can't use male Y chromosomes to achieve the same results as the female X chromosome?"

"I, ah, haven't gotten that far in my research to answer those questions," Pucci offered in the more subdued tone of a man who had been found out.

The two virologists smiled, nodded, and, without another word, walked back to their quarters. Along the way, they decided to end their participation in the projects at The Preserve as soon as possible, for fear that Pucci's inadequacy as a scientist would jeopardize their safety and the safety of others in the lab. If some pathogen should inexplicably escape the laboratory, all hell could break loose worldwide.

THANKS TO AN UNDETECTABLE NEMESIS AI PROGRAM that tracked all transmissions into and out of the Yucatán plantation, Liz was privy to every one of them. Tipped off by her agents inside, Liz took advantage of a miscalculation Magus made. He had allowed Dr. Pucci to update the monitoring features in and around his precious Preserve. Independent contractors had to be brought in to install the sophisticated equipment. Sprinkled among those techs were Nemesis specialists who installed their own dataveillance hardware around the plantation.

Now that she had two sets of agents working on the inside at The Preserve training grounds and her super-sleuth equipment to surveil her suspects, Liz wondered what the next move was going to be from the exalted one and his goons. Judging from the latest data, it could be anybody's guess, seeing as things weren't all that chummy at the top of Nuevo Mañana.

WHILE HIS BIG SISTER MULLED OVER the events going on in Mexico, Davis McCall was hitting golf balls on the practice tee at The Circle M range. On sabbatical from his grueling cyber tutorials provided by Levon Vargas at The Monastery, Davis basked in the warm Texas sunshine and laughed his head off. Since he no longer had to prove himself on the Tour, the youngest McCall was having fun just messing around with some of the tried-and-true tips his father and grandfather had shared with him over the years. He was hitting his driver long, working the ball right to left, then left to right—high, then low—at will. He caught a glimpse of a shadow slip in behind him, then he defensively whirled and planted. But he relaxed when he saw Novél Vargas filming his swing from behind.

"Whoa there, Ninja master," she exclaimed. "Sorry, I just had to get your action on film. Your swing is the best I've ever seen. What have you done? Any changes you'd be willing to share? Honestly, it's poetry in motion."

"Thanks, Novél. Coming from you, that's incredibly high praise," Davis said shyly. "The answer is nothing. I'm not doing anything other than what we've both been taught. But instead of putting pressure on myself to make it happen, I'm just letting it happen. Does that make sense?"

"You know what? It makes all the sense in the world," she said with a huge smile. Would it be okay if I bring my clubs over here and hit balls next to you and mirror your rhythm? I've struggled a bit of late with tempo. Do you mind?"

"Be my guest. It's not often a Hall of Fame player asks to mimic my swing," he said with a wink and a wide grin.

It was true. Novél Vargas was an LPGA Hall of Fame member with thirty-two wins, including four majors and two Player of the Year awards. And she was still one of the nicest individuals in sports. After their practice session, she bought Davis a tall Arnold Palmer—iced tea mixed with lemonade—and sat down with him in the shade.

"Thanks, Davis. I believe you've put me back on track," she said excitedly. "I wonder if I might infringe upon you for one more favor. I've decided to chronicle all the tips your father and grandfather shared with us in a journal—not for publication, but for our own personal use to refer to when necessary. Would you check over my notes to see if I've left out anything? I'd like to have a written record—something special to share with my kids someday."

Novél Vargas was part of The Circle M extended family and loved by all its members, including Davis, who was more than glad to peruse her notes. They went down the list from the grip to the full finish of the swing. Davis added one or two suggestions. Between them, her notebook comprised a masterful collection of golf swing know-how that had been overlooked or misinterpreted by a host of guru theorists—the grip, the waggle, continuous motion, the role of the right foot and hand, and the left leg at impact, to mention a few.

That evening, Jefferson McCall finished his review of the journal, smiled at Novél and Davis, and remarked, "Wow! I'm impressed. You two really paid attention. I can't think of anything else at the moment. We keep this in the family, right? It might put a lot of know-it-all teachers out of work. And that would be a crying shame," he added with a sly grin.

CHAPTER 14

WHILE CONFLICTING FACTIONS FOCUSED on the Yucatán Peninsula in Mexico, a long-forgotten player in the overall scheme of things was horizontal on a chaise longue beside the pool outside his condo in Indian Wells, California. Miles Stewart, alias Marcus Ward, who was technically still in witness protection (WP), walked away from his new life in Flagstaff, Arizona, leaving everything, including his false identity, behind. In his carefully orchestrated escape, Miles and two WP agents he had befriended went on a weekend camping trip in the mountains nine miles west-northwest of Flagstaff.

BEFORE DAWN ON SUNDAY MORNING, Miles quietly sneaked away from camp, expertly covered his tracks, and hid in a cave he had discovered months before. Unbeknownst to the deputies, he packed extra water and canned goods in his rucksack, along with a change of clothes and bedding—enough for three to four days. His escape route provided him with optimum cover from above and terminated at an ancient mining road that led to a paved county road outside Bellemont, Arizona, and intersected with Historic Route 66.

Four days later, a filthy, sunburnt, physically sapped wreck, Miles hitched a ride with a trucker to San Bernardino, California. He caught another ride to Palm Springs, then another over to Indian Wells. It felt good to be in familiar surroundings.

Finally, he arrived at his condo in a dated development on the outskirts of Indian Wells. Miles Stewart unlocked his front door with the key he had hidden outside years before and was pleased to find the maid service had done a top-notch job of keeping the place clean and presentable. He had paid cash for the place—property taxes, condo fees, and incidental charges were taken care of via autopay, set up years earlier on an established account under an alias. In a concealed space under a floorboard in the master bedroom suite, he had squirreled away $250,000 and the key to a ten-by-ten safe deposit box in a bank in Palm Springs that held $2.2 million more—enough greenbacks to make another fresh start.

The next thing on his agenda was to get cleaned up. The stares he got from other residents when he let himself into his place were enough to convince him of that.

Miles took a cab to a barbershop near the bank. After a haircut, shave, and manicure, he walked over to the bank. Delighted that everything was just as he had left it in his safe deposit box, he closed the container, replaced the box in its numbered slot, and pocketed his key. After that, he deposited into a new account $50,000 from the stash he kept at the condo, less two grand for pocket money. The teller handed him a book of checks and the $2,000 in cash on his way out and told him it was a pleasure doing business with him.

He proceeded on foot from the bank past a pizza joint, a dry cleaners, and a mom-and-pop drug store with an old-fashioned soda fountain inside, where he stopped to enjoy the first root beer float he'd had in ages. Back outside, he continued past a pawnshop across the street from a Lexus dealership. He hustled across the street against the traffic light to browse the used cars on the lot. A savvy salesman showed him his inventory and let Miles decide which vehicle he preferred. That proved to be a clever tack, commission-wise, for the salesman since, after a test drive, Miles chose an LX 470 SUV—the most expensive preowned vehicle at the dealership. He wrote a check for it, then drove it off the lot and back to his condo.

Once inside, he put half his cash and his checkbook under the floorboard in the condo. Then, before he went down for a power nap, Miles took a long look at himself in his bathroom mirror and contemplated whether or not to change his appearance again. It was something to think about, given there must be a gazillion plastic surgeons in the desert to choose from. How would he know if a doctor he chose was reputable? It wasn't something he wanted to just jump into.

An idea popped into his head: *Why not go to one of the private golf clubs on the pretense of joining?* He had been a decent player at one time, so he knew his way around country clubs, where to find countless men and women who had gone under the knife. Miles could pose as a recent retiree from Ohio looking for a friendly club to join, where he could play golf and enjoy the other amenities. He was still a fine figure of a man who would attract some of the unattached or unhappily married ladies in the country club set. Indian Wells Country Club would do. It was convenient to his condo.

THE LADY AT THE RECEPTION DESK of Indian Wells Country Club didn't take her eyes off the man inquiring about new memberships until she introduced him to a Ms. Diana Filburn, a knockout in her early forties who still had that mystical sparkle in her eyes. Ms. Filburn waved him into her office and invited him to sit down, then asked if he'd like coffee or a drink. Miles declined.

"Very well then. My receptionist, Astrid, tells me you are looking to join Indian Wells. I must say, looking at you, my first impression would be that you are just what we are looking for in a man. Sorry, I mean a member," she said with an intentional Freudian slip. She smiled wickedly. "Of course, you would have to be vetted. We have strict but *flexible* parameters to work within. I believe you understand what I'm implying."

"Yes, Ms. Filburn, I believe I do," he said and held her stare until she blinked.

"Good, then please call me Diana. Why don't you tell me about yourself? And please don't leave anything out," she replied, unconsciously licking her lips.

"Very well, *Diana*. My name is Ryan Allen Miles, but all my friends call me Miles. Anyways, it's an alias I assumed years ago to avoid any further contact with my ex-wife and the name stuck. I'm now a happily retired divorcé from a no-account wife who tried to take me to the cleaners but failed miserably. Over time, I doubled my net worth, recently sold my business for a huge profit, and came to California for some fun in the sun. Indian Wells came to mind because I saw my first pro golf tournament here when I was a younger man. Back in 1979, I watched John Mahaffey birdie the final hole to beat Lee Trevino by one on this course at the Bob Hope Desert Classic. I thought this was such a cool place to win a tournament, and it stuck in my mind."

Diana frothed at the mouth with the prospect of having Ryan Miles as a new member. "What a coincidence. It so happens we have a picture of that day on our wall of honor here at the club. Wow, small world, huh? As far as your name goes, we can easily work around that. I assure you, it's not the first time we've made *allowances*."

He nodded as she continued. "Let me give you an application form and my card to look over. Any questions you have, call me day or night. I'll make myself available."

Ryan took the application and her card, then stood to leave. Diana followed him to the door with a longing look in her eye. As he opened the door to leave, the yearning expression on her face told him he'd scored big time. "She confirmed it when she said, "Don't be a stranger, Miles."

She watched him as he walked to his Lexus SUV and drove past her window on the way to the exit. He waved, and she smiled.

Miles took a left on Highway 111 and headed northwest. Before he reached Rancho Mirage, he turned left on Highway 74. Two miles up the road, he took a right into his dated condo complex. In total, it was less than a twenty-minute trip. While he was driving, Miles admired the contrast of the mountains against the desert floor and the brilliant green of the multitude of golf courses that dotted the landscape. He thought about the bewitching gaze Diana gave him during their meeting and wondered what kind of hoops she would have to jump through to make him a member of the country club. The background associated with his alias would easily pass any vetting process, if she even bothered. But there must be a long waiting list for new members. Time would tell what kind of pull she had.

THE INITIAL STOP MILES MADE when he cleared the door of the condo was his bedroom to check his hidey-hole. Satisfied that all was in order, he plopped onto the bed. It had been a long, satisfying journey leading to this day, and he was worn out. His mind raced as he coveted sleep; regrettably, he was unable to let things go for the moment.

After an hour of tossing and turning as he reminisced about his and Moon's futile projects, Miles finally fell fast asleep and didn't wake until half-past nine the next morning. He threw back the curtains and stared out over the mountaintops at a cloudless blue sky. Sunshine bathed his face. The promise of a glorious new day lay before him. Indian Wells, California, would be a dandy place to hang his hat until whatever came along to tickle his fancy. A good night's sleep, along with a hearty bacon, egg, and toast breakfast, perked him up even more. His first business of the day was to fill out the country club application.

Miles opted to give it a few days before he dropped off the membership application with Diana at Indian Wells Country Club. He was curious to see how she reacted to him after she'd had time to think about their meeting. In the meantime, he checked out some real estate in the area. His condo wasn't suitable for a well-to-do retired business tycoon, although he would keep the old place as a safe house in case he needed it.

Why not? It's paid for in full.

A JUDAS TO THE TRUE MAYAN CAUSE, Kai Camal worked from the shadows at The Preserve. Filled with loftier aspirations that he kept to himself, he applied lessons in deceit and manipulation he had gleaned from Ari Moon, aka Magus, and Anton Pucci. It came as no surprise to him that after the first year, things at The Preserve hadn't turned out as Magus anticipated. Kai and his mercs saw to that by covertly undermining the plantation magnate whenever possible. As for his constant source of aggravation at the plantation, Kai publicly stifled his hatred for the imbecilic maggot Pucci, desirous of personally dealing with the phony scientist at a later date—in private.

DISENCHANTED WITH THE NUMBER OF NEW RECRUITS, Magus shook his head in dismay. After three training sessions, with nearly one hundred fifty graduates sent around the planet to draft members for Nuevo Mañana, the list of new prospects was disappointingly small— down to a mere trickle rather than a flood. Perhaps Magus had gone to the well too often with the same tired sales pitch. To make matters worse, his favorite paramours, Britany and Sloane, were nowhere to be found. After a meeting at The Preserve, his chief means of finding relief in times of anxiety had gone missing.

When Magus questioned him about their disappearance, Pucci confessed he had no idea what could have happened to the two women. Kai was beside himself and rolled his eyes after Magus blankly accepted the researcher's lame explanation, as if what became of those women wasn't as obvious as the bulbous nose on Pucci's face.

Unknowingly betrayed by those he believed to be his most trusted allies, Magus was mired in a nebulous state of flux. Adrift alone in a sea of highs and lows, he was desperately in need of a miracle to stay engaged.

WELCOME NEWS THAT THE GOLF PROJECT was near completion came just in time to reenergize Magus. No longer did he dwell on his misfortunes. Instead, he eagerly looked forward to the future. There was no doubt in his mind that the development would attract droves of wealthy prospects for his cause. But more importantly, it would provide him with the revenge he sought for so long. He cracked a smile as he visualized the trials and tribulations his primary adversaries would face in the days ahead, titillated by the anticipated outcomes slated for Bryce Lonagon and his bride, Liz McCall Lonagon.

Overwhelmed by his unexpected good fortune, Magus *gave* Kai a predated copy of a handwritten obituary—one Magus penned expressly for the special occasion. I was a costly miscue for the overzealous charlatan. It read: *Shortly after Lonagon Golf Course Design and Development completed construction on La Buena Vida Club de Golf Resort, a rogue faction of radicals kidnapped developer Bryce Lonagon and his wife and held them for ransom. In a brave escape attempt, the Lonagons disappeared into the jungle and fell prey to its predators. Our deepest condolences go out to the surviving family members for their loss.*

KAI ACCEPTED THE GIFT, KNOWING FULL WELL it furnished him with an ace in the hole to use against Magus should the occasion arise. That, in turn, would allow him the freedom to move forward with a strategy of his own, *without Magus's knowledge or permission.* To fit his narrative, Kai modified the original abduction theme.

Bryce Lonagon was kidnapped. But instead of holding him for ransom, Kai's guerilla faction freed the victim and returned him to Texas. Reverting to the initial outline, Kai blamed a rogue group of rebels for the incident. Assured he had pulled one over on Magus, the Mayan descendant sent his sincerest regrets to Bryce Lonagon for the incident and begged him to return to the plantation, promising armed security to ensure his safety—plus $2 million for damages and personal aggravation. Kai hoped his concessions would appease the elites at Nemesis.

In timely fashion, Kai received an email from Texas. Bryce Lonagon agreed to return to the plantation. It was time for Kai to initiate step two of his game plan while Magus busied himself entertaining the out-of-touch beautiful people of the jet-set world.

DESPITE HIS WIFE'S STRONG OBJECTIONS, Bryce Lonagon played a hunch and agreed to fly back to the Yucatán Peninsula to meet with Kai Camal. During his stay, he was given the royal treatment, including around-the-clock armed guards and accommodation in a megasuite with complimentary food and beverages. Kai presented him with an addendum to his original contract, providing for a nuisance fee of $1 million and another million tacked on the existing bonus for early completion.

Bryce signed the rider and flew back to The Circle M to pack for an extended stay in Mexico. Well aware of the risk from an earlier visit, Bryce approached his upcoming trip to La Buena Vida on high alert with his eyes wide open.

LIZ MCCALL LONAGON was dead against it.

"Damnit, Bryce. Are you insane? Those people down there are fucking nuts and would just as soon murder you as swat a fly," Liz erupted. "I don't give a shit if they rolled out the red carpet and kissed your feet last time you were there. Those bastards cannot be trusted. Why can't I get that through that thick skull of yours?"

"You know, it kind of turns me on when you get all worked up and nasty about things," Bryce said in response in an attempt to change the subject.

"Don't even go there with me, Bryce Lonagon! I won't have it. This is some serious shit, and you want to blow it off as nothing? Damn it to hell, I don't … won't … can't lose you!" Her voice quavered as her eyes teared up.

Bryce embraced her and quietly whispered in her ear, "I have an idea."

She pushed him back and glared into his eyes. "What? You have a *what*?"

"An idea. One I think you might like if you'll hear me out. Here's how I see it. Because our adversaries at La Buena Vida have plausible deniability and reasonable doubt in their favor, I believe they are going to kidnap me for real this time to draw you down there. If we both go missing, all they have to say is the radicals made good on their second attempt."

Liz rolled her eyes, shook her head vehemently, and sighed deeply. "That's precisely—"

Bryce interrupted. "Now, listen closely before you lose your cool. It's not me they want. It's you. You and Nemesis are their worst nightmare. As soon as they take me prisoner, they'll figure they have complete control over you and the freedom to proceed with whatever schemes they wish."

"And this is a good thing? How? You're not a trained agent. Or have you overlooked that fact?"

"Granted, I'm not a trained *Nemesis* agent. However, I am a retired army ranger. With your permission, I'll continue. I'll need your techs to implant a GPS microchip under my skin so Nemesis can track my whereabouts at any given time. My guess is they'll hide me in an isolated location at The Preserve, or maybe even Pucci's dungeon. Follow me so far?"

She hesitantly replied, an expression of bewilderment covering her face. "Yeah, well, sort of … but still—"

He cut her off again. "All I need to know going in is who and how many assets you already have in place at the plantation."

She cocked her head and gave him a sideways stare. "Hold your horses there, cowboy. We're not even close to that point yet. First thing that comes to my mind is that it's an awfully risky undertaking for an inexperienced person such as yourself. What's the upside? Is it worth it in the long run?"

"Liz, I say it is more than worth the gamble. This guy we are after is responsible for countless crimes against humanity and has been on the lam for decades. With me as bait, Magus is sure to show his face if only to gloat. What an excellent opportunity for Nemesis to nab him for kidnapping, right?"

Hmm, she thought. *At present, Magus is linked to a multitude of heinous crimes, but even if he's caught in the act of committing a felony, with the justice system as skewed as it has become, there is no way to ensure a legitimate trial. Bryce has a good idea—brilliant in that it gives me options to deal with Magus on Nemesis's terms. Best of all, it might just work.*

Impressed with her husband's creativity, Liz agreed to go along. "Okay. *If* you pass muster from my team, you're in. Only then will I share the information you need relative to our target and his facility in Mexico."

Four of her best Nemesis agents were on the grounds, and a plethora of surveillance systems operated twenty-four-seven in and around the plantation. Isla Paraíso, the Caribbean branch headquarters for Nemesis, was less than forty-five minutes away by Jetcopter should serious reinforcements be needed. All the bases were covered as far as manpower and spyware went. Innovation was paramount if an assignment like the one Bryce proposed was to succeed. *No problem there,* Liz thought, grinning as she reflected. *My man is as quick minded as they come. Spontaneity is his specialty.*

MEANWHILE, WHILE BACK IN SOUTHERN CALIFORNIA, Ryan Miles was living it up with Diana Filburn in Indian Wells, California. Diana moonlighted as a real estate agent, and when she discovered Miles was in the market for a new place, she showed him around—mostly properties in or near her neighborhood. Admittedly, she was a terrific agent who listened carefully to his critique of every place she showed him. The look in her eyes when they scouted out houses was that of a predator baiting her prey. As of yet, he had not succumbed to her feminine wiles.

After many open houses, they came across just what he was looking for, and it was not too far from the club or her place, for that matter—a ranch-style stucco structure with a tile roof and a fenced-in pool with an attached hot tub. It was a little larger than he needed, but for the price, he couldn't resist. The place came tastefully furnished, including all new appliances. He and Diana just so happened to be in the spacious bedroom suite when he told her this one was it. With a broad smile covering her face, she brushed by him on her way to the California king bed.

Diana bounced up and down on the mattress and patted the bedspread next to her as a signal for him to join her. "I think you are really going to enjoy this place," she said. "What say you and I give this new mattress an initiation, just to make sure everything suits you?"

"Well, if you insist," he replied as he took his position beside her.

"Oh, I insist all right. You can bet your ever-loving sweet ass I insist," she said as she tore off her blouse, ripped open his shirt, and clawed at his belt.

It must have been a while for Diana, because she was insatiable. Miles had experienced a dry spell as well, so he was happy to oblige. By the time they were totally exhausted, the bedspread was in shambles and the sheets and pillows in complete disarray.

When she caught her breath, Diana laughed. "I must say, you were a challenge, but well worth the effort."

Miles stared into her captivating eyes. "If I'd known you were this incredible, we'd have done it in your office that first day." The funny thing was, he meant it. The woman was gorgeous, with a firm, trim body, and she knew how to use it. "You know, I'm not sure we gave that new mattress the full initiation," he said. "Think we ought to give it another shot?"

In a low, steamy, sultry voice, she purred, "Only if you think it's necessary."

"Oh, I think it's necessary. You bet your sweet ass I do." Ryan laughed as he smothered his face between her lovely breasts.

After an hour's nap to recoup, they cleaned up and salvaged what clothing wasn't destroyed. Miles said, "Diana, I feel I know you well enough to ask you a personal question."

"Of course. Yes, they're real. Blessed from birth."

He snickered. "No, that's not it, but I figured as much. I'm getting a few wrinkles and things. Anyway, I wondered if you knew someone around the area who could do some work on me. And don't be kind and say I don't need it, 'cause I do."

Diana didn't bat an eyelash. "Yep, I've got just the guy. Dr. Mike Morgan, who worked on my late husband and made him look fabulous until the cancer finally killed my poor Frank. If you want, I can take you to see him tomorrow. FYI, Mike had a crush on me back in the day, before I married Frank. Now we're just good friends. And he's a member of Indian Wells."

It wasn't long before Miles was comfortably settled in his new casita and was a brand-new member of Indian Wells, thanks to a special package his new lady friend, Diana, created. Best of all, he'd had just enough cosmetic work done to make him unrecognizable as Miles Stewart. He still thought it a good idea to keep his old rundown condo, the one nobody else, including Diana, was aware he owned.

Most mornings, Miles played golf with Doc Morgan, who was a pretty good stick, and two of Doc's golf buddies, who liked to gamble but weren't overly good at either. Miles and Diana did the town almost every night and made love at his new hacienda until they were spent. She shared the huge walk-in closet with him, keeping enough outfits there for work when she slept over.

Every now and then, Miles wondered how things were going with the Mayan project in Mexico. Then he blew it off. It was best to leave the past where it belonged—in the past. Anyway, Miles figured the folks in Mexico most likely had no clue that he was in California. Besides, he no longer wished to associate with the malignant, sordid elitists of that world. He'd seen them for what they were—sociopathic, egocentric pariahs. They were never happy, whereas he was happier in California than anywhere else or at any other time in his life.

First and foremost, he had all the money he would ever need and a cool-as-hell woman who made him laugh and loved him dearly. Last of all, he played golf almost every day in a regular foursome at Indian

Wells. Miles and Diana hung out with some of the most established locals in the Coachella Valley—often going out to dinner, playing cards, or taking in a show or a movie. He was even asked to run for city council, which he immediately laughed off as a practical joke.

MEANWHILE, ON THE YUCATÁN PENINSULA, Dr. Pucci was burning the midnight oil in his laboratories at The Preserve. At present, Dr. Pucci cared about little else than his precious research. The mad doctor enhanced his menu of illicit substances to include hallucinogens, deadly virus chains, and a new powerful mind-twisting drug he was currently testing. Only a few drops of the tasteless solution in a drink or mixed in with a meal would quickly place a subject in a mind-altered state during which they could be directed to do anything the doctor suggested.

Purely by accident, Kai overheard Pucci brag about his new discovery to one of his lab assistants and say that Magus was his preeminent test subject. *It must have been Pucci's whispered suggestion to Magus that brought Bryce Lonagon on board for the golf course project,* Kai thought, as he wondered about the timing. Pucci's lecherous facial expression gave him away, and the Mayan figured it out—Pucci was dosing Magus with some heavy shit. *No wonder the fucker didn't know where he was half the time.*

In order to play out his hand, Kai had to tolerate Anton Pucci for a while longer. His spies at the infirmary lab confirmed the existence of the drug cocktail Pucci covertly slipped to Magus. It was imperative that Pucci continue to dose the leader with regularity. A clear-headed Alberto Magus did neither of them any good.

WHEN ANTON PUCCI HEARD THE NEWS that Bryce Lonagon was coming back to La Buena Vida, he pranced around his lab, gleefully rubbing his hands together and giggling like a kid who got the present he asked for at Christmas. There was no doubt in his mind that Liz Lonagon would fly in routinely to see Bryce, which gave Pucci time and opportunity to cook up the worst possible scenario to torture the head of Nemesis—perhaps a dream cocktail of fatal hybrid viruses she could harbor as a host, then infect everyone she encountered.

Under the influence of Pucci's psychoactive drug and in response to another of Pucci's suggestions, Magus abandoned the search for his former courtesans, Britany and Sloane. Instead, he settled for quantity over quality in his current harem, which was Pucci's self-serving move to ensure himself a continuous supply of female recruits for his experiments, among other things.

WHEN BRYCE ARRIVED BACK IN YUCATÁN, he walked the La Buena Vida Club de Golf property again, checking here and there to make sure things were done properly and playing his role to a tee—business as usual. Topo maps didn't do the spectacular property justice. He took time to smell the earth, ogle the movement of meandering streams, and take in the sounds of wildlife. In the bottoms, surrounded by dynamic rock outcroppings and spectacular waterfalls, there were enough natural corridors present in the dense vegetation and waterways for him and his team to build a spectacular eighteen-hole championship golf course without having to move an excessive amount of dirt. To top it off, there was more than enough room for a clubhouse with all the amenities on a picturesque plateau overlooking the marsh. The golf course development was one of a kind. Now he'd returned to finish it.

At least twice a day during his boots-on-the-ground assessment, Bryce spotted Kai peering over rocks or from behind razor-sharp blades of thick marsh grass, checking out the architect's progress. Working diligently, his crew and a considerable number of workers Kai provided took advantage of good weather to move ahead at a rapid pace.

SEVERAL TIMES DURING CONSTRUCTION, Jefferson McCall arrived by helicopter to lend his input to the course design. His visits were a show of good faith to make everything appear on the up-and-up to Kai. On occasion, pretending to be interested parties, the four Nemesis undercover agents would show up at the project. Rich Martel played the role of a big fan of Jefferson McCall's. he even got his autograph on a golf ball for his supposed collection. Samantha Smithwick took a picture with the Hall of Fame member's arm around her as she secreted a note into his pocket for Liz. Seth Collins and Becca Evans dropped by to marvel at the progress and ask Jefferson and Bryce all sorts of amateurish questions about the golf course design business. Their conversations were in code to keep Bryce abreast of proceedings inside The Preserve.

Jefferson McCall even gave Kai a signed golf glove as he climbed aboard the Jetcopter to leave, and he wished the Mayan good fortune for the future. Kai never suspected a thing.

LIZ LONAGON AND HER NEMESIS TEAM monitored the situation at the Yucatán plantation from Nemesis HQ on Isla Paraíso. Her not-so-little brother, Davis McCall, and cybercrime genius, Levon Vargas, joined them on the island to work on their current top secret drone innovation designed for Merlin. Using her husband as bait to lure Magus into their net did not exactly thrill Liz. Although, it was comforting to know that her two teams of undercover agents at the plantation had Bryce Lonagon in sight at all times. Moreover, several trustworthy men from Nemesis ally Carlos Morales's Mayan faction embedded in the construction crew were there to keep an eye on him as well.

AS THE GOLF COURSE CONSTRUCTION neared completion a good month ahead of schedule, Bryce became more conscious of his surroundings. Early one evening, he received a note under his door from one of Morales's men, warning him that he could be abducted at any time. A prompt at the end of the note reminded him to put up enough of a fight to make it believable.

It wouldn't be long now. Bryce was ready.

CHAPTER 15

A FEW MILES AWAY, IN MAGUS'S OFFICE at the resort, Magus and Kai reviewed the Lonagon abduction guidelines.

"I say we expedite the timetable while the golf course construction is still underway," Magus proposed.

"And why should we do that?" Kai retorted in the confrontational attitude he'd adopted as of late.

"Puts us in a better light with the Federales. Why would we want to kidnap the guy *before* he finished the golf course project?"

Whatever. After all, it's your idea, the Mayan thought. Then he scoffed, "Makes no difference to me."

"Then it is settled, my little Mayan friend. The hour is nigh to begin the reclamation of our heritage. Give the order to take Mr. Lonagon captive."

With a scowl on his face and hatred in his heart, Kai obeyed. "By all means. It gives me great pleasure to do so, my lord. I have waited far too long *for this glorious moment*."

Oblivious to the implicit meaning in Kai's final words and his petulant air, Magus nodded ceremoniously in response before he dismissed his number two with a flick of his wrist.

BRYCE LONAGON HAD HIS FEET UP in his leather recliner, nursing a beer in the living room, when five masked men burst into his bungalow. He gave a good account of himself but eventually succumbed. Zip-tied and blindfolded, he was dragged outside to an idling diesel SUV. After a twenty-minute drive, they arrived at a deserted cabin that smelled of fresh paint and disinfectant.

After his blindfold and restraints were removed, Bryce looked around the small living area, then at his masked abductors, who made their way to the front door, exited, and locked the door behind them.

Free to wander about, he checked out his surroundings and was pleasantly surprised to find an updated bathroom with a shower, a small kitchen with a microwave, a refrigerator-freezer combo, and a two-burner propane gas stove. A Murphy bed with fresh linens pulled down from the wall. Inside the refrigerator, he found food and drinks. Ice and frozen dinners filled the freezer. A bar was set up on the kitchen counter. It was not exactly what he expected as a kidnapping victim. Confused, Bryce sat on the edge of the bed to consider the situation. The phone rang on the nightstand, breaking up his jumbled thoughts. Curious, he answered it.

"Good evening, Mr. Bryce Lonagon," said a voice he recognized from the past. "I am the esteemed leader of the Nuevo Mañana, known to my throng of followers as Alberto Magus, better known to you as Ari Moon. I've called to crow a bit about my ingenious strategy that brought you here. My motivation is one of pure revenge against your wife for all the angst Nemesis has caused me over the years. You, of course, are what is called collateral damage. With my approval, Dr. Anton Pucci has created a most unpleasant end for you both in his basement laboratory. By the time Nemesis can regroup, I'll have achieved my lofty position on the world stage."

Lonagon listened but did not respond. After more than a minute of silence, he sensed anguish on the other end of the phone.

"Are you there, Mr. Lonagon? Did you hear what I said? You are at my mercy. Don't you have anything to say?" Magus screamed.

Dead silence from Bryce.

Magus slammed the phone down and summoned Kai Camal to get to his office ASAP. "Kai, I know that asshole heard every word I said. You've got to tell me where you have him. I want to see the man face-to-face."

Kai replied instantly. "Now, we talked about this early on. It's imperative that you *not* know where we have him for your own protection."

The steamed leader reluctantly relented.

Kai left Magus's office with a grin on his face, aware that Liz McCall Lonagon heard every word the exalted leader uttered to her husband during their phone call.

As part of his grand scheme, Kai's men moved Bryce to a Mayan ruin in a remote portion of the property later that night. Then, under the cover of darkness and via a circuitous route, Kai brought Dr. Pucci to the ruin for a chat with the prisoner. The Mayan chieftain was well aware that Dr. Pucci wouldn't be able to resist the temptation to one-up Magus and brag to the supreme leader about his visit with Bryce Lonagon.

NEMESIS HEADQUARTERS ON ISLA PARAÍSO and at The Circle M were buzzing with news coming from Yucatán. A ransom letter landed on Liz Lonagon's desk demanding $4 million in cash to be delivered by Chairperson Lonagon in person at the La Buena Vida Hotel. Anticipating the note, Nemesis was already ahead of the game with a stand-in for Liz waiting in the wings in Texas to fly to the plantation on the Nemesis Cessna Citation. Liz was kept up to date on all fronts in her Isla Paraíso quarters.

Rich and Sam staked out the plantation ruler, who appeared confused and disoriented. *Not surprising,* thought Liz.

Adhering to Liz Lonagon's directive, Seth and Becca shadowed Dr. Pucci, who was a lot more active than usual. They tailed him and Kai Camal to what remained of an ancient Mayan temple, where Bryce was being held, and waited outside in the underbrush until Pucci and Kai came out half an hour later. Then they followed them back to the plantation grounds. Becca followed Pucci, who made a beeline to the mansion, most likely to rub it in about whom he met with at the old temple. Liz found that to be *predictable.*

By means of one of the mini microphones Nemesis agents planted in the mansion, Liz overheard a most interesting exchange between Magus and Pucci.

"Really, old boy. Bryce didn't seem that much worse for wear. Not nearly as bad as he'll be when I get through with him and his bride," Pucci boasted to the exalted one.

Magus could hardly speak because he was so livid. "Wait until I get a hold of Kai, that little Mayan Judas. How dare he take you to see Lonagon without my permission. That's treason, that's what it is. Where is that little bastard?"

Pucci shrugged and gloated.

Well, well, malcontent among the chosen. What a pity, Liz muttered to herself sarcastically.

PRESENTLY, KAI WAS NOWHERE NEAR the mansion or the temple. Under clear skies and a full moon, he was on his way back to the old cabin to remove any incriminating evidence that might have been left behind. Stretching on a pair of neoprene gloves, Kai wiped the place clean of fingerprints and took with him anything that could have Bryce Lonagon's DNA on it. Next, he hand-washed and dried glasses and plates, then emptied the garbage can into a huge plastic bag, along with any of the other items he found in the bathroom or on the floor.

Following by the light of the full moon, Seth kept Kai in sight as the Mayan left the cabin and circled back to the crumbling Mayan temple to go through a similar but less taxing ritual. Kai even took an old straw broom and swept out the footprints on the dirt floor when he left the temple. Now without a single piece of evidence to the contrary, Kai could deny he'd ever heard of the cabin or the temple—much less been there. His goal was to drive a wedge of resentment between Magus and Pucci. However, he'd been tailed by an experienced Nemesis agent who could prove otherwise if necessary.

Upon his return to the resort hotel, Kai lied to Magus, refuting any knowledge of a meeting between Pucci and Bryce Lonagon. He said the allegation was absolutely absurd. Why in the world would he agree to something as asinine as a meeting at some ancient ruin that, as far as he knew, did not even exist?

"It seems to me that Pucci is playing you. He must have something sinister planned. If I were you, I'd be very careful around our good doctor. Watch his every move," Kai cautioned the supreme leader in his most sincere tone.

Scratching his head, Magus thought for a second, then replied, "You know, you could be right. Lately, I seem to get confused, even forgetful, when he's around. I'll make it a point to be unavailable to him for a while and see what happens."

"Sounds like a good idea. Seems to me his attitude of late has been most disrespectful toward you. Maybe a little comeuppance is in order to put him back in his place," Kai slipped in to reinforce his narrative.

DR. PUCCI DID NOT APPRECIATE the cold shoulder he received from Magus. It meant the leader's frequent dosing would be interrupted. Not that he cared too much at this point since he'd already gotten what he'd desired from the delusional ruler. Still, he liked having power over his subjects. To take his mind off the big picture, Pucci locked himself in his lab to perform some experiments on a couple of recruits he'd held captive in the soundproof cells. Britany and Sloane were special since they had been Magus's favorite paramours. It was only fitting to test his latest drug cocktails on the girls as a means of revenge against the promiscuous pope of the plantation.

Acutely focused, he watched his test subjects writhe in anguish as the mad doctor approached them and carefully prepared the syringes. So committed to the task, Pucci didn't hear the door slowly open behind him. Nor did he feel a presence closing in until they were on top of him. A hand held a cloth doused with chloroform tightly over his nose until he passed out. Kai Camal and his two compatriots laid the unconscious doctor in a body bag and zipped it up. Next, they released the girls from their restraints. Then, as a group dressed in hospital scrubs and lab coats, they wheeled the body out of the building on a stretcher and loaded it into the back of a Land Rover.

Still unconscious, Pucci was hauled to the same Mayan ruins where he'd met with Bryce Lonagon earlier—far away from any populated areas, where curious ears could not hear screams. Kai brought three vials of liquids he'd found on a tray closest to the doctor in the lab, along with syringes, cotton balls, and alcohol to administer injections to their prisoner.

When the doctor woke up, it was pitch black outside. Glancing around the dimly lit relic of a temple, he saw a handful of faces, one of which he recognized—Kai Camal. "What the hell do you think you're doing? Magus will have your fucking head when he hears about this," the arrogant, pissant doctor admonished.

Kai cracked a wry little smile. "You have more to worry about right now than what Magus might or might not do. He has no idea that you are even here and couldn't care less. This is my way to pay you back for the anguish you have caused me and my people. The boys and I thought it would be interesting to test a few of the drugs you created on you, so you could experience the full effect of your work. Oh, and we brought along a couple of spectators to watch your reactions."

The look of horror on Pucci's face was unmistakable. "Please, I beg you, don't do this. The drugs are experimental. You don't understand what they can do."

"You're right. At this point, we don't. However, before the night is over, we'll have a pretty good idea. I'm sure the girls will get a kick out of it. What say we find out? No time like the present. By the way, we appreciate that you left detailed notes on the highest nonlethal doses for each vial. You best get ready for the ride of your life, Doctor. See you on the other side of hell."

Dr. Anton Pucci squirmed uncontrollably as the first injection was administered, the effects of which were nearly instantaneous. This particular drug affected the brain's central nervous system, leaving the mind and body totally receptive to suggestion. The doctor's eyes glassed over, and his mouth drooped open as he drooled down his chest. Kai ordered him to perform certain ridiculous tasks, which the man did without hesitation. Each of the others gave the narcotized doctor a command, astonished that he responded in like to the order.

After the novelty wore off, Kai injected Pucci with the other two drugs almost simultaneously. One created horrific hallucinations; the other, total indifference to grievous bodily harm. They watched the man thrash around until he passed out from exhaustion. Kai decided to perform an experiment of his own by combining what was left of the three drugs into one massive dose for his doctor friend. However, that could wait until morning. So they each took a two-hour shift, guarding their prisoner while the others slept.

THE PREVIOUS EVENING, Seth Collins and Becca Evans rendezvoused after following their prospective subjects to The Preserve labs. It was now dawn—not the first time the two agents had spent the night in their car while on a stakeout. The only activity the previous evening was when a group of lab assistants wheeled out a body bag, stuffed it in the back of their vehicle, and drove away.

This was not an unusual occurrence, since Seth and Becca had witnessed the same thing on several occasions. Wild pigs that had not survived the doctor's experiments were routinely placed in bags and taken into the jungle to be disposed of by predators. When afternoon rolled around, the two agents became concerned. Becca went inside to check that everything was all right. Mum was the word. No one had seen or heard from Pucci or Kai. Troubled, Seth reported their findings back to Liz in Texas.

"Okay, you two stay put at Pucci's lab for now. I'll have Sam contact Kai," Liz said, then rang Kai.

When Sam broached the subject of Dr. Pucci with Kai a few hours later, he replied, "No, ma'am. I haven't seen the little weasel since midday yesterday."

Which wasn't anywhere near the truth. Just that morning, Kai had given the doctor the triple-strength injection of blended serum before he and his companions fled the scene. When the drug cocktail wore off, Pucci's brain was fried. Completely disoriented, a pathetic blob crawled out of the temple and into the bright sunlight, which blinded it. Crying out in anguish, it scrambled deep into the surrounding forest and whimpered until it fell asleep in the dense jungle shade.

Rumors spread quickly about a manlike creature that lived in the jungle near the Mayan ruins. There were a few reported sightings, but no one gave them much credence, figuring it was local hearsay to boost the tourist trade. *Karma!*

One down, one to go, Kai thought, gloating to himself.

MAGUS WONDERED WHERE HIS SECOND-IN-COMMAND might be. He'd tried to raise him several times to no avail, a common occurrence lately—one that played on his every last nerve. Spies operating on Kai's behalf picked up that Magus was getting edgy with an overzealous need for attention—a side effect of the mood-enhancing drugs Pucci developed for him. Paranoia took hold as Magus pondered whether Pucci and Kai might be conspiring against him.

When he glanced out his second-story window to find his security detail was not in position, Magus felt a serious rush of anxiety. Panic set in, and his mind raced. *Kai. Good god, man. Where in the hell are you?* Again, he tried to reach the man with no success. Out of the blue, a one-word text message popped up on his phone—*¡Vete!* ("Get out!")

Too experienced not to retreat, Magus retrieved his go bag packed with travel documents and miscellaneous essentials, like a flashlight, matches, a Swiss army knife, photo IDs, and credit cards bearing his aliases. Hastily, he removed two nine-millimeter handguns with extra magazines from a wall safe and shoved them into the bag.

Everything became deadly quiet. He took that as a bad sign and fled as fast as he could for his escape tunnel behind a wooden panel in his downstairs library. Twice, he stumbled coming down the stairs. He made it just before Rich and Sam crashed through the front door. The experienced agents heard a sound in the library and dived inside. Expecting to face a barrage of bullets, they incurred nothing but silence. After a thorough search of the library, they came up empty, with no sign of Magus or his means of escape. *Nada. Zilch.*

Sam stopped dead in her tracks and said, "Hang on. There's something fishy going on here. Based on his history, tunnels are his thing—a kind of fail-safe for Ari Moon, aka Magus. I'm willing to bet that somewhere in this room, there's a concealed entrance. And an underground passage that leads to the private airport here on the property."

FOLLOWING HIS NARROW ESCAPE from Nemesis, Ari Moon, aka Magus, stood motionless in the pitch dark of the underground passageway. As soon as the hatch closed and the lock engaged, the lights and air-filtering system were supposed to switch on. Only they didn't.

Removing the flashlight from his go bag, Magus scoped out his surroundings as he moved slowly down the tunnel. At some point soon, he expected the emergency generators to kick the lights and air on, but five minutes had already passed, and the stagnant air in the tube had yet to move. *Why didn't I pay more attention to Kai when the man brought me down to walk the tunnel years ago?* he thought. There were all sorts of auxiliary systems to fall back on, but for the life of him, he couldn't recall a single one. He'd forgotten where the emergency phones were located.

But there was something he did recall—there were six numbered markers on the walls and floor, one for each quarter mile of the mile-and-a-half trek to the exit. As he trudged along, it became harder to breathe. *Why aren't the generators coming on?* he wondered. Looking down, he saw the number 2 in reflective paint on the floor. That meant there was a mile to go before he reached the end. It might as well have been a thousand. It was stifling inside the tunnel. Magus broke out in a cold sweat. His lungs ached and heart pounded as if it were about to explode in his chest. *What about the air vents? There were supposed to be air vents, just in case.* Exhausted, the broken man was moving at a snail's pace when he saw the number 3 on the floor.

Only halfway. How could that be? He looked at his watch. *It has taken over half an hour to go a quarter of a mile.* No way. He wasn't going to make it. The only sounds in the cylinder were his shuffling feet, heavy breathing, and the rapid beat of his heart getting louder with each step.

In desperation, Magus fumbled for the phone, but he'd left it on the nightstand by his bed. And the canteen he'd filled with water was still by the sink—both overlooked in his rush to flee. Nothing in his life made sense anymore. Maybe it never really had.

Resolved to his fate and with little else to do until he expired, Ari Moon, aka Magus, reached into his bag for his iPod. He flipped through his saved music to a category he'd labeled Crash and Burn Rock—music that had to be turned up as loud as possible to achieve its full effect. It contained his personal classic rock collection performed by his favorite artists and groups that lived on forever in their music. Songs by Creedence Clearwater Revival, Guns N' Roses, Bob Seger and the Silver Bullet Band, Cheap Trick, Led Zeppelin, Journey, Van Halen, Lynyrd Skynyrd, AC/DC, and ZZ Top highlighted his selections. He pushed the Play button and cranked up the sound. At first, it almost blew out his eardrums. *But what the hell.* He'd be dead soon, and it really wouldn't matter.

CHAPTER 16

TWO DOWN AND NONE TO GO! Kai crowed.

Magus's disappearance was a mystery to all but Kai Camal. No one discovered the remote-controlled sliding panel that concealed the tunnel entrance in the mansion's library. Kai saw to that the day before Magus vanished. Dressed as an electrician, Kai had sneaked in to the library to activate the auto lock on the panel that sealed the entrance permanently. Once the lock engaged, no one could get in or out of the entrance or the exit. Kai thought it a fitting going-away present for Alberto Magus, the magician.

After weeks of searching and coming up empty, the weary authorities unofficially threw in the towel. Officially, they kept the case file open, but there was no sense of urgency to close it. As the lone survivor of his partnership with Magus, Kai Camal assumed sole ownership of the property and all the improvements.

Kai's proud and dedicated hotel staff saw to it that La Buena Vida resort continued to thrive on its reputation as one of the finest vacation destinations in the world. The Mexican tourist bureau was overjoyed to have another draw steeped in legend to lure visitors to the Yucatán Peninsula. Local politicians were handsomely compensated for perpetuating the myths surrounding the disappearance of Anton Pucci and the even more intriguing puzzle of Ari Moon, aka Magus, who had so many lives that cats were jealous.

EPILOGUE

BACK IN TEXAS, LIZ LONAGON saw things in Yucatán for what they truly were—corruption masquerading behind a smokescreen of success. No matter how often Nemesis exposed the criminal element as the predators they were, the cybercrime giant was never able to get ahead of the curve to prevent those responsible from repeating the same atrocities over and over again. Greed and corruption continued to grow at an alarming rate. Nemesis played by the rules while its adversaries made their own. Expanding on a proven tactic while manipulating the criminal justice system internally, Liz believed that Nemesis could turn the tables. Confident her operatives could pull it off, she set about to map out the two-pronged approach.

Although it was looked upon as an impossible task, Liz Lonagon's cyber genius, Levon Vargas, in collaboration with her younger brother, Davis McCall, created an undetectable pathway into a site known as the DOE, or the Department of Excision, located deep in the bowels of the dark web. Specializing in termination, the DOE catered to a select group of influential clientele. Steeped in wealth and political power, the entitled used the wet-work site to dispense their brand of justice on those who threatened their sovereignty. Utilizing the cybercrime unit's skills, Nemesis sought to turn the wet-work network into an internet black hole that ultimately collapsed in on itself.

Then, capitalizing on the expertise of a fearless pair of Nemesis lawyers, Maxwell Silver and Chloe Devonshire, Liz proposed to draw on their unique talents to battle a twisted justice system by attacking it from within.

As far as Mexico was concerned, Liz figured the authorities in the Yucatán were about to close the books on Anton Pucci and Ari Moon, aka Magus. Which was all well and good—except …

The End

ABOUT THE AUTHOR

JOHN MAHAFFEY WAS BORN in Kerrville, Texas, and attended the University of Houston, where he was a two-time All-American. John was a member of two NCAA national championship teams and the individual NCAA champion in 1970, a feat he accomplished one week after he tied for low amateur in the US Open at Hazeltine National Golf Club in Chaska, Minnesota. He graduated from U of H with a psychology degree in 1970 and turned pro in 1971.

Mahaffey is a ten-time winner on the PGA Tour, including the PGA Championship and the Players. In 1978, John won the individual title in the World Cup and partnered with Andy North to win the team competition at Princeville on the island of Kauai in Hawaii. The following year he partnered with Hale Irwin to win the World Cup for the US in Athens, Greece, and was a member of the victorious 1979 Ryder Cup team.

After playing the Tour for over three decades, John enjoyed the role of announcer/analyst on Golf Channel; broadcasting live golf for the Champions Tour. During his tenure as a commentator, Mahaffey wrote his first book, *Hogan's Boy—A Journey in Golf*, an autobiography of stories and recollections of a career that spanned from the end of the Ben Hogan, Byron Nelson, and Sam Snead era to beginning of the Tiger Woods and Phil Mickelson era—a time in which Mahaffey was fortunate enough to have Ben Hogan as a mentor.

Inspired to write more, Mahaffey embarked on a mission to author a collection of fictional works—the Nemesis series. *Shafted* is the first of the cybercrime thrillers. Golf takes a holiday when the McCall family is plagued by a corrupt narcissist who seeks to bring the golf star Trey McCall's world down around him. The ingenious family of survivors stands up to fight for what is right.

Unfinished Business, second in the Nemesis Series, chronicles the exploits of a disjointed group of unscrupulous disciples, steadfast in their belief that a reengineered master plan of their deceased mentor will bring them wealth and power. Their ultimate goal—to destroy Nemesis and the McCall dynasty.

Dead Quiet, book three in the Nemesis Series, centers around Trey McCall's son Robert and Nemesis's arch enemy Desiree Richards. How were they able to slip the dragnet set up by the most elite crime fighting organizations in the world? Where were they now? And what were their intentions?